J.A. ST. THOMAS

A STEPHANIE BEROE CHRONICLE

Cat Tales Publishing Los Cerrillos New Mexico 87010, USA www.CatTalesPublishing.com This is an original publication of Cat Tales Publishing.

Cover art design by Todd Yocham – Tuff Dog Studios

Cover photograph by Bella Bucchiotti

Library of Congress 2023944426

ISBN 979-8-9886188-0-5

This book is dedicated to my daughter Elektra Bella Nyx St Thomas, the bravest person I know. You will always be my brilliant, beautiful light.

Acknowledgements

Teach-er

The definition of an educator, is a person who helps students to acquire knowledge, competence, or virtue, through the practice of teaching. Informally the role of teacher may be taken on by anyone. Wikipedia

I would like to acknowledge all of the "teachers" who have left an imprint on my life, and thank them for their passion, bravery, guidance, and altruism.

Mrs. Mertie Dorko, Miss Coney, Mrs. Sandy Young, Tina Alikas, Tommy Alikas, Margaret Alikas Smith, Richard Francis White I, Joan Patricia White, Barbara Weber, Russell Weber, Patrick Mangold White.

The world is a better place because of you.

Author's Note

Written at a time when the world as we know it was upside down: public-school shootings, Black Lives Matter, insurrectionists storming our nation's capital, women's rights revoked, LGBTQ losing decades of ground, migrants caged at the border, nationwide mental health crisis, drug addiction endemic, Climate Change on the brink of collapse, hypocrisy on the highest courts, and the threat of yet another world war that made surviving a global pandemic inconsequential, if not smiteful. This novella, the third book of The Stephanie Beroe Chronicles, was a catharsis for processing isolation, fear, and the ramifications of distrusting mankind while living under long-term duress. As life imitates art, not unlike my heroin, I homeschooled my daughter during COVID, creating a micro-school with several other families. This experience became so incredibly surreal, that I paused the completion of my manuscript Class 7, book II of The Stephanie Beroe Chronicles to write, and complete Pot Luck, the story unfolding immediately before my eyes, demanded my full attention.

I learned through this process, that even in the darkest place we persist. Our children give us hope and purpose through their strength, humor, love and light as they find their path; carving an inexplicable future for themselves and the world they're re-imagining.

Life is about being out of our element, it is what gives us strength and challenges us to do better and be better.

Chapter Title List

The chapter titles in this book are named after each song that inspired sentient action, mood, or dialogue. All e-book chapter titles have live links to the songs that are related to the dialogue or action of the chapter. Scan this QR Code to listen to the book playlist for experiential drama. E book chapter titles are live, just click to go.

Contents

Prologue

Who knew one of the scariest topics known to women would be educating our children? Purring up Gold Mine Road in our 1971, VW van Trixie, pretending she was made for dirt roads, the red and white paint job is a dead giveaway. *They'll see me coming; but I have a plan.*

Danielle, is following me through a satellite GPS tracker attached to my hat on her phone, a lovely gift from my husband Remy last year before all hell broke loose. It has a built-in panic button. *I hope I won't need.*

Armed with more gadgets than a cold war spy, the only thing I don't need is a gun. I'm excited about a new micro-droid that looks more like a fly than a machine. It records video and sound through a satellite link, giving a whole new meaning to the term bug. My husband Remy buys most of these things from a mercenary catalog. *Which is why, I'm sure, our mail lady is terrified of us.*

Running through a checklist, I also have my Hello Kitty stun ring, a smoke bomb lipstick, a stun gun cell phone- ready and charged, and my new electrified "no-touch" jacket. *Of course, if all this goes wrong, and I'm just delusional about this woman, I'll be in jail. So, no pressure.*

At almost five o'clock, the long shadows, emphasizing the low autumn sun, saturate everything around me in golden light. *It's deceivingly beautiful.* The panorama of the Sangre de Cristo mountains in the rear-view mirror bumping along, is alienating as our home, indistinguishable in the distance, no longer anchors me. Wiping my sweaty palms on the thighs of my pants, I take a long, deep breath. *Stay cool, Steph.*

Turning right at the third juniper tree, past a painted rock on the side of the road, I see Chatura's house; a sprawling one-story with a living roof, wind turbine, and three-car portale covered in solar panels comfortably nestling her Tesla, harbored within a stunning, thousand-acre property with breath-taking views. The main house is casually formidable, surrounded by an adobe wall, protected by an ancient gate from a forgotten temple in India that's barely blue, and left permanently open.

Parking, I gather my thoughts for a moment, then roll down the passenger door window; the fresh air feels good. Pointing to a spot next to the sliding door in the back out of sight, "Sit, Soter," I command, giving him the hand signal for watch and a pat on the head. His Egyptian eyes are intent with purpose. At full attention, our German Shepherd will not move unless I call or whistle for him.

I don't see Holly's car, which is a relief. Activating the micro-drone, it's inaudible to me but curious to Soter while it hovers between us. Ideally, it will follow the locator in my hat, somehow, guided by sonar.

Pulling my tracker cap down over my ears, my pockets full of toys, I slap my cheeks, riling them out of a pallid, anxiety response. Slipping my phone into the back pocket of my jeans, I prime the safety button in the liner of my jacket. During an attack, all I need to do is press the button in the pocket, and KAZAAM! 150,000 volts to anyone who touches me. "I'm ready, and I'm not fucking around."

Walking the path to the front doors guarded by two enormous hand-carved pots with towering cactus protruding out of each, I'm suddenly distracted. *Have they been de-prickled?*

Looking closely in disbelief, I raise my hand to knock when the door opens, "Stephanie, I'm so glad you're here. I was getting nervous." Chatura exclaims. We hug like it's been years instead of hours, tears in both our eyes.

"Please, come in. Sit. I can only imagine how stressful this is for you. I made a relaxing tea from my Chinese doctor; it's valerian, skullcap, and passionfruit. I think you'll like it," she rambles nervously.

Tea is laid out for three on her Balinese coffee table that's so big I could use it for a stage, and it's practically on fire from a copious array of candles she's put to task cleansing the space.

"Thank you, Chatura, your home is lovely." I take a deep breath allowing the lavender, tea tree, and orange aromatherapy to settle me before an unpleasant but vaguely familiar aroma breaks through. *It's almost fishy. Definitely at odds with the vegan surroundings- so clean and fresh.* "Your house has such an openness about it. It's really energized," I move into the delightful space, acknowledging the trouble she went through to make me comfortable.

"Thank you. Well, as you know from my vlog, I've had a virtual Feng Shui master working with me for weeks pushing energy around, but I think we finally did it. It feels good. Right?"

"Definitely." Everything, beige or green, it's soft and organic, dreamlike even, I'm almost at ease. The two giant, picture windows on either side of the front doors face the Santa Fe Mountains standing majestically in the background as the entire mountain range to the west transforms into a silhouette against a fading orange sunset; it's sexy and powerful.

Led to an enormous balsa sofa surrounded by hanging basket chairs, I'm soothed by the low-key- Balinese chic as heated, rammed earth floors warm the space naturally, accentuating stands of exotic plants in every corner. Between the kitchen and living room, an array of different-sized, hand-blown glass, bubble planters coddle air ferns hanging from the ceiling in a pattern that create a light and playful wall division. To the left of the kitchen is an area dedicated to her vlogging. Tripods topped with cameras and lighting rigs face a haphazard, multitude of chairs and props in disarray.

"So, what's the plan?" She asks anxiously, sitting across from me.

"We need to get Holly to talk."

"Ha! That'll be a feat."

"Yeah. It's not going to be easy, but listen, whatever I say? I need you to just go with it. It may… get messy."

"OK, Stephanie. But what if… she really did murder Gabriella?" She whispers, eyes wide with fear.

"I'm prepared for anything, Chatura. Don't worry. But keep your phone nearby in case we need back up."

"I hope you know what you're doing." She pours tea nervously as Holly pulls into the drive.

We both watch silently as she gets out of her car contemplating my van for a moment but, Chatura opens the front door on cue. "Holly, I'm so glad you're here." Successfully collecting her before she bolts, she shuttles her up the path.

Stopping in her tracks at the threshold, Holly iterates, "Why is she here?" The characteristically gruesome, monotone she's famous for, lays in the air like ether.

"We need to talk." I pick up my cup, hoping she'll ease in.

"No." She turns to leave.

"Wait, Holly." I smile gently. "We really need to talk."

"Stephanie, you're under suspicion for murdering Gabriella. You tried to kill Delia, mothers from our home school group!" She continues, almost smiling, then whispers, "You're a sociopath." Swinging her Goyard purse playfully at her side. She adds, "Of course, it's no surprise to me or anyone else." Her voice flat and righteous she's on a roll, "Do you want to know why?"

I raise my eyebrows.

"Because you're reckless. Everything you do is counter to society," She confirms rhetorically, her nostrils flaring as her face turns angry, and dark.

"I believe the term is counterculture."

Her bag drops dramatically to the floor as the introverted, non- verbal woman we had come to know evaporates, "It's all a joke to you, isn't it? I mean, you sell marijuana. Why would anyone take you seriously?" She stammers, her features pinching all over her face, like a defiant tween.

"You know what, Holly? You're right. My life is reckless but not because I sell marijuana." Sipping my tea quietly, has a calming effect on her. "I was born reckless. I learned early, never to surrender. It was me against the adult world as a child, like Charlie Brown for god's sake, and now, as an adult, it's me against the conformity of society, just like you said."

Moving towards the couch, she's pleased to be proven right.

"I'm not like you, Holly. I *never* will be," I resume. "I'm less trusting… I *despise* routine. I'm hard to please; and *so* much more because I *have* to be. My life is different. I have *no* safety net, and I have to take huge risks *every* day. But most importantly I enjoy feeling alive, really alive, out of my comfort zone."

Silent, her eyes narrow.

Time for the attack. "Whereas, at times, it's been hard for me to decipher whether you even have a pulse. You're disengaged, morbid, and entitled."

Rage bottlenecking in her face, I'm a steam roller, "You've given up. Whatever spark you had, it's gone. You're lost to fear and the unknown like you've been stripped of your instincts and senses."

"Stop," she hisses. "This better not be an Asian thing."

"Seriously?" I stand up, my hand on my chest, "There's a life force inside of me, and I don't take it for granted. Some people create, some people consume; that's the real difference between you and me, not our race."

Holly smirks, but Chatura nods her head in agreement.

"You know what I mean, Chatura. You're on a similar path. Look at the dedication you have to your vlog? Sharing all that wonderful vegan information with the world around you, making the world better than you left it. You get it, don't you?"

"Yes, Stephanie. I get it." She smiles, topping off Holly's cup.

It's time to amp this up. "You may not understand this but creating things makes you vulnerable." Turning towards the counter that separates the living room from the kitchen with my cup in my hand, I buy time admiring a couple of succulents next to a pile of bills. *Where is my bug?*

Chatura stands up. "I couldn't agree with you more, Stephanie." Tears in her eyes, she surprisingly professes, "Being a content creator isn't easy. Everyone makes fun of you. And being counterculture," she looks to me, "makes you an outsider and a target. I know you all think I'm nuts with my solar oven and Earth Ships and Veganism. I know you don't agree with me. But I'm making a difference in my own way. And that's the thing! Just when you think you're doing something amazing, letting people in on something they should know, someone comes along and calls you crazy! It's thankless!" She throws up her hands and flings herself back on the couch in frustration.

"I know about being vulnerable," Holly replies, pulling viciously at a button. "You don't know me!" She looks to Chatura, "I don't need to pretend to be a social media superstar to feel fulfilled." She grimaces, cocking her head back in my direction with disgust, "Or make a living selling drugs to justify coping."

So, it's the marijuana that bothers you. It all comes down to that. I sit down placing my empty cup on the table like punctuation. *There's only one place to go from here.* "Let me ask you something? If I'm a drug dealer, what's your husband?"

"Nate is a surgeon! He went to medical school." Appalled, she screams, "He helps people!" Mirroring my punctuation, she slams her cup down. "You don't even have a college degree. You're just nobodies! Dropouts!"

Chatura's gone Tweetie Bird for a moment as I set my gaze on Holly. "At least I don't lie to people. I don't treat symptoms to create long-term patient returns, and I don't charge incoherent prices for natural remedies. There's a statement on our cannabis coffee bags, 'Good karma always tastes good.' It's there for a reason."

"How dare you!"

Pacing to the large palm next to the fridge, I drive it home, "Really, Holly? You told me yourself you moved here to get away from the HMOs that capped Nate's salary. That came out of your mouth, and you said it like it was OK! You're in some serious denial if you can't see how insurance companies and medical costs kill people. Look around you. The same medicines in over thirty-five countries in the world cost 250 times less than in the U.S.! Two hundred and fifty times! That's a fact. You can look it up." I lick my lips, "Your husband is part of the biggest Ponzi scheme that's ever existed, and you couldn't care less as long as your shopping sprees aren't interrupted and the endless sea of Amagog boxes piling up at your front door arrive in two days. You're a cliché."

"Shut up!"

"You think you're helping animals by not eating them? What do you think you're doing to their habitats shopping online? Where do you think all that cardboard comes from? It'd be ironic if it weren't so sad."

Blistering, she looks to Chatura for backup, but Chatura ignores her, quietly picking up Holly's coat and bag from the floor and placing them on the kitchen counter.

Cornered like an animal, Holly glares, her eyes dilating wildly, "I'm warning you, Stephanie." Pointing an irate finger, she yells, "You're just belittling people who are really making a difference!" Moving aggressively towards me, she adds, "You think you're making the world a better place by opening legal drug stores on every corner? Near schools? Normalizing drug addiction? You're the one that's delusional! You need to be stopped!"

That's what I'm looking for. "For the record," I reproach, "there already are drug stores on every corner and with the help of doctors like your husband, over ten million Americans a year are now hooked on opioids. Your sacred doctors murder more than 128 people a day! Every day! These people aren't old and dying, Holly. They're healthy, twenty-five to fifty-year-olds with families and lives! The fall of the American Empire is on your family's head!"

Chatura's eyebrows peak as Holly plots her next move, self-consciously panting.

"You claim to be a vegetarian to stop animal suffering?" I hammer the last nail, "What about human suffering? What about all those people whose lives have been decimated for a golf club membership and a condo on the ski mountain? Shame on you! I don't know how you can live with yourself." I take a sip then add, "Maybe you can't? Maybe that's why you're always checked out? Maybe you took all that anxiety out on Gabriella because she fed you bugs."

Part One

1

What's inside?

Walking into the PTA meeting, I know there could be hiccups. Number one, I'm not a parent and number two, I sell weed. I'm a glamping version of the corner drug dealer for sure. I'm not handing out dime bags or selling to minors, and considering it costs a minimum of over a million dollars to start up in the cannabis industry these days, *it's glamping on steroids.*

OK, Steph, let's find a seat somewhere. Wow! It's all women. From grandparents to barely twenty-somethings, the age span is incredible, and I'm stunned at the attendance, until I remember the school has 1800 students. Amidst an array of hairstyles, yoga pants, sweat shirts, pantsuits, and power heels, *I hope we all have something in common.* Working the most unassuming resting face I possess; I write my name on a tag like a stranger in a strange land and soldier on through a sea of neatly lined chairs smoldering in battleship gray. Quietly commandeering a vacant seat, I place my bag underneath me in an attempt to fit in. The cavernous, quasi- modern gymnasium is as cold as it is bland, fluorescent lights hovering above, wildly humming. *I'm glad I threw my puffer jacket on over my turtle neck.*

At six o'clock precisely, Mrs. Cox, the principal, a portly, no-nonsense woman in a tan pantsuit, steps up to the podium centered among thirty or so parents. The energy of the room momentarily abates, "Hello, everyone, and thank you for making this meeting tonight. As you know, the PTA organizes and funds all of the extra-curricular activities for the school as well as language, music, and arts programs. Without your help, we would be lost, so please give yourselves a round of applause."

The gym erupts around me. *They must raise some serious cash.* I clap like everyone else, then the minutes from the last meeting are read by the secretary, a timid woman in her thirties with gallerist glasses. After she steps down, there's a long pause.

"Gabby, we're ready for you," the principal appends into the microphone, looking around.

Gabby Menckawitz, the President of the PTA, is a terrifyingly large woman with a booming voice. This is only my second meeting, but I can tell her heart is all in. A hush overcomes the room waiting for her to take her place at the podium.

"Gabby?" She repeats, confused.

Fleeting footsteps rush forward in the form of a svelte, casually dressed gal with a power ponytail who covers the mic and whispers in Cox's ear.

"Oh, my goodness!" Cox responds, her voice shrill, in shocked disbelief. "Are you sure?"

The woman nods then whispers something else I can't make out, but it's not pleasant; that much I know.

"Ladies, I don't know what to say. It seems there's been an unfortunate accident. Gabby is dead."

"Dead?" The gal sitting several chairs over to my right repeats as Cox fights for composure, the air around us a murmuring swarm.

"I'm sorry," she continues, "but we're going to have to postpone our meeting. Thank you for your understanding. We will post a new date and time later this week." Clearly rattled, she clads off in hairdresser clogs, avoiding all interaction.

I turn to my neighbor, not knowing what to do. "Wow, that's crazy. The poor woman," I offer.

"Well, she wasn't poor," she looks over, "but it is shocking. I wonder what happened?" Respectfully silent for a moment, she then reaches out her petite, manicured hand, "I'm Chatura." The no more than thirty-two-year-old in yoga pants and a beautifully handwoven, ice blue wool coat that sets off matching crystal-clear eyes, offers delicately.

She's a knockout. Even without makeup, and her blonde, streaked hair is in a flawless chignon. *I suddenly feel under dressed.* "Lovely name."

"Thank you; it means…."

"Wisdom?" I venture.

"Yes." She smiles radiantly.

"I'm Stephanie, Stephanie Beroe. Nice to meet you."

"Nice to meet you too. Is this your first meeting?" Her demeanor is genuinely poised, a perfect match to her diminutive figure that might have been slightly augmented. *But who cares? I would kill for her waistline.*

"No, it's not my first," I respond honestly while kaos erupts around us. "But I am new to all of this. Does it show?"

"Not at all. What grade is your child in?"

"Our niece is in the sixth grade. She started here last month," I reply raising my voice over the screech of folding chairs being hurriedly whisked away and stacked at the door.

"How wonderful. My eldest daughter Satara is in the sixth grade. Maybe they know one another." She moves gracefully over to the chair next to me. The echo of mom shoes fills the air distractedly, as she continues, "My youngest is in kindergarten, and Tamira is in the second grade. Do you live near the school? I find the problem with charter schools is the kids come from everywhere, so there's no real community. Everyone is always in such a hurry to get home after pick up."

I never thought about that. "We live in the village."

"Really? We're up on Goldmine Road."

"We look on to Goldmine Road. Small world."

"Or divine intervention." She smiles perfectly straight, white teeth. "It's nice to meet you, neighbor. We should get together," she proposes, waving to several women behind me.

"That would be great."

"Here's my card," she hands me a luxurious linen card with an embossed lotus through the words "Ayer Vedic Life Specialist."

It all makes sense. "Thanks. This is my cell." I hand her mine and wait for it.

"Cannabis and CBD? This is synchronistic."

"I was thinking you'd appreciate the ingredients in our products."

"You have no idea." Grabbing her things, we walk towards the steel gym doors as another gal approaches.

"Hi, Chatura." The well-dressed, forty-year-old almost whimpers.

"Hi, Holly. You look great. I love that dress." Noticing the woman's distress, she asks, "Are you OK? That's terrible news about Gabby."

"It's horrible news." Tears collecting in her large, doe eyes, every aspect of her Asian features are perfectly in balance if not discomposed. She's impeccably dressed in a slim Ann Taylor dress with a wool, neutral Burberry overcoat and Louboutin boots. *Definitely a professional.*

"This is Stephanie."

She nods, "I can't believe this. An accident?" Reaching in her bag for a tissue, she falls apart. "I should go." Shuddering, her shoulders convulse as the remaining attendees throng out to the parking lot.

"Are you OK to drive?" I ask, worried she might fall down.

"I just don't want to cause a scene," she says, bracing herself on a rubber trash can.

"Don't be silly. You're not causing a scene." I place my hand on her arm. "Hey, would either of you like to join me at the pizza place down the road? We could sit for a moment."

"Sure," Chatura responds.

"OK."

Gathering Holly up, we place her in Chatura's white Tesla before they follow me to the pizza place. Bracing the cold, we're in luck. The table in front of the rock fireplace is open and makes having to watch a hockey game worth it. On a Monday night, the restaurant is empty. Rust and gray colored stone walls close in, insinuating an abandoned previous life. Shedding my winter coat, I'm acutely aware of its synthetic sound, suddenly feeling a bit out of touch while both women are so elegantly showcased in hand-woven garments in this natural setting.

"Hey, Stephanie, nice to see you again. A glass of pinot grigio. Right?" The young waiter my husband Remy and I tip well asks, pulling out my chair.

"Thanks, Perry. That would be great."

"Ladies, what can I get for you?" His tall, chiseled, millennial- mountain man charisma entices through a frieze of facial hair that's endearing, if not colloquial.

"I love pinot grigio. I'll have a glass," Chatura responds, unknowingly captivating.

"Sure," Holly also acquiesces, searching in her bag unsuccessfully.

"Stephanie has a niece in the sixth grade too, Holly."

Perking up, Holly mops her eyes with her napkin, "Maybe you know my Seraphine?"

"What a lovely name. I'm familiar with the male version Seraphin or fiery ones, and I know a Seraph is an angel of light and purity. What does Seraphine mean?"

"I have no idea. I named her after the brand. I thought it was pretty."

"What brand?"

"The holistic maternity line," Chatura explains. "Are you a teacher?"

"No, I study the classics and have a penchant for ancient languages and mythology." Both ladies raise their brows. Thankfully, drinks arrive in the nick of time. "Would either of you like to split something? I don't like to drink on an empty stomach."

They both jerk their heads back before answering, "Sure," in unison.

Handing them menus, I ask, "What looks good?"

"I don't eat animal products. I'm a plant-based vegan," Chatura states, clearly affirming herself in her seat.

"Well, pizza probably wasn't the best idea. Sorry," I cringe, as Perry stands by at the ready.

"It's fine. I'll have the chopped salad, no meat, no cheese, no egg, no croutons, and no dressing. Do you have any peanuts at the bar?" she asks. "My herbalist recommends I consume a minimum of a hundred grams of protein a day."

"Sure, I can get you some peanuts." Nodding, he looks to Holly.

"I'm a vegetarian. So, I'll have the Caesar salad with anchovies; I do eat fish," she explains to the table, "but no croutons. I'm gluten free, and no eggs in the dressing. I'm allergic."

"The dressings aren't house made, so I can't remove the eggs. Can I bring you a balsamic dressing?"

"Fine. Just put the anchovies on top."

"The anchovies are also in the dressing."

Disappointed, she places her napkin on her lap, visually bracing herself as Perry looks to me for relief.

"I'll have the Margherita pizza, please." *I'm feeling guilty about the cheese, but it's too darn cold out for a salad.* He totters off, and an uncomfortable silence ensues. Hoping to manage it, I offer, "Where do you live, Holly?"

"Santa Fe."

"How long have you both lived in New Mexico?

"We moved out here almost two years ago after my divorce; we were in Austin. That's where my girls were born," Chatura offers.

"Are you from Texas? You don't have an accent."

"Well, Austin isn't Texas." She laughs. "But you'll hear it, after this wine!" Picking up her glass, she takes a sip with a wink.

I smile, "That's how I am too. I grew up in New Jersey."

"Really! I would have never guessed. That *Jersey Shore* show was over the top. You don't fit the bill at all." She pauses, "That's a good thing!"

"Yeah, well. I escaped. How about you, Holly?" I ask in between sips.

"Oh. We relocated after my husband Nate finished his internship in New York. He's a surgeon. We moved to Santa Fe from the South to escape the HMOs; it was insane," she responds, clearly pained while I mull over her response.

Raising a glass, Chatura states soberly, "To Gabby."

"To Gabby." Holly and I state in unison, clinking our glasses.

There's a pause while Holly collects herself, then Chatura picks up the conversation, "So, does your niece live with you full time?"

"No. My husband Remy's sister is an archeologist. She and her daughter have lived all over the world. In December she was offered a job in Iraq. Usually, she would bring Imogene with her, but it's so unstable there right now, it just wasn't safe."

"Iraq‽" Holly blurts out. "Why would anyone go to Iraq on purpose?" Shock clearly written all over her face, she snatches a handful of peanuts from the bowl Perry just deposited in front of Chatura.

"Esme´ is in Iraq in an attempt to save magical manuscripts that are in danger due to the region's instability. They date back seven hundred years before Christ," I say to hoisted brows. "Imogene will be with us for seven more months," I add.

There's another silence before Chatura concurs, "Well, someone needs to care for our past."

"Yes, exactly. And in the meantime, we get to be a real part of Imogene's life. It's awesome."

"That's lovely." Draining her glass, Chatura looks around for Perry.

"I confess," the wine loosening me up, "I'm a newbie to all of this parenting. Except for our German Shepherd, Soter, I've had no experience with kids. In fact, I've never even babysat before." Laughing nervously, I continue,

"When Esme´ couldn't take Imogene safely with her into the desert, we volunteered. It's only nine months. What could go wrong?"

A hunger driven silence isn't uncomfortable, but it isn't comfortable either before our food arrives. *People with kids are so sure of themselves. I guess twenty-four hour a day exposure will do that.* The reality that Remy and I won't ever have children, rushes through my subconscious, silently filling my eyes. Lowering my head, I pretend to wipe my mouth, drying the tears. *This topic is a no go. Not even Remy and I discuss it.*

"Sounds like she's an interesting little girl." Chatura smiles warmly looking for our waiter who has completely disappeared.

"She is. She's a precocious eleven-year-old. Sweet, smart, eager to make new friends." Imogene's, Beroe hazel eyes come to mind, changing with her mood and the clothes she wears, just like her uncle's, that offset her light brown, Cleopatra style tresses. *I can tell that the come in your favorite t-shirt and sweatpants ala' Americaine has brushed off sadly, and perhaps even squashed her once unique costuming style we had grown to love via social media. She is such a light.* "I'm constantly reminding myself she's not a grown-up. She's learned languages and customs most Americans don't even know exist. For an eleven-year-old she has a keen sense of independence and maturity that cannot be cultivated, but she's still very much a little girl." Suddenly, I realize, I'm bragging and stop myself, before throwing in, "I was afraid she would find our old house in New Mexico provincial; but she's taken to the solitude and grown to love the vulnerable nature that defines this magical place. It's not for everyone."

"That's for sure," Chatura adds. "I remember telling my ex, before we divorced, that I wanted to move up here. He told me I was crazy!" She laughs comfortably through her second glass of wine. "I will never forget the look on his face when I showed him the land I wanted to buy. He said, 'There's nothing but dirt here!' And he's from Texas!" She shakes her head. "When did your niece start school?"

"Imogene arrived in January. We enrolled her at the charter school just after winter break, and I joined the PTA. Resisting the urge to tell them how nerve-wracked we've been about a school shooting; I take a breath. *I don't want to appear as if I'm judging them as parents by admitting my own weakness, but we're throwing our children to the wolves! I've lost Holly; her stare is definitely other worldly; poor thing.* To keeping the ball rolling, I add, "We've only lived in New Mexico for a little over a year ourselves. We know a couple of people, but no one with kids. It's funny how we clump into friend groups."

Chatura gives me a smile.

"Anyway, there was no one to ask about all of this. I find myself talking to moms at the grocery store." They both smile, silently pushing their salads around on their plates. "We're doing a lot of things with Imogene we wouldn't have done without her, like skiing." *Why I'm talking so much?*

Just as I think Holly's gone for good, she refocuses, "We ski."

Chatura and I wait for her to embellish her statement in vain.

"What a hoot! Right?" I add coaxingly.

"I have been wanting to get the girls up the mountain for ski lessons. But I just don't have the time with my vlog schedule on the weekends, and the holidays were beyond crazy for me. I just couldn't do it," Chatura confesses.

"Well, I hadn't skied since I was sixteen. I don't even want to think about how long ago that was."

They both laugh.

"But it was like riding a bike, and it's so peaceful up there on the mountain. We've had a blast. Now we find ourselves looking for special events, like the father and daughter Valentine's Day Dance."

"Oh. Nate and Seraphine went to that dance." Holly perks up. "I had to shop online for her dress. There was nothing in these small stores around here. But you know if you can't find it? Go to Bergdorf's online." She interjects with what can only be described as hindered enthusiasm before she's entranced by her salad again. Chatura dismisses her indifferent behavior with a smile, but I find myself thinking back, knowing Imogene's never met her father. When she asked Remy to take her to the dance, it meant the world to him. *I still see her in that beautiful violet, full-length gown with a sequin neckline she picked out with stars in her eyes, and Remy in his shark-skinned suit with a matching tie and hanky. It melted my heart.*

"Stephanie is in the cannabis industry," Chatura interposes.

The hair on my neck stands up.

Holly, clearly unsure of how to respond, squeaks, "Oh?"

Another uncomfortable silence ensues, a déjà vu, reminding me of when Remy and I started out in the cannabis industry in 2007, way before all the hoopla. We would never tell anyone what we did for a living. Most of us had very real concerns about the DEA breaking through our windows at night. *We've come a long way; in fact, now, some civilians consider it a glamorous occupation, oddly enough. If they only knew. Selling cannabis beverages has been an honest-to-goodness trial of wits and stamina with my husband abducted and shot at, me being kidnapped, corporate sabotage, and a long list of catastrophic events in the past two years alone that almost drove Remy beyond the point of no return. But I'm not going to tell them that. They wouldn't believe me if I did.* "Oh, yes," I respond, thinking about all of the conversations we've had about getting out altogether.

"And you manufacture CBD products as well?" Chatura's ardor is honest and inviting. Not the usual response in a world of tailored taboo.

"Yes. Yes, we do. We specialize in beverages."

"How interesting. We need to talk more about this. I'm a Momtrepreneur! I have a vlog. I'm a branded broadcaster! I have almost eleven thousand followers," she proclaims, pausing, allowing me to soak up her enthusiasm.

It all makes sense. The clothes, her hair, the makeup; everything is perfect. "Wow, I'm impressed."

"What I really want to do," she continues, "is create a line of sumptuous CBD skincare products."

"They sure are trending right now. It's one of the only CBD products that big box stores will allow regardless of the farm bill that protects hemp in this country. Edibles are another story. We're grass roots-ing our products at farmers' markets and small retail shops in the meantime." I smile, noticing the miserable look on Holly's face while she tortures a tomato on her plate.

"I'm so glad we met. Can I call you this week? I'd love to talk with you more about my ideas." Chatura's eyes so clear and bright are glowing from across the table.

"Sure. Anytime," I respond.

"So, why the charter school and not the academy?" Holly, oddly alert, changes the subject.

"Well, it seemed like a better fit for Imogene. She's academic but not regimented. She's done a lot of home-schooling while traveling with her mother, but most of the work has been project based. The academy was a little too formal."

They both nod, then Holly raises an eyebrow, "And what does the school think about your business?"

Adjusting myself in my seat, I take a moment to assess Holly's intentions, but she seems purely inquisitive before I respond, "I must admit enrolling her in school wasn't as easy as I thought it would be. Medical marijuana is legal in New

Mexico with a prescription and recreational marijuana is on the ballot, but school drug policies and social service interventions still tell a very different side to our story. Cannabis is still very much a taboo as far as schools are concerned and that is understandable."

Holly laughs, then catches herself as Chatura pushes her plate aside nodding her head, checking her phone for notifications.

"Remy and I thought this through and decided to meet it head-on. So, we met with the principal, vice principal, and all of Imogene's prospective teachers to nip it in the bud. No pun intended." *That goes over their heads.* I slide the rest of my pizza into a to go box. "Anyway, we brought our contracts and licenses in to prove we work within the legal confines of the cannabis industry here in New Mexico and half a dozen other states, before we proceeded to inform the entire administrative staff that our niece, as an eleven-year-old, may tell other students what we do, and that she may talk about cannabis."

Holly nods sardonically, picking up her purse, rummaging through it like she has a point to make. Both Chatura and I wait for it. Then she pulls out her lipstick.

With a disapproving glance towards her friend, Chatura intercedes, "That's crazy Stephanie. How humiliating."

"Yeah, well, we pleaded our case to a room, informing them that Imogene perceives marijuana as a healing plant without stigma attached, and that she might counter misinformation about its uses. It was a lot."

"What did they say?"

"No one at the meeting objected to anything we said, but there was a definite shift in the room. I'm still hoping our transparency hasn't made her a target."

"Ladies, is there anything else I can get you?" Our waiter appears, briefly, depositing our check. "Here's your bill. No rush." He turns away, distracted by his phone, furiously typing with his thumbs.

"Here's your hat. What's your hurry?" I joke as the restaurant is absolutely dead, reaching for the check.

"No, no. This one's on me." Chatura extracts the check from my hand.

"Are you sure?"

"Yes. Absolutely."

"Thank you. Hey, why don't you both come over this weekend with your girls? Imogene could really use some girl time."

"An impromptu playdate?" Chatura's eyes light up.

I look to Holly slowly suffocating in the faux pashmina scarf she's hiding behind, "We may be at our condo skiing in Colorado," she croaks, "I don't ski, but Nate and Seraphine do." She states more clearly, tucking a stray highlight with a perfectly French manicured hand, her wedding ring dazzling.

"Oh, darn it!" Chatura looks up from her phone. "My stream schedule is out of control this weekend. How about the following weekend?"

Holly shakes her head no.

"Come on, Holly, you need a ladies' day, and you know it," Chatura coaxes.

"If we're not skiing," she adds, indifference liberally punctuating her reply.

"Great! We'll talk soon." I stand up. We all pull on our coats. *Some louder than others.* "I wish the circumstances could have been different, but it was really nice to meet you both." Grabbing my to-go box and my purse, I head out. *Who knew having kids made it so easy to make friends?*

Dancing in the moonlight

Soter, sitting sentinel in our driveway as I pull up, playfully pounces in front of my car. Leading me in, his thick winter coat makes him look twice his size, and he's already a large German Shepherd. "Hey, boy." Giving him a good scratch behind the ears, he licks my legginged calves before directing me towards the bedlam coming from the opposite side of the house that's obviously, the bane of his existence.

At 7:30, it's pitch dark and eighteen degrees in February, but that's not stopping Remy and Imogene. With their cell phones bungeed to the trampoline net, strobing blue light, King Harvest is playing just a little louder than their shrieks of joy as they bounce counterclockwise like whirling dervishes around the tramp. Smile on my face, watching covertly from the patio outside our back door, the milky way entreating me. *Life is good.* I savor this moment and this feeling of happiness because I know, *the other shoe usually does drop.*

Imogene's giggles are truly contagious while Remy bounces her repeatedly up and down a couple of dozen times. Once they collapse from exhaustion, I yell, "Hey, anyone want a piece of pizza?"

"Yes! Pizza!" Imogene climbs over Remy's back and up the hill in seconds.

I hand her a piece. She's in a red and black striped, short-sleeve shirt, a miniskirt with shorts underneath and red stockings. "Aren't you cold honey?"

"Nope. Yum. Thanks, Aunt Steph." She runs inside with Soter at her heels.

"Hey, sweetie." Ambling over, Remy plants a kiss on me, his long blonde hair in streaks against his broad shoulders as he adjusts the light blue ski cap his eyes are competing with.

"You two are crazy!"

"She needed to blow off steam. She's having a hard time with a kid at school. Damn, you're right. It is cold!" He shivers.

"Is she OK?"

"Yeah. She's OK. You might want to talk to her about it, though. I think it may be more of a girl thing."

"All right, I will."

He gives me another kiss and whispers, "Do you remember waking up in Costa Rica and having to look for our warmest swimsuits?"

"Ha!" I laugh, knowing he's not kidding.

Opening the pizza box and the back door simultaneously, he asks, "Since when do you eat Margherita pizza?"

"Oh, I went out for drinks with two moms from the meeting who have kids in the sixth grade. One is a vegetarian of sorts and the other is vegan."

"A vegan at a pizza place? That's interesting. How was the meeting?" He asks through raised brows and a full mouth.

"Talk about crazy. The meeting was canceled. The president of the PTA is dead! And the principal didn't know it until after she introduced her!"

"Awkward."

"You think?" I unzip my coat and noisily throw it on the kitchen chair with determined abandon. "Anyway, I met two interesting ladies. One is a Momtrepreneur."

He stops in his tracks. "A what?"

"Yeah, I didn't know that was a thing either. It's like a whole different language." Following him into the warm glow of our kitchen, I continue, "The other mom, Holly, was really upset about the PTA president; they must have been close. She was noticeably quiet but seemed nice. I invited them both over with their girls next weekend for a playdate."

Remy nods, placing the pizza box on the enamel kitchen table. "I hope one of them isn't named Seraphine."

Oh, shit.

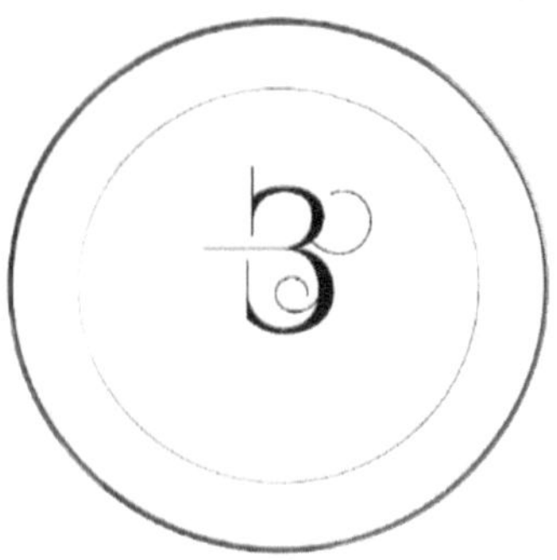

Accentuate the positive

Waking up to unpredicted snow, I'm naturally drawn to the opportunity of first tracks down our country road. Opening Imogene's bedroom door quietly, coaxing Soter out with a jangle from the leash, I then slip on my boots, coat, GPS locator hat, gloves, and fist mace. *I'm ready.*

Our previous exploits with billionaire-sociopaths, taught us to always be prepared. Now, I always carry a variety of self-defense items on me and have become alarmingly proficient at Hapkido. The locator pin on my hat is one of many safety gifts I receive from my husband every year. *Initially I balked at the idea, but they've come in quite handy.*

The sun, nowhere near the edge of the hills to the east of our house yet, rigidly reminds my body of the almost single-digit temperature. My breath is a mysterious fog, but Soter, wholly unaffected, is ready to go. His beautiful black and tan coat, and dark eyes are a stark contrast to our blanketed surroundings. The slope of his back and his gait maneuver through four inches of perfect powder without care as he leads the way through the untouched and pristine snow-covered road.

It's so peaceful. My mind completely still. *This is a rare moment indeed.* What our new, little village lacks on Saturday and midweek, weed whackers compared to our townhouse in California, it more than makes up for in coyote howls and owl songs. *This is not the suburbs.* No sirens or planes or neighbor's cars revving; or neighbors for that matter. It's quiet, except for a bird or the wind between the trees and my own thoughts. *It would unnerve most people. But for us, it's the perfect abandonment.*

Heading up to the state park behind our house, there is no differentiation between the hiking path and its rock border; everything blanketed in white, is one large plain. But Soter knows the way, and after the second mile, we've got a groove on. *I don't know what it is about the snow that makes me feel playful. I guess it just reinforces the presence of magic in the world, something I rarely have time to look for anymore, purifying everything, if only for a brief moment. It's a gift in a world full of spreadsheets and conference calls that I wish I could make disappear.*

The last six months we have been mired in our new business plan, deck, and financials; I have been creating for our first round of expansion-fundraising. *It's been a learning curve. And even though I'm more than familiar with preparing taxes and creating budgets for projects, these algorithms for future projections are absolutely, ludicrous. Seriously, how does anyone in the cannabis industry project sales five years from now, honestly? Anything can happen and usually does. It's mind-blowing that the cornerstone of corporate economics is based on a math formula and a positive attitude! Even with the slog of Fast Book tutorials and business vlogs I've been binge watching to get a handle on this, I'm still at a loss. When you boil it down, it just seems like lying.*

The prospect of not handling new contracts and partnership agreements correctly, is defining the additional and apparent stress in our daily life and at the end of the day, taking on partners is absolutely frightening. *I cannot fuck this up. Thanks to Bank of Americans tagging our social security numbers as high risk, we're considered financial non- grata due to our industry. So, the reality of paying over a million dollars for a short-term, $500,000 loan has become a stark reality.* Even with the steady stream of associates of associates of associates introducing us to armies of investors and financial brokers that are eager to be in the cannabis industry. The momentum stalls at almost exactly the same point each time during the pitch. Because at the end of the day, no one wants to take on any risk. *Oxymoron anyone? Or maybe it's just me?*

Like a twisted, matchmaking game show, we meet via Schloom because they inevitably live in New York, California, or Arizona. Remy and I repeat the exact same pitch we pitched to their broker and sent over by PowerPoint the week before. Then like clockwork, they ask me to break some figures down so they can "better understand it," or my favorite request, 'create a new P and L so we can read it better, and we'll get back to you.' *Whatever that means.* In the meantime, their desire to press upon us how financially voracious their careers have been is unrestrained. Usually, a retired CEO of some kind, always from the financial industry or a descendant from a long line of financial gurus, they ironically, value a spreadsheet, *my nemesis,* precisely the same way I admire a sunset, a beach, or a meticulously crafted song. It's mind-blowing! We have nothing in common, and although that may be necessary as they have something we don't, the notion of being swept into an ocean of debt is not necessarily our long-term goal. *We are walking a tightrope, but if we don't expand… we'll lose everything.*

Our present talks focus on three brokers and five different groups of investors for the same loan and although the financials are identical, they must be tailored for their different perspectives. Hoping to put an end to all of this next Thursday, with an in-person follow-up pitch to the main group of investors that our friend Burgess introduced us to, keeps me going. *I need to remember to check on the conference space I rented in town for the meeting after they tour our New Mexico, cannabis licensee's, manufacturing facility, as neither of us are comfortable meeting them at our home-office. I love Burgess, he's the real deal, his heart is always in the right place, but my muse is feeling a little trodden upon the corporate politics his networking has exposed us to. Or maybe it's just the reality of how thuggish capitalism really is?*

Running over my schedule, I'll be shackled to my desk after I drop Imogene off at school. *Not a happy prospect, but at least we have prospects.*

On my return, Remy is up and guarding the coffee pot. With a sleepy kiss, I head to the shower as Soter waits at his feet for his morning treat. Walking through the drafty back hall into the bathroom, I'm eerily aware of the door at the top of the stairs that leads to our offices, *like it's watching me, or maybe I should be watching it?* On the floor in front of me, there's something black. *What is that?* Bending over, I scoop up a baby cricket with one hand, she tickles my fingers climbing around, looking for god knows what in the dead of winter. Placing her in the geranium in our bathroom window, *I hope she's a good omen.*

The hot water is a welcome cleanse. I enjoy every ounce of moisture our newly black and white, honey combed, tiled bathroom collects in this arid desert, mindful of my water usage. Toweling off, glancing in the mirror, my long, dark hair clinging to my head and back, I take a minute to pluck a couple of embarrassing hairs on my chin through a fogged mirror. *They seem to get longer and longer in shorter intervals.* My brown eyes dark as ever, have never been as clear as Chatura's, *it must be a Mediterranean thing. I'll chalk it up to my Greek heritage.* But my eyes tell a story for someone looking. Life has been a challenge. Losing my grandparents and parents early, living life on my own, dealing with stepfathers, surviving the music industry and now the cannabis industry, not to mention H.S. and all his mayhem. Remy and I know that living outside our comfort zone has become the new norm. *Watching civilians go about their daily business un-impinged, is like gazing through an impenetrable looking glass. A completely different reality, and while we're clamoring around at Defcon three with new regulations and legislation threatening our livelihood on a daily basis, I'm always a step behind. Desperately trying to stay one step ahead. The ad nauseam banking fiascos, ill-willed licensee relationships, and absurd, biased, cannabis legislation vibrating at hyper-speed is getting old.*

Meanwhile, everything is so peaceful on the other side, it always seems like I'm working ten times harder for a quarter of the stability everyone else has around me. Maybe it's time to ask some sobering questions?

Slathering obscene amounts of coconut moisturizer on, it's hard not to notice, *things are shifting.* I still look good, but my classic more than thirty-year-old figure is a little more hourglass than my summer memories suggest. *Less comfort food really isn't an option in the winter.* With a sigh, turning sideways before wrapping up in a towel, the stress of living on the edge is showing. *Living by the beach in California made working out a hell of a lot easier.* Preparing for the chill of the hallway, I trot through the house, purposefully avoiding my phone until a reasonable hour. Picking out something warm, cozy, *and loose*, I'm hoping to offset the looming spreadsheets with whatever crutches I can employ, dressing on autopilot.

Once I'm in the kitchen, I place four strips of bacon in a cast iron pan with a sizzle, then slather mayo on two slices of homemade bread to toast on the griddle of our 1940's Wedge Wood stove. I feel comfort in my new element, *this stove is an inspiration*; it demands you pay attention to it, power it up, experiment, splatter it, clean it, *and I am a willing devotee.* I keep a dozen cookbooks in the bathroom and subscribe to cooking shows and websites that literally excite me. Cooking for Remy and Imogene is always a pleasure; they both love food, and the togetherness preparing a good meal creates, is what life's all about. *This is where I come to manifest happiness.*

Unlike the rest of our house, the kitchen has been meticulously renovated with beautifully leaded glass cabinetry by local woodworkers, fresh bright watermelon colored paint, a cheery yellow ceiling and its racy, red, linoleum floors. A pendant, school lamp from the 1940's, hangs from a Model T, Ford hubcap, ceiling medallion over the white and blue enamel kitchen table I use to make bread on. It's a delight to be in here, especially in the morning with the sunlight casting fresh hope on the hills around us. But this is the only room that has been touched. So, we've spent the last year slowly taking on new electrical, plumbing, and flooring. It's been a labor of love that our eclectic tastes for antiques and found objects was designed for. The house has lovely bones. Built in 1884, it is a Victorian, adobe hybrid. She stands proudly against the small hills behind us, and the views are astounding.

"Good morning, Aunt Steph."

"Good morning, sweetheart." Imogene is dressed, but clearly not happy. "Did you sleep well?"

"Yeah." She shrugs.

Handing her a glass of milk, I broach the subject. "I heard you had a tough day yesterday."

"Yeah."

The sigh says it all. "So, what's up, buttercup?" I ask, slicing an avocado.

"I don't know, Aunt Steph.

"You don't know what?" I say, placing her plate of bacon and avocado toast down, before sitting across the kitchen table from her.

"I don't know. Why nobody likes me," she cries.

Moving quickly to her side, I offer "Oh honey, that's not true." Wrapping my arms around her.

She sighs, nodding her head, with a heave.

My mind racing for a remedy, draws a blank. *How do I help her?* "I don't believe that."

She looks up her eyes swimming with tears, "Maybe one."

"Of course. See?" I say, catching her face in my hands, wiping her eyes. "Listen, most of these kids have been in this school together since they were four. Give it a little time. We've lived here a year, and Uncle Remy and I only have one other couple we really jive with," I say stroking her hair gently, "It just takes time."

She nods full of discouragement, "I just always feel like I'm the freak in the room." Wiping her tears, she draws in a deep with rattling breath. "That's what they call me at school."

"Imogene, honey. You are not a freak," I say, holding her close. "You are amazing! You're kind and funny and smart."

"You think so?" She looks up at me.

"I know so. Amazing! These kids just need to get to know you. Now, name one thing you *like* about school?" I ask, hoping she can.

There's a long pause, before she claims, "I like the library."

"OK, that's great! Sometimes focusing on the positive makes the negative not so bad. You know what I mean?"

"Yeah. But we're never in there. I like to read during recess, but the lunch monitor is always yelling at me to play some stupid game I don't want to play. And no one picks me for the teams because I don't know how to play them." Her body shudders.

"Do you want to play the games?

"No."

"Is it mandatory for you to play a sport at recess?"

"No."

"Then why is she telling you what to do?"

"I don't know." Exasperated, she wipes her eyes on her sleeve.

"I'll talk with the school about that today. But you know, playing games is a great way to meet people."

She shrugs, her shoulders tight and anxious.

"Sweetie, listen to me. You are a remarkable young lady. You brighten everyone's day. I am so proud of you for starting over and embracing all this change. My money's on you, kid!" I tag her nose playfully.

"Thanks."

"You gonna make it?"

"Yeah." Readjusting herself on her chair, she absentmindedly disassembles her bacon from the stack in front of her. "What type of shoes do kidnappers wear?" *Her Beroe resistance comes through in humor.*

I immediately visualize polished men's loafers but know that's not correct, "Um, I don't know."

"White vans."

"Ha!" I'll have to remember that. *God knows it might come in handy one day.* "We've got ten minutes till it's time to brush teeth. Can you pull it together?" I give her another hug and a kiss.

"Yeah."

Walking into our bedroom for a warmer pair of socks, I see Remy leaning against our bed, phone in hand, texting furiously.

"Everything all right?" I ask.

"I just spent the last two and a half hours on the phone with these guys, and it's barely eight o'clock in the morning. They're telling me their fucking life story! I know more about their ex-wives, drug addictions, and spiritual annals than they're analysts."

"Wow, all they ask me for are spreadsheets."

"You're lucky." He smiles, happy for a distraction from the investor group. "How's our girl?"

"I think it's the new kid on the block syndrome. She's used to one-on-one attention. A classroom must be quite a shift. Plus, she's so much more mature and traveled. Most of these kids have never left the state, and she's lived all over the world. I think it's making her stand out, but maybe not in a good way."

"Did you tell her about your *playdate*?" He raises his eyebrows.

"No. But I will."

"Good luck with that." He pats my butt and walks out texting.

Turning onto Hwy 14 on the way to school, I take a deep breath, "I met a couple of moms at the PTA meeting last night," I say, checking Imogene in the rearview mirror before continuing, "Do you know Satara?"

"Yeah, I know her. She's not in my class, but I know her."

"Would you be comfortable if she came over with her mom next weekend?"

Her eyes rapidly scan across the back seat as she silently deliberates. "Yeah. Yeah, that would be OK."

One down. "I also met Seraphine's mom, and I unknowingly invited her over too." I cringe in the mirror, so she sees how mortified I am.

Silence and a rigid mouth are her only response.

"I would have never invited her over if I knew she was causing you problems. Believe me, I can cancel," I confess.

More silence. *Just like her uncle.* Two songs later, she's ready, "I've been thinking."

I turn down the radio.

"The longest I've ever lived anywhere, is two years. So, just when I'm making friends, I'm leaving. It's always just momma and me." Looking out the window, she looks so lonely it breaks my heart.

"It's OK about Seraphine. I can handle her. Besides, I think she's only like that when no one else is around. On my turf, it shouldn't be a problem."

"And if it is? She's out!" I say, shifting the car into park at the drop-off curb. I walk around and open the door for her. "I love you, sweetheart. You are an inspiration."

She wraps her arms around my waist and hugs me like she's never going to let go.

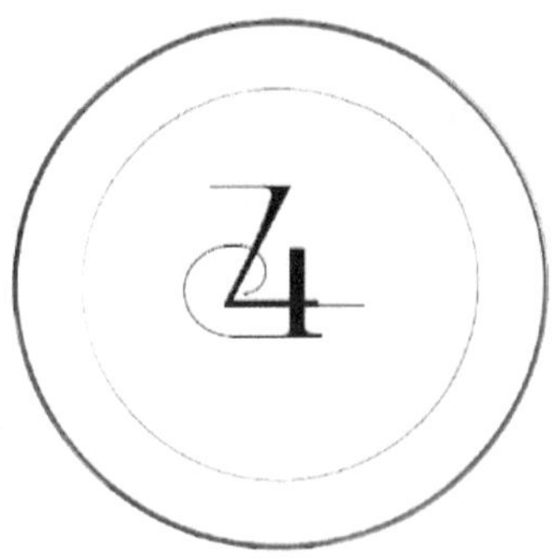

A taste of honey

Donning a hat, fingerless gloves, shearling boots, and a wool button-up sweater over Remy's Gap sweater I permanently borrowed. I'm ready for work upstairs in my office. The second floor's never been finished off or even insulated. *It's on our list.* There's a rumor in town that a man died in the bedroom I converted into my workspace, *which may account for the creepy feeling surrounding the stairwell. It feels full, like all the space in between has been filled, the air is thick and heavy, but not necessarily malignant. I'm hoping he likes what we're doing with the house and he'll behave.*

Only two large rooms up here were ever framed out, one facing east and the other west, with two, floor to ceiling windows on either side of chimneys opposite the door. They both have wide planked floors, they were lathed, and plastered but were never finished or even painted, so the plaster, brittle as bone, was falling off in clumps. It sounded like rats in the attic before we were brave enough to pull all that out and drywall when we converted them into our offices but the other two-thousand square feet up here is barely floored and un-insulated, so it's cold; see your breath cold.

Danielle, Remy's assistant, is interned in a small room between our opposing offices that sits directly over the front doors. It's insulated, but she doesn't have a wood stove, just a portable heater. Luckily for her, it faces south, collecting an incredible amount of passive solar gain through a wall of windows. *I think she's better off than both of us, actually.*

My space to the left, *always go left,* looks warm at least, with the eastern light. A mahogany sewing table I use as a desk and beautiful old wooden file cabinets glow in the overhead opaque, mid-century fixture we suspended from the twenty-foot pitched ceiling. *It's eclectic.* The 1940's, green and pink jungle fabric, black-out curtains I made set the mood with simple sheers diffusing the morning light silhouetting the mountain ridge that frames the sunrise. Like most days, the cloudless New Mexico sky will turn rich periwinkle as long shadows throw themselves onto the rolling hills sparsely covered with pygmy juniper and pine. The lack of neighbors on either side of us, is a welcome buffer to the clamorous cannabis world, and a wonderful sense of safety.

Remy started the woodstove for me today, so my office is almost warm. As I settle onto my yoga ball chair that needs inflating, I'm distracted by a conversation across the hall. *There's a little too much inflection going on in there.* I strain my hearing as I take the five steps over to Remy's office to confirm a serious problem. Poking my head in, the air is strife with tension. "Hey, what's up?" I sit on his stainless steel, 1950's doctor's desk that takes up most of the room, and watch him pace at a furious rate. *That's not a good sign.*

"These guys coming in next Thursday," he ejaculates, "for the last four months, have flat out stated they would be partnering with us. No loan, just equity! Right?" His agitation is combustible.

"OK." I relent.

"The outlines and prelims all state that!"

"Yes." I look to Danielle spontaneously but she's characteristically impossible to read.

"Well, ten minutes ago, Jimmy clearly stated he's submitting our financials with theirs for a twenty-million-dollar combined loan!"

"What? That doesn't make any sense. You mean these millionaire, financial geniuses don't have any money themselves?"

"Not that they're willing to part with, apparently."

"I'm not really interested in a twenty-million-dollar loan."

"Neither am I! And they don't make anything! Not a thing! They don't have a grow! They don't hold any THC licenses! Not one product! They're just piggybacking off us!"

A gruesome, familiar silence fills the room as I massage my forehead, "You'd better get the story straight before we meet with them on Thursday."

"Yup."

Turning to leave, Danielle, who has been pragmatically silent and motionless interjects, "Stephanie, a woman named Chatura called."

"Thanks, Danielle." My relationship with my husband's incredibly beautiful assistant is complicated. I admire her and like her as a person, *all six feet of her*, but last year, I put the brakes on a budding friendship when I thought they had been emotionally involved during Remy's abduction at the park. Honestly, I understood being placed in the unspeakable situation they faced together might have required human contact to maintain balance under the extreme duress they were subjected to. I could handle that. *Even as striking as she is with her golden eyes, and beautiful chocolate skin.* But what I couldn't handle was the thought that they continued to be romantically involved under our roof. *Nothing happened, of course. I was mistaken. But a wedge was driven, like a nightmare you believe so intensely, it leaves you with a hangover you can't shake. I'm just not ready.*

Running my finger tip over Chatura's embossed card, I pick up my phone and call her back on speaker.

"Hello?"

"Hey Chatura, it's Stephanie."

"Good morning. Thanks for calling me back."

"Sure."

"Who answered the phone before?"

"That was Danielle, my husband's assistant."

"I would love to have an assistant. I am so busy. My schedule is insane. Anyway, we are so looking forward to next weekend. What day works for you?"

"How about Saturday? We'll be skiing on Sunday."

"Skiing, what fun. I want to take the girls up there, but my posting schedule is slammed. Saturday is perfect, though. Is it a potluck? Should I bring something?"

"Bring whatever you like. It's been so cold; I was thinking I might make chili. Vegan of course."

"Sounds delish. I'll bring some healthy snacks. That reminds me. Did you receive the invitation to my vlog?

"I don't know. Did you send it by text? I haven't been online yet."

Scrambling quietly through my texts, I find the invite.

"I think you'll love it. Don't forget to subscribe. And I'd love to talk with you more about your CBD products. Do you have any time today?"

"Sure, if you don't mind watching me eat lunch."

"Not a problem. Just tell me when."

"Eleven-thirty-ish?"

"What's the address?"

I give her the address, smiling as we disconnect. *There's synergy here. It would be great to make a new friend, as lame as that sounds.*

My closest friend Laure, who seems like a war time assistant, has been hard to reach. She sends me honeymoon photos every couple of days or so from her husband Tyler's, family home in Cairo or from some exotic locale. I'm genuinely happy for her, even though Tyler is the son of our real-life arch-nemesis. It was a hard pill to swallow at first, but he's proven himself to be honorable. They're well suited. I think they'll be happy together. *But I miss her.* She is the sister I never had. The brutal reality is, I'm going to have to hire someone else to work with me, as I can't imagine Laure working for fifty-grand a year as a consultant while she's married to a billionaire. *The whole thing's depressing.* Shifting my focus to the financials in front of me, I plug in.

I hate spreadsheets! Three torturous hours later, that seem like three days, I've dissected this spreadsheet twenty different ways. *What is the point of these ridiculous projections?* The familiar pang of being out of my comfort level stings yet again! Looking at the clock, I'll have just enough time to watch Chatura's vlog and make a quick sandwich before she arrives. But first I need to shoot Imogene's principal a quick note about lunch time.

Dear Ms. Cox,

I hope you are well. It seems Imogene is having difficulty fitting in at school and presently her only safe place is reading in the library. She has been informed by the lunch monitor that she must play an activity, and reading is not allowed. Is this true? Is there any way she can have access to the library at lunch time? I know you are busy and appreciate all you do, thanks for your response on this.

Stephanie Beroe

Knocking that off the list I click the link to Chatura's channel. ***The Crazy Vegan Wife.*** Today's stream is titled; ***Figs – Not a Vegan Snack?***

The video opens with Chatura sitting in front of the camera in a comfortable, beige Indonesian chair. A wall of handblown-glass, teardrop planters with air ferns hanging from the ceiling behind her creating a beaded curtain affect. Her stunning crystal-clear blue eyes and flawless skin radiate health. She's wearing a dramatic, diagonally cut, one armed, gray sweater that highlights her perfectly smooth chignon. A painter's easel with a beautiful watercolor of a fig is positioned next to her.

"Hello, vegans! If you're like me, snacks are an essential foundation of your day, and choosing the right snack can make or break physical and mental stamina." Her voice is warm yet playful, like a kindergarten teacher, disarming me immediately as she continues, "Fruit is one of the most convenient snacks for a vegan, and seasonal fruit can add an element of luxury to spruce up any table." Beautiful watercolors of dragon fruit, rambutan, lychee, and figs sift through my screen.

"Figs," she continues, "have been coveted as a delicacy for centuries outside their native habitat, and they have been cultivated for over eleven thousand years. That predates wheat and other crops our world depends on by a thousand years! Knowing this, it's hard to believe that a fruit most vegans and vegetarians have sustained themselves on, if not treated themselves to, due to cost, are literal cemeteries for insects!" A slamming sound accompanies a slide across the screen with the picture of a black, flying ant-like insect, the words "Fig Wasp" in blood-red letters across the top.

"That's right, fig wasps are the sole reason figs exist! They pollinate the fruit! But unlike common fruit trees that flower and create fruit from the pollinated flowers, fig flowers are inverted, meaning they bloom inside the fruit.

That's where the hacker comes in, the Fig Wasp or Fig Hacker, a female fig wasp is genetically designed to penetrate the skin of a fig, climb inside, and lay her eggs, pollinating the multiple flowers inside that create the tiny seeds called achene."

This is uncomfortably startling. Another beautiful watercolor of a lime green, premature fig cross-sectioned, shows multiple pods of micro buds and disturbing black ants crawling around inside as she proceeds in frame, "The female wasp is drawn by the sweet scent of the fig and lays her eggs where ninety-five percent of all larvae will mature into females. The minority males are born blind and wingless; their sole purpose is to burrow out of the fig, leaving holes for the females to escape after mating."

Chatura holds a fig cut in half over her mouth, teasingly, then drops the fig in her hand, "Fear not! Reproduction only occurs in the male figs, and we don't eat them!"

Instantly, the words **But Pollination Occurs in all Figs!** covers my screen.

"That's right, pollination occurs in all figs!" She continues rhythmically, "So, when a female wasp enters a female fig, her wings and antennae are broken off as she climbs in, trapping her inside! Although she's unable to reproduce, she inadvertently pollinates the tree, leaving her carcass behind! So, every fig is a virtual cemetery of wasp exoskeletons!" A watercolor of dozens of dead wasps inside a fig slides, across the screen.

I catch my breath.

"My take away?" She surmises, putting the fig down. "Figs are not on my vegan table, and they shouldn't be on yours." Smiling her perfect smile, her chignon the perfect crown, she adds, "Until tomorrow, stay vegan safe and remember to subscribe."

Wow! I'm not sure I can unlearn that! Clicking "subscribe" as any good friend should, I'm impressed and can see why she has over eleven thousand followers. Looking at the clock, *I need to boogie.* Popping my head into Remy's office, obviously, on a Schloom call from hell, I catch his eye and make the feeding myself gesture. He nods "Yes". I also confirm with Danielle, who also acquiesces to a sandwich.

Turning on the flat screen my husband installed over the sink so I can watch *Columbo* while I cook, I pick my favorite song playlist, and Barry White's inspiration gets the tuna melts finished in no time. Making sandwiches is one of my favorite things to do. There's an art to arranging condiments for flavor and balance, and my new trick for spreading mayo on the bread before grilling, is worth every calorie. After delivering lunch upstairs, I stoke the fire in the living room and sit down as Soter trots through the house silently before sitting at the front door, which means my guest will be knocking any second. My phone vibrates, and I open a response from the principal,

Mrs. Beroe, Thank you for reaching out. The lunch time staff is concerned that Imogene may be using her books to not engage socially, which is why she is being encouraged to participate. You may want to discuss this with her.

Thank you, Amelia Cox, Principal

Hmm. I speed type my response. ***I assure you, Imogene is not anti-social. My concern is a free period should be just that, if she wants to participate great! If not, that should be fine too. Creating a safe space for children should allow them that flexibility.***

Thanks for your understanding. Stephanie

Opening the door and slipping my phone in my back pocket, I smile, "Hi, Chatura, welcome."

She passes through the threshold, the smell of peony trailing behind her. "Thanks. What a beautiful house. This view is amazing! I've always wanted to see inside this house. You can see it for miles."

"Thank you. This is Soter." He checks her out and sits by my knee.

"Hi, Soter. Look at you. You're beautiful." She pats his head. "My kids have wanted a dog for so long, I wish I had the bandwidth for it. I just don't have the time to train a dog, and puppies are so much work. Right?" She adds, floating into the living room.

Nodding, I take her indelibly soft woven jacket I find myself caressing before placing it on the foyer chair. "I was just about to eat. It's a ridiculously busy day for me. Can I get you something? Tea? Coffee? I know you don't want a tuna sandwich, but I have nuts."

"Tea would be great. I'm not that hungry, thanks." She follows me into the kitchen and stops. "Wow, this is beautiful."

"Thank you. Herbal, OK?"

"Perfect. Your stove is awesome." She runs her delicate hand around the edge of the chromed stove top. "I love the griddle. You know, I published a post about solar ovens last week."

"Oh, I just watched your fig post! That was crazy! I may never eat figs again!"

"Right? I mean, who knew?" She turns towards me with her eyebrows raised. "I feel obligated to share this information, Stephanie. This is crucial for vegans."

"Well, it looks like you're doing it right. You have a lot of subscribers."

She smiles humbly. "You should check out the solar oven post. They are so amazing! No fossil fuels! You literally just put the food inside and leave it alone for a couple of hours as it cooks in the sun. You would love it!"

"A solar oven? I guess it would be good for camping?"

"Oh no, not at all, it's for every day. You can cook everything in it! And it's completely sustainable. I think it could save the world!"

I love her enthusiasm.

"Is this stove natural gas or propane?"

"Propane." I smile, pouring two cups out from my morning teapot. *Do vegans eat honey?* For a moment I'm' mesmerized by the golden liquid, the color of our woodwork pouring off the warm spoon into my cup, "Did you know honey never goes bad? A jar can sit for over three thousand years and still be edible. Sugar?" I ask, knowing the answer.

"No, thanks. I have Stevia in my purse." She pulls out a small tin box and proceeds to spoon the white powder into her cup. "Propane *is* better than natural gas," She continues redirecting, "What's this?" she points adoringly to the citrine colored, glass-molded chicken next to the stove that's caught her eye.

"That's bacon fat. I keep it around to elevate my potatoes and onions." *Oops.*

She discreetly covers a frown.

"Let's sit by the fire," I offer before she zeroes in on my liquid gold, knowing full well how uncomfortable I'll be explaining why I have rendered duck fat in that jar. We move into the little TV room off the kitchen and take a seat on the couch; the crackle of the fire is a welcome distraction.

"This is so cozy, a back-to-back fireplace. That's not something you see every day."

"We love this old house. We're really enjoying fixing her up."

"I can see that. There's a lot of love in here. You can feel it. Have you thought about solar? I have a great guy." Looking into our guest room just off the library, she bounces, "Is this Imogene's room?"

"Yes."

"It's adorable."

"Thanks. We had her help us decorate when she arrived. We thought it would be fun for her. She picked out the paint and fabric, and we made the drapes and the canopy for her bed."

"I've wanted to paint the girl's rooms, but I've been so busy. There just isn't enough time in the day."

"Well, you have outnumbered yourself." I tease with a smile.

"Yes. Yes, I have." She laughs, amused. "What was I thinking?" She takes a sip of her tea, and places her cup down without a sound. "Anyway, my solar guy? He created the system for my house. I should connect you." Whipping out her phone, she texts me his contacts.

"We're still busy updating all the electric from old fabric lines one room at a time. If you can believe that?" I respond, feeling self-conscious about both the tuna, and my lack of sustainable awareness.

"Please eat." She smiles, as if she's read my mind.

Relieved, I pick up my sandwich. "My husband Remy was a vegetarian when I met him," I manage between bites. "He was actually more like a fruitarian addicted to hummus and peanut butter."

"Wow! Really?"

"Yes. He says I won him over to the dark side with my sandwiches."

"That's funny."

Stopping myself from making a yum sound, I get to the point, "I'm sorry, I don't have much time today. How can I help?"

"Well, I have this incredible idea for a CBD company."

Her enthusiasm is contagious. "Great!"

Readjusting herself on the sofa, she begins her pitch, "I've…." Then she stalls.

Chewing silently while she collects her thoughts, I wait patiently, encouraging her with my eyes.

Shuffling papers in a folder, Chatura shakes her head after an even longer pause and looks down.

"Is something wrong?"

Visibly struggling with something internally for a moment, she reluctantly submits, "How do I know you won't steal my idea?"

Wait. What?

She just looks at me.

"Seriously?"

Again, with the stare.

What the…? Stunned, several responses immediately come to mind. It takes a great deal of self-control to swallow snark as I toss my sandwich on my plate. "You're serious?" I ask with my napkin in front of my mouth.

She nods silently.

"Chatura, we have our own CBD company. And I have more work than I can handle. I'm not looking to steal your idea. You asked me for help." *Why am I explaining myself? Breathe Steph.*

Her face turns bright again, "You're right, of course. Sorry. I don't know what I was thinking." Painfully clear eyes yield to a familiar, charismatic smile as if nothing happened.

"It's all good." I throw Remy's favorite line out there like a buoy.

"Well, I've met this gal that's designed an Ayer Vedic line of sensual lotions," she begins again.

"So, you're going to partner with her?" I ask, trying not to sound as disappointed about this conversation as I feel.

"No. I'm going to buy the product from her as a white label and rebrand it."

"Is the line already infused with CBD?"

"No, but how hard can it be?"

Alphabetically or chronologically? "So, what do you need my help with?"

"I want to know how much money you think it'll cost to get this going?"

"Have you laid out a business plan yet?"

Her stare is my answer.

"OK." I push my plate away. "I'd suggest asking yourself a couple of questions: What's your mission statement? What's your budget? Who are you selling to? What demographic? How many stores do you plan on launching with? What's the cost of goods out the door with packaging and shipping? Is there outside labor included? Is your brand label ready? Print-ready? And most importantly, how are you going to infuse your product?"

Wide eyes stare back. "Can you write all that down for me? I didn't bring a notebook."

"Sure, I'll email you later today."

"Thanks. Do you have a design person?"

"Yes. He's local, I'll send you, his contacts."

"Who do you use for packaging?"

"Well, since we manufacture coffee and tea, our packaging is very specialized, and we're ordering in large MOQs," I clarify, "minimums." Then offer, "But the internet is full of jars."

"How do you infuse your products?"

Wiping my mouth, I crumple my napkin in my hand. "If I told you, I'd have to kill you."

She jerks back on the couch, her eyes wide as saucers.

"Ha! No, seriously, that's proprietary information. Anything else?"

"I mean, do you just add the CBD oil to your drinks?"

"We use isolate, actually."

"What's that?"

"It's a powder derived from extracting an isolated cannabinoid oil from the entire plant."

"So, you just add the powder?"

"It's a little more complicated than that." *It's time for her to go.*

Eyes suddenly brimming with tears, she states humbly, "I really appreciate your help, Stephanie. My husband has been paying alimony and child support for the last two years until the estate is split evenly. I want to invest in something smart for my girls' future."

"That makes sense," I say, reaching out my hand, placing it on her leg for support, "Let me know if you have any other questions. I'm happy to help. Really." Guilt from losing my patience bubbles up. "You're going to be just fine. You already have a built-in clientele."

Placing her hand over mine, her vulnerability showing, she whispers, "Thank you, Stephanie."

After closing the front door behind her, I totally relate to what Imogene is going through. Remy meets me midway up the back stairs, and asks, "Who's Tesla?"

"What? Oh, one of the moms I met last night at the PTA meeting." I tell him how she was worried about me stealing her idea.

"Sweetie," he says, brushing a hair from my cheek, "be careful."

Karma police

Sometimes karma is instant, and today feels like one of those days. Staring at the Schloom screen in front of me in disbelief, I'm speechless.

"No, really. Stephanie, we need to get to know one another. I'll go first. I've done some background research on you." He smiles, his voice showing decades of leadership skills and team-building conferences not gone to waste. "I found out you were in the music business before Mad Hatter." The leader of the investment group we are working with beams.

Nodding slightly, I'm hoping not to encourage Jimmy. This isn't a difficult fact to find. Like most cannabis companies that have been around for almost a decade, we've been profiled. Women in weed have been paid attention to; *Forbes*, *Time*, *The New York Times*– I've been in all of them. The sheer number of female CEOs in cannabis was an anomaly for years, outranking any other industry. Unfortunately, once Recreational twenty-one and over was legislated, male-weighted investment firms, and corporate infiltration, stymied the feminine growth.

"Well, I'll go first," he continues with eerie self-confidence, "I want to play you something I think you'll enjoy, and you'll have a better understanding of who I am and what I stand for."

"OK." *If this isn't the weirdest Schloom call I've ever been on, I'm vegan.*

Jimmy stands up from behind his desk, a petite stature silhouetted by a monstrous, white marble-slabbed desk, as he moves his laptop to follow him, he grabs a guitar. The sixty-something, short but handsome man is now in front of a giant world map that covers the entire wall behind him; impaled with pins of cities conquered. Oddly, the red pins are the only discernable items in the stark white room flushed with light. *I'm feeling Déjà vu.*

Attaching his guitar strap, he coughs, "Can you hear me?"

"Yes." I nod, looking around my office to see if anyone else is catching this.

"I'd like to play you a song I wrote several years ago, just after I found transcendental meditation. I was lost Stephanie, and it guided me to where I am today. It helps me find myself every day. You should really look into it. It could really help you."

Blinkingly unaware of how lost I truly am, I nod again, mute to a Johnny Cash syncopation. My confusion is difficult to suppress. *I'm sure my restrained response would be audible if he wasn't singing so loudly over the guitar.* At his request, this call, way too early on a Saturday morning, is a follow-up to our in-person meeting from Thursday, which was a complete disaster! Remy and I watched as Jimmy and friends attempted to explain their way out of using Mad Hatter as a vehicle to raise money for a cannabis company that only exists in their minds. They suddenly want to launch their own company in partnership with ours instead of investing in ours. This has come after months of negotiation and literally hundreds of Schloom calls later, finding ourselves as far away as possible from where we thought we'd be. Like so many others we've met along the way, this group has no idea of the risk, monopolies, or regulations that makes this business so uniquely challenging. Obviously, they just see a cash cow, and absolutely all of them believe cannabis is just another industry their expertise can commandeer; it's mind-boggling!

Placed in a difficult position in person, we had two choices at the meeting, leave or go along quietly to see what they were really up to. Our mantra, "It only takes one person to change our destiny," is a constant source of tolerance. *But this is ridiculous.* This call is supposed to be addressing the ROI that's plugged into my financial breakdown for equity that all of the brokers we're working with are using to shop our expansion loan. The one positive thing about the cannabis industry is that the rate of return is still growing exponentially across the country, and it looks good on paper. But because these algorithms are all hogwash to me, I tend to configure less than average numbers for return of investment. *Because anything can happen!* It seems safer to have a buffer when you're paying a premium for investment capital. *But not to brokers.* Which is what Jimmy has become. For the past month, he's been arguing with me over my stance, "The more juice it has, the better," he's repeated a dozen times like a Zen sales meditation, *and now I guess he figures a serenade will sway me*?

Remy pops his head in. I look over my screen, eyebrows raised. "Who is that?" he mouths.

I write ***Jimmy*** on a sticky note.

"What the fuck?" he shakes his head and walks out texting.

Immobile, I feel like someone's strapped me to my chair. My mind racing to interpret this. *Have I missed something? Has the past almost fifteen years of working for myself placed me at a disadvantage? Is this some kind of corporate team-building tactic that's lost on me? Or is this guy just over-sharing? God, I hate the era of virtual interaction! What's wrong with a good old-fashioned phone call?*

The song ends somewhat abruptly. I find myself shaking my head "no", but saying, "That was great. Thank you. Thank you for sharing."

"Yes, yes, I thought you might enjoy that." He unhooks the guitar and brushes the front of his Polo blazoned, button-up shirt with his hand. "You know, I have a couple of songs that aren't finished, I would love you to listen to them. Maybe we could work on them together?"

"Oh. Well, I'm not really writing music right now."

"Just give them a listen. I would love to know what you think."

"Well."

"I can send them over to you. It's no big deal."

"OK," I acquiesce.

"Out of sight," he actually whispers to himself before asking, "How would I send them to you? Do you have a cassette deck?"

Oh lord. "Umm, an MP3 would work."

"I'll have to figure that out." Sitting back in his chair, readjusting his computer so he's perfectly aligned within the world again, he recollects himself, "Now it's your turn."

"What?"

"It's your turn to share."

This can't be happening.

Eager to get as far away from my computer as possible I hang up, relieved I narrowly escaped an overwhelming performance anxiety. I send Jimmy a link to my old videos on You Boob and run downstairs for a desperate change of atmosphere and something hot and chocolaty.

Remy intercepts me, pouring another coffee for himself, "So, what was that all about?" He eyes me over his cup, with profound curiosity.

"If I never have to take another Schloom call again, I'll be happy! I get that it's important for us to see the people we're partnering with, but when does it end? Do I really need to be Schlooming with my web designer or our tea purveyors or packaging manufacturer or hordes of investment bankers I'm never going to work with? Do I need to see Jimmy every time I talk to him?" I ask rhetorically. "No! I don't! For literally thousands of years, businesses have survived without meeting every single person within their network. This is just–overstimulation!"

Smart enough not to patronize me, my husband waits in silence with a genuine look of concern on his face as my ranting dissipates, before offering, "Can I make you a tea?"

"No. I'm good."

He kisses me on the forehead and walks out, determined not to be amused.

Standing alone in the kitchen I recall last year, when Remy and I had no contact with the outside world, it was bliss. Twice, Laure and Danielle ran things for us while we recuperated in the tropics from our trials with H.S. and his cronies. *Why do we need to carry phones around all the time anyway? Who needs to be that reachable? I remember life before cell phones and answering machines. It wasn't so bad!*

Slathering peanut butter on an English Muffin, *I've given up trying to get a good bagel in New Mexico.* My head still shaking from Jimmie, Danielle walks in behind me, "Don't tell me he has you working on Saturday?" I ask with my mouth full.

"Just an hour or two. It smells good." She involuntarily walks over to the crockpot on the counter. "I hear you're having a get-together today. Anything I can help with?"

"It's really just a playdate for Imogene. I put the chili on last night, and we'll make cornbread in a bit. I'm good, thanks."

"I heard you made vegan chili. How does one do that?"

"I manhandled a jackfruit."

"A what?"

"A jackfruit. They're huge, like the size of a watermelon and green and covered in bumpy knobs. When you cook them with beer and chili spice they taste just like meat."

She nods dubiously. "Well, I love cornbread. My mom's cornbread is amazing. She makes it on top of the wood stove in the winter and lines the pan with bacon fat."

"Sounds like my kind of gal. I'll have to try that. How is your mother?"

"She's good. She and my auntie keep each other company. They live for the day I have kids." She laughs, but her face turns rigid as she pours herself a cup of coffee. "Not likely. Anyway, have fun. Enjoy your Saturday."

"You too." I sigh. Knowing Danielle bears inconceivable scars. Abducted and brutalized by a real villain, she survived a sick and torturous game for over a year. Only after a scare with cysts last year did her doctor confirm that she had been sterilized by her captors, the procedure irreversible. She hides her anger well. *We all do. It's amazing she's intact. I can't imagine the barbarous reality she endured; how many people she watched die, and the fear she had to live with at the park.* When Galax, the only other survivor from the park, had been told the same thing by her physician. *I knew it was my fate as well. Remy and I don't talk about it. They stole our future from us, and we will never forgive them.* Wiping a tear from my cheek, it's hard to look at Danielle and not be triggered.

Soter, staring at me from across the room, intuitively knows my heart hurts and reminds me of our walk. *I definitely need to clear my head.* Without further delay, we hit our mountain trail hard, the sky clearing with the rising sun. *I know it's going to be another beautiful day, regardless of anything else. That's the beauty of nature. It doesn't pay any attention to our folly.*

Imogene's awake and ready to conquer the world by the time I'm showered and changed into a pair of yoga pants and the plushest angora sweater I own to combat the morning chill. My abalone pendant, a dramatic contrast to the forest green pile, gives me strength.

Imogene's happy face instantly turns me around. *I love how refreshed she is in the morning. She just wakes up, and it's full steam ahead. Kids are amazing.* "Good morning, sweetheart."

"Good morning." She wraps her arms around me and gives me a hug, I take an extra second absorbing her. "So, how did you sleep?"

"Good." Hair mussed; she unfolds herself onto the kitchen table. Her hazel eyes, peaked by the smell of food, glow with the opportunities of the day.

"Are you ready for our guests?"

"Yup. How about you?"

"Yeah." I give her nose a playful tap with my finger. "Let's have some oatmeal, then we'll make cornbread."

"OK." She smiles. "What do you call it when you have 50 pigs and 50 deer?"

"Umm. I don't know."

"A hundred–sowsandbucks."

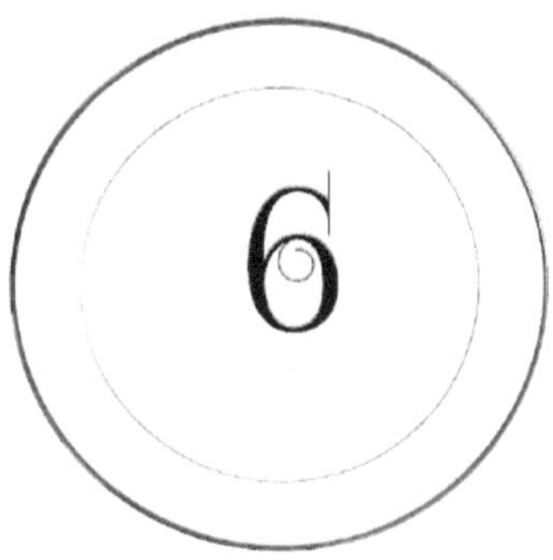

Know your chicken

The sun, as I predicted, is shining, and it's almost 50 degrees out. All the snow is gone, and puffy white clouds are literally swimming by. It feels like spring.

"This is crazy weather," Remy states, tying off a clamp to a cable he's pulled between the two huge cottonwoods in the backyard. "Can you believe it was negative twenty, for two days last week? Everyone in town broke a pipe! Danielle said the plumbing wreckage is still the only talk at the coffee shop."

"We are so lucky none of our pipes broke."

"What do you mean luck?" he states indignantly. "Sweetie, I dug a trench around our entire house, changed out every pipe, insulated them, and even wrapped them with heated coils! It has nothing to do with luck." Dejected his response does not go unnoticed as Imogene and I place cups and a thermos of our sober–uninfused hot cocoa on the picnic table just outside our back door.

"You're right! Luck has nothing to do with it," I say, eyeing Imogene with a wink as she giggles, "Anyway, it feels good to be outside."

Remy's eyebrows lower, and we go back inside to arrange plates and silverware on the kitchen table while my underappreciated spouse finishes the installation on the brand-new, glow-in-the-dark zipline he's talked about for weeks.

"What do you think?" I ask Imogene.

"I think we're ready."

Remy appears, "Where's my test pilot?"

We pile outside. Imogene climbs up on the round plastic seat, her feet where her bum should be and grabs hold of the cord above her head as Remy pushes her.

"Wheee!" Taking off like lightning, she heads full steam for the other tree, Soter chasing after her.

"How does it stop?"

"It has a built-in brake. Relax."

Of course, it does. Five feet before she careens into the tree at the other end of the cable, it magically shuffles through low gears, coming to a halt. *How could I be such a doomtard?*

"That was so cool, Uncle Rem!" She runs back with Soter jumping at her side. "This time I want to try a running start." She pulls the seat back to the other end and jumps on, propelling herself, Soter bounding after her as a car pulls up.

"That was a success. I'm going for a bike ride." My spouse states pumping his eyebrows.

"Escaping?"

"Definitely." Kissing me on the forehead, we walk up to the parking area.

Chatura alights from her car like Mother Goose, her three little girls in tow, in matching white, Roxy snow parkas with fake fur trim, are adorable.

"Chatura, this is my husband, Remy."

"Hello, Remy. Nice to meet you."

"Nice to meet you."

Her radically blue eyes are desperately attempting not to linger, and thankfully Holly's arrival breaks what could have been an awkward moment.

"Holly, thanks for coming. This is Remy."

She's dressed in a neutral ensemble from H&M, topped with an open tan Burberry jacket that matches the expression on her face, ironically.

"Hello."

"Hi, Holly. You must be Seraphine?" Remy smiles with a pause, "Nice to meet you." I know his tone. It's genuine, but I definitely see a warning there.

The girls all drop their jackets on the ground and run off towards Imogene. Remy heads to his mancave/lab-studio-barn for his bike. While I attempt to lead the gals over to the cocoa, but the vision of my husband kick-starting his dirt bike is overwhelmingly gravitating. Reminding myself I have a crush on him too, I smile.

Once the purr of the engine wanders off the property, we all sit down at the table, unzipping our coats. "Well, it's a beautiful day. We lucked out," I offer.

"We sure did."

Silence.

"Have you been out here before, Holly?"

"Oh, yes. Seraphine plays with Chatura's girls all the time. You have chickens?" She asks over the crow of our rooster, riled by the squealing mayhem the girls are causing in the yard.

"Yes. Yes, we do."

"How many?"

"At any given time, about twelve. I like to know where our eggs come from."

"You don't eat them." Her question is more like a statement.

"The chickens? *Umm.* Yes, we do, mostly the roosters. In the spring, we'll get new chicks, and the extra roosters will have to go." Feeling a look of discernment, I add, "We use everything. We eat the meat and use the bones for soup. I render the fat for cooking, and we make dog food for Soter out of whatever's leftover. I even send the feathers to Remy's brother, who makes fishing flies. Nothing goes to waste."

"Is that a duck, I hear?"

"Yes, we're raising two ducks for Christmas." Horrified looks, stop me in my tracks. *My animal husbandry definitely not the fine point I thought it might be.*

Holly nods without comment, expressionless like she's in deep thought.

"Well, they look like they live a very happy life," Chatura states genuinely, "That's a huge coop, and look at the size of that pond, Holly. Those ducks are having a blast."

"I really enjoy spending time with them each day. It's calming," I say, watching the ducks climb in and out of the water excitedly.

Holly removes her jacket as another long, uncomfortable silence, painfully washes over the group until two of Chatura's girls start screaming at each other over a hula hoop on the trampoline. *It sounds violent.* Chatura reluctantly jumps up to intervene, embarrassed but channeling her inner mediator. We hear her calm and thoughtful voice terminate the quarrel immediately below us.

"I watched your music videos on You Boob," Holly admits quietly.

"Oh? Well, that seems like a lifetime ago." *Am I the only person who doesn't look up prospective friends online?*

"They're very good." She smiles nervously. "My husband is in a band. He plays guitar and sings."

"Really? That's great. What's the name of his band?"

"The Cohorts. They play the Cowboy bar occasionally. Nothing like what you did."

"That's very cool. I would love to see his band. Please tell me when he's playing next."

She nods then becomes suddenly animated, but not in a good way as she asks, "Have you been following everything that's happening in China?"

"Yes," I respond, noticing she's wringing her hands, before I continue, "But in my line of work, every day is a red-letter day, so I try to take international news in stride." *Not entirely true; I have watched several videos released from Wuhan. It's so dystopian watching people fall to the ground; I want to believe it's fake.*

"I'm so anxious all of the time. I know this sounds silly, but I feel like the end of the world's coming."

I put my hand over hers. "Do you have family there?"

"No, they're either here or dead." She takes a deep breath; her face turning dark. "My husband isn't helping. He told me if it is a virus, it could be just like the movies, spreading exponentially across the globe with international travel and commerce the way that it is. He's saying millions of people will die. I'm so frightened for Seraphine."

"All we can do is guess right now, but luckily science is on our side. If it is a virus, this would be the one moment in history for pharmaceuticals to shine."

Ignoring my statement as though she didn't hear it, she continues, "Anyway, Nate's been recording on his days off from the hospital. He's made a recording studio in the garage. That's where they practice."

"Wow, a real garage band." I smile but it goes over her head.

"He's been writing some really interesting songs." The expression on her face borders agony.

I nod. *Where is this going?*

"Maybe you could shed some light on this for me." She scoots closer, checking quickly to make sure Chatura, who is now jumping in the middle of the trampoline surrounded by all of the girls laughing, is out of range. "Nate played a song for me he's been working on the other evening; I didn't quite know how to take it."

I wait as she looks around anxiously, her hands red from friction.

"It mentions something about how painful it is to love," she pauses, "me."

Drawing my head back, not knowing her, her husband, or their relationship. *This is a can of worms.* But Pablo Neruda's, *Tonight I Can Write the Saddest Lines* comes to mind immediately. I begin gently, as an artist, "Love is the language of the arts, Holly. Songs you hear on the radio, timeless books, ancient poems, Masterpieces, they're all about love because love is so dynamic, so personal. So intrinsic."

Childlike perplexion is her responds.

"I'm sure you've read Shakespeare, Neruda, Marquez?" She doesn't register so I keep offering, "Austen, Fitzgerald, Lawrence, Poe?"

"I went to Duke, Stephanie. I got a BS in accounting. That's where I met Nate." She shakes her head, "I hate Shakespeare. Never did anything for me. I don't know who Neruda is, but I read Poe. I just can't say which book."

Silently shocked, I try another tactic, readjusting my bottom on the wooden picnic bench, the warmth of the sun on my shoulders, I take a deep breath, "Have you ever listened to a song on the radio and cried?"

"Yes!" she answers overly excited. "I cry all the time! In the grocery store! Making the bed! Making dinner! Sometimes," she looks around, "I sit in my car and cry in the driveway!" she confesses.

OK, that's probably not good. "Well," I offer gently, "I find myself crying to songs when love is felt so deeply it's both pleasure and pain."

"That doesn't make any sense, Stephanie. How can love be painful?"

"To be tortured by love is the greatest love of all, Holly."

She blinks. "I'm a highly sexual person, Stephanie, but I don't go in for the kinky stuff."

Chatura returns while my eyes blink, and immediately picks up she's missed something as the conversation ends abruptly.

OK, where do I go from here? "Would anyone like a hot chocolate? It's our own special blend."

"Sure."

I pour out three mugs of our luscious caramel cocoa.

"This doesn't have any pot in it. Right?" Holly asks.

"No, of course not." *What the Hell?*

"Then I'll have a cup."

My mind races as I hand her a mug of the rich dark liquid. *Who does she think I am? A drug dealer? Ouch.*

They both decline the vegan whipped cream and marshmallows I bought as I sit down on the bench swallowing hard.

Chatura changes the subject, her face turning dark. "Have either of you heard the terrible news?" her voice hushed as she looks over her shoulder for the kids.

We both shake our heads.

She looks at Holly dumbfounded for a moment, then corrects herself, "That's right, you were in Colorado last weekend. Well, I ran into Warren, the head of the fire department at The General Store. He's such a nice guy. Anyway, he told me that they found Gabby dead in her hot tub!"

"Was it a heart attack?" I ask.

"No." She takes a sip from her cup and places it down dramatically, "She drowned!"

Holly lowers her head.

"Was she drunk?" I ask. "I mean, how do you drown in a hot tub?"

"Maybe. I don't know. But the worst part is that she was in the tub all night, at 110 degrees!"

"Eww, that's not good."

"Oh my god!" Holly exclaims, her head shaking as her fingers viciously begin to bite into her hands.

"Warren said her flesh was coming off the bone," she nods towards the coop, "like a chicken in a pot."

"Oh my god! Stop! I don't want to hear anymore." Holly places her hands over her ears.

"I'm so sorry, Holly. You must have been close," I say, placing my hand on her arm, eyeing Chatura.

"We were. We were close." She breaks down out of breath, verging on traumatized.

Running inside, I grab some tissues. The thought of poor Gabby or rich Gabby stewed in her own hot tub visually clinging to my conscious, is dreadful.

Handing Holly, the box, I sit back down next to her, "I am so sorry."

"She was a good friend. I mean, she could be challenging at times, she was so driven and bossy, but she was a good friend."

"We were at her house the night it happened." Clearly macabre-intrigued, Chatura professes.

"You're kidding?"

"No. We had a committee meeting for the spring fling dance. It was a potluck. She was the queen of potlucks. We had a couple of bottles of wine and finished all our work by eight. We all left by what? Eight thirty? Nine? Right, Holly?"

Holly nods, reaching for another tissue in slow motion, mascara running down her face.

"I can still see the line-up of her crockpots."

"Her what?"

"Crockpots. She had at least a half a dozen of them. We used to joke that the PTA was a coven, and our meetings were full of bubbling cauldrons." Chatura shakes her head, talking to herself, "You know, she didn't seem drunk when we left. But who knows what might have happened later?" Lowering her voice, she continues, "I heard she and her husband weren't getting along, and there was a ridiculous amount of money involved if they divorced."

"So, the police think it's homicide?" I ask, my overly informed new friend.

"Well, the fire department does. Have you been questioned, Holly?"

"No."

"Me neither," Chatura adds, disappointed.

Taking the ladies inside to change the morbid subject, the overwhelming chili aroma greets us at the door as we enter the kitchen.

Holly takes a moment in the bathroom.

"You know, in New Jersey, chili has a whole different meaning," I offer. "The recipe I grew up with was ground beef mixed with beans and tomato puree that all came from a can with a dash of cayenne powder. It took me awhile to warm up to the New Mexico version, everyone asking for red or green chile. It took me a while to understand what they meant. I know now it's a type of salsa picante."

"I know. They put it on everything! It's delicious."

"This chili is southwest style, without meat, of course; I added jack fruit to the beans for flavor."

"I've never had jack fruit." Chatura trails her finger around the edge of the kitchen table.

"Let's hope it tastes as good as it smells," I add.

"I'm sorry, I didn't have time to pick anything up," Holly confesses, rejoining us in the kitchen.

"Not to worry, there's plenty of food."

"Is this all organic?" She retorts, using her finger as a pointer.

"Umm," I run through the list of ingredients quickly in my mind, "Yes. Yes, it is."

"It looks delicious, Stephanie," Chatura offers.

"Is it non-GMO?" Holly appends.

"I know it's organic, but I'm not sure about it all being non-modified."

She looks at me, her eyes impedingly wide. "It's crucial to know nowadays, Stephanie. There are studies linking GMO pollution to chronic flu-like symptoms."

The look on Chatura's face is priceless. I nod my head, not knowing what to say. Rolling her eyes, Chatura empties the bag of baby carrot sticks she brought onto a plate next to the cornbread Imogene cut into neat little triangles. I'm trying not to act as inadequate as I feel as the kids come in and practically scrape the plates clean in less than a minute. Whatever was going on with Seraphine and Imogene at school is taking on a different life today; they are inseparable as

Chatura's kids play together out of familiarity. *The house feels good, so much laughter and noise. It feels happy.*

"Stephanie, I want to show you something." Chatura pulls out a folder from her purse, setting her untouched plate down. "You have inspired me. I have been working on this since I left your house the other day."

"This cornbread is amazing," Holly manages between two pieces. Thankfully, her demeanor has changed for the better.

Opening the folder, I smile and sit down next to Chatura. There's a mock-up of a logo. The brand is impossible to read, scrolled illegibly across the top of a blue butterfly on a red background.

"Does that say Perfection?"

"Yes! Don't you love it? It's sexy right?"

"It's great! Did you work with my layout guy on this?" I ask, knowing she didn't because my layout guy rocks.

"No. I did this on my own to give him an idea."

"Oh. Well, it's an excellent start."

"I think it's perfect, no pun intended. I mean, I wouldn't change a thing. Would you?" Her excitement is precious and makes me rethink my instincts.

"It may be a little hard to read. The script …."

"Oh?" She retracts instantly.

"I love the butterfly." *It should be centered to give it more space.* "Why Perfection?"

"Because it's perfect in every way."

I nod, wanting to help but afraid of going over the line of helpfulness. "You know, since you're a You Boober and an influencer with a following, you could brand it "Chatura." Your name is so beautiful and exotic, and it has a double meaning – wisdom. It could play off the Ayer Vedic platform."

"That's a great idea," Holly adds with a full mouth.

But Chatura recoils.

Now, I know I've gone too far. "I like what you've done. Really. You should take it to my guy and see what he can do for you," I add genuinely. *Because this mock-up is a hot mess.*

"I will." Chatura closes up.

"Can you give me the recipe for this?" Holly interrupts, "This is the best cornbread I've ever had."

"Thanks. Yeah, it's really simple: cornmeal, flour, baking soda, salt, a little sugar. I used coconut milk instead of cow's milk for Chatura and olive oil instead of eggs or butter, and I lined the pan with…." *Oh, shit. Bacon grease!*

Part Two

Every day is exactly the same

"Well, today started like every day has for the past 180 days. We eat the same thing, do the same thing, wear the same thing," I complain to Laure, "I'm just thankful not to be on a Schloom call." I laugh. "This quarantine is blistering my muse, memory, enthusiasm, and all hope for the future, seriously!" I add exhausted for no apparent reason.

"Girl, tell me about it! Who could have guessed? Who could dream this shit up? What's next? Zombie apocalypse?" Her Jersey accent spilling out of the speaker phone breaks a smile on my face.

"I know!" We both laugh, it feels good and weird. "Oh my god I was in the store the other day with my mask on, of course, because, thankfully, our Governor mandated masks in public, and this couple from who knows where is shopping for produce, and she has what looks like a retainer strapped around her head with a three-inch by five-inch clear plastic shield in front of her mouth."

"What the hell?"

"I know. Like her nose doesn't emit droplets of moisture when she breathes? And her husband was holding a bandana with one hand over his mouth while he was picking out apples with the other. Talk about zombies."

"What did you do?"

"I pulled a Karen, and told the manager, who did absolutely nothing. Then I went over and told woman she didn't have a mask on. She said, 'Mind your own business.' I said lady, I am minding my own business. You're not wearing a mask for your protection. You're supposed to be wearing one for mine!"

"Crazy!"

"Ha! The whole thing makes my head spin. I remember asking Remy what was going on. He was swearing up a green streak in his office, which seems like years ago, literally. I'm in such a fog. I'll never forget seeing the headlines on his phone."

The United States Confirms First Covid Death in Seattle.

"I had no idea what it meant." I continue, "I was in a complete state of ignorance. And frankly, it wasn't such a bad place. Our date nights now, consist of buying a beer at the grocery store behind two masks and sitting in the parking lot in our car, watching people walk in and out of the store. It's unbelievable! How about you? How has it been in Egypt handling lockdown?"

"We're in Singapore now."

"Singapore?"

"Yes, it's beautiful here."

"Isn't that where they filmed *Crazy Rich Asians*?" I ask, sitting on my new Covid day bed in the front yard, the light magically changing through the leaves of the large elm I'm under as a flock of birds line up for a pre-dusk drink at our pond in front of me. It's dreamlike.

"Yeah, well, they got that right! I've never seen so much money, seriously. People buy lifetime memberships to restaurants here! It's fuckin' crazy!" Her Jersey slips-in again, making me laugh.

"How were you able to leave Egypt? I thought all international travel was restricted?"

"Not for private planes. Not here."

"And they're letting non-nationals in?"

"We have citizenship now, thanks to a family investment. How's Imogene?" My oldest friend changes the subject, uncomfortable talking about her new married wealth. *And frankly, it's none of my business.*

"She's so frightened with the airports closed and international travel non-existent," I respond hurriedly, "the worry of not being able to see her mother is having a serious effect on her. I see it on her face. They talk once a day when the satellite is over the encampment Esme´s held up in. But I don't think she's giving us the full story about what's happening there. I really wish she could get the hell out." Pausing, I weigh in on economic disparity.

"Where is she, Steph?"

"Outside Kuyunjik in Iraq. Anyway, Imogene's like a different kid nowadays. No more of her sweet jokes."

"Oh, no! You're kidding! I love her jokes."

"She sleeps in." I continue, "She's hard to wake up. She's hard to motivate all of a sudden. She's depressed. She's in her room all the time! And the kids from school have a group chat, but all they do is pick on one another. She's in tears most of the week. I'm terribly worried."

"That sucks. I remember middle school being hard, but that sounds awful."

The last six months blur before me. "It's so crazy here Laure. When we signed her up for public school, we worried every day about a school shooting. It was terrifying. Remy even gave her tactics for hiding and lined her backpack with Kevlar. Can you imagine having to talk to a child about this as a reality?"

"No. No, I can't. School was always a safe place for me. In fact, I spent more time at school than at home for that reason."

"Exactly! I'm so glad we pulled her out of public for this new year. I mean, at first, a mandatory vacation was fun; you know, board games, hikes, bike rides, playing with Soter, and karaoke at home, but life needed to go on. School needed to go on. So, I reached out to her friends' moms, and we created a micro-home school."

"Oh my god, what a brilliant idea!"

"Well, I was surprised I didn't have to talk them into it. We were all looking for safe alternatives. It's a truly diverse group. I'm hoping that's a good thing."

"Spill it, girl."

"There are five of us, five families. Four moms, me, and our five kids, so we are under the mandatory limit for groups gathering in New Mexico, and they can have class in person outside, masked of course. Two of the moms I already know from Imogene's charter school, but the other two are new."

"Is Chatura one of them? I've been following her vlog."

"Yeah. She's prolific, right?"

"I'll say. She's intense. But I pick up great tips from her vlog."

"Me too, and I'm not vegan or vegetarian. I didn't have to talk her into it at all. She's been incredibly enthusiastic. But Holly, her friend, has been a hard sell. She already had her daughter fast-tracked for Ivy League at twelve, and at the same time has this blind belief in public school that it's the end-all. It's been difficult to get around. But her daughter Seraphine was a key element for me since she and Imogene have become fast friends. I needed to secure that relationship for her, especially now with all of this isolation."

"This is such a brilliant idea. Oh, my god. What are the other moms like?"

"Chatura introduced us all. Gabriella, one of the new moms, and her son are from an old New Mexico ranching family. The fifth family moved here from Southern California a couple of years ago; her husband's a teacher and a surfer."

"Oh, that's a good fit for you."

"Yeah! Well, it should be, but the Californians are a bit… conservative. The Grandma's cool, though. Grandma Josephine is a big-time benefactor at the Santa Fe Opera. She's hired several small groups of out of work musicians to play for the kids, outside, and even catered it."

"That sounds amazing! Where are the classes? Who's teaching?"

"We were holding classes at our house at first; the kids were outside under the elms in the front yard. We have so much outdoor space, you know. It was great. I bought a ton of patio furniture to accommodate the class and the teachers." Staring at the now empty chairs around me, my enthusiasm deflates. "But Delia, the Californian, caboshed it."

"Why?"

"I'm not sure." I pause, "Honestly, I think it has something to do with…."

"Cannabis." Laure finishes my sentence.

"Yeah."

"That sucks. Why can't people just get over themselves?"

"Her husband is a recovering alcoholic. Now they're very Christian. I get it. Anyway, it's at Delia's house for the time being. We hired four teachers, I interviewed for math and science, one for English and history, one for arts and performance, and one for French. They had all been let go from a private school that went bankrupt during quarantine, and they're happy to have a cash-paying job; they're all very dedicated. We bought a curriculum from a home school that's been around since the seventies and created a school calendar based on the public-school calendar but better thanks to the teacher's input, with longer holidays and more breaks for the kids since they're moving through so much work so quickly and the small class size is so intense."

"And who's Gabriella?" She instinctively unravels my tale.

"Yeah, Gabriella. She's a challenge. A bit entitled, very wealthy, but she also works hard. She's the CEO of a small private firm related to cattle ranching; I think. I don't actually know what she does exactly, but all she does is work."

"Why is she a challenge?" Laure asks, amused, sipping something.

"I don't know. It's like she has oppositional disorder. We come up with a plan, and she throws a wrench. It's been difficult." I sigh. "Ironically, her job is decision-making. And she never has time to do anything except attend the weekly planning call and basically cause kaos. Seriously, my anxiety levels are rising just talking about her. My real concern is that all this frustration I've been bottling up, will influence Imogene. She absorbs everything. I'm trying to stay focused and positive."

"Well, if anybody can do it, you can!"

"Thanks."

"How's business?"

"Oh! All those hot-to-trot investors calling a dozen times a day pre- lockdown, who couldn't get us to sign a contract fast enough?

They've completely disappeared. Ha!" I laugh. "It's a good thing. Putting the brakes on is giving us a new perspective. That one group we were talking to with the serenader?"

"Oh my god, that was so crazy!"

"They tried to convince us that a loan for half a million dollars was a great deal with a million and a half return! Three times! They wanted three times their money back!"

"That's fucking extortion!"

"Don't get me started, Jersey."

She laughs.

"Anyway, I think Remy and I both know now, if we can't do it as a mom and pop, it probably shouldn't be done. We're just not that. I don't want to be in a room full of suits questioning my strategy for survival in an already volatile industry. We're going to keep it simple for a while."

"Amen, Sista. How are sales?"

"Better. Now that they've listed cannabis as an essential business, but for three months, we were completely closed up like everyone else. Go figure, it takes a global pandemic to make the cannabis industry seem necessary and normal! It's almost disappointing."

"Dude, that's crazy!"

"Yeah, it is! But sometimes I feel like Covid is finally giving the world a taste of what it's like to be in the cannabis industry. I mean this is how business is ***every, single, day for me!"***

"Ha! A little retribution?" She laughs.

"Maybe." Glancing at the clock, *I've lost track of time.* "Listen, sweetie, I have to go. I have a parent meeting in five minutes."

"No prob, honey. It was good catching up."

"I didn't' get to hear about you and Tyler at all, but it's good to hear your voice. Keep sending photos; they're an inspiration for better days."

"Next time, let's Schloom." She laughs.

"Oh, no!"

"Love you, sista. Ciao."

"Love you too." Hanging up, the simple act of talking to someone outside of my Covid bubble infuses me with happiness. *We really are social animals.*

The light filtering through to the ground around me, casts a peaceful reminder that if one good thing comes out of this pandemic, it's focusing on living in the moment. Watching another small bird enjoying a bath at the edge of our pond is precious as nature becomes a centerpiece for me again. With less work and more time on our hands, doing nothing guiltlessly has been good for us. Remy and I were working six days a week before the shutdown. *Now, we barely work three.* I'm enjoying seeing the simple world around me. Danielle had said, "We'll be safe out here in the middle of nowhere." *She was right. We have been virtually unaffected with so much open space around us and no daily mandates for masks or social distancing to adhere to because it's just us. But we are really isolated. I think it's getting to all of us. Cabin fever.*

I'm looking forward to Remy and me taking the micro-school kids camping this weekend for a class field trip in our '71 VW camper van. We are hoping to give them something they desperately need, normalcy. Trixie is already packed up with all our gear, and the coolers are full of the kids' favorite snacks and drinks. But running through what seems like a "brilliant idea," waiting for the parent meeting to convene, the reality of all five kids and five families being happy is becoming apparent.

"Hey, who was that?" Remy asks, plopping himself down on one of our new Covid nesting chairs opposite me on our new brick patio that was a family pandemic effort in preparation for the micro- school.

"That was Laure."

"How is she? How's Egypt?"

"She's great! She's in Singapore."

"Yeah, that's not a surprise. Are you OK?" His look of concern is endearing. "Oh, let me guess, a parent meeting?"

"Yeah."

"So, whose head is on the chopping block today?" He asks, crossing his long legs in front of him, taking in the breath of nature around him casually, his long hair framing his shoulders and back.

"Mine." I shake my head, "Gabriella will take up half the meeting, telling us how busy she is, like no one else has a life. It's infuriating. And Delia has taken over bossing everyone around. She has no consideration for the group. It's all about her son Gerry, and what he needs. And from what Imogene tells me, he's a complete bully, and he's not happy unless he has all the attention, all of the time."

"Just like his mom."

"Yeah, well, what really troubles me is she's using her religious beliefs as a shield for everything she doesn't understand. So, every decision we make about curriculum or choice of literature or music is affected by this very stringent if not archaic view of the world. But even though she's the odd man out, she's so loud and unyielding, she's bending us to her will. We give in to her, just so she'll stop talking! I don't know what I like less, the fact that she's using a Presidential tactic to control us or that she's so narrow-minded! It's a real conundrum." I place my computer on my lap with one minute to spare. "Why are you smiling?"

"I'm just glad it's not me on the call." He smirks.

"You should be on the call! You wouldn't put up with their nonsense!"

"Neither should you." He gets up, sauntering off towards the house knowing full well, I'm watching every muscle in his sumptuously toned body. *Men are such a pain in the ass.*

Logging into the Schloom call with two seconds to spare, everyone's voices are already pitched and talking over each other. My screen fills with three small squares of moms in their homes against a wall. All of them dressed in some form of leisure-outfit, verging on pajamas, combined with lousy lighting that emphasizes their lack of personal care that's riveling the epidemic itself. The one thing they have in common, is they all look miserable, except Chatura. Her smile is unyielding. I count on her as a shining light and take a cue, adjusting mine to match. No one says hello. The conversation is already heated.

"I'm not comfortable with Gerry at a party in person! It's too much of a risk!" Delia proclaims, her masculine features and heavy brow mimicking her irritating, husky voice.

I interrupt, knowing they're talking about the Halloween party ***again***. "The reason we kept the class to five kids was so they could meet in person to interact and socialize under Covid guidelines. They're already meeting three times a week for school. How is this any different?"

"It depends on how stringent everyone is about their Covid bubble," Delia propounds, her forehead pursed. "We have elderly parents to consider. Anyone allowing outsiders into their home is placing us all at risk!"

That's aimed at me. "I don't see how Danielle being included in our family is any different than Grandma Josephine is to your family. She's been in our bubble since lockdown."

"Whoever she is, she's not almost 80 years old."

"Your mother is 62."

"Exactly, she needs to be protected."

Knowing Holly's husband is a surgeon at a hospital, and Delia's husband is a public-school teacher who is back at work two days a week, I'm scratching my head. *This better not be about race, or we're going to have a real problem.*

"I think we're treating this pandemic a little too much like a vacation," Holly interrupts. Her voice exclamatorily, monotonous, "FEMA is on the move. They're building cages. And once they start tracking us through 5G, people will start disappearing," she churns out alarmingly.

The group silently stutters.

"It's all part of their plan to take over," she continues, unprompted.

Dare I ask? "Who's they, Holly?"

"FEMA!"

"Holly, FEMA can barely distribute tarps to hurricane victims."

"They're going to take over."

"Take over what?"

"The world. They won't stop until we're all in cages!" She's gone from zero to a hundred in two seconds. There's another audible silence.

"Who would profit if we're all in cages?" I ask, regretting my question as soon as it leaves my mouth.

"Wake up, Stephanie. This is genocide!"

The meeting comes to an uncomfortable halt before Chatura morphs into the voice of reason, "I believe a party, masked, outdoors is as safe as anyone could ask for. Don't you think, Holly?"

Prompted, she moves back on track, "Oh, yeah. I guess so."

And that will be the last five words we hear from her. "It's just a Halloween party, for goodness sakes. Outdoors with masks!" I plead.

Gabriella logs in, and somehow, she's configured her own introduction every time she joins the call; we're silenced, by a robotic voice stating, "Gabriella

Cecilia Garcia Fernandez del Olmo Lopez, mother of Alejandro Juan Carlos Garcia Fernandez Del Olmo Lopez, has joined the call."

"Ladies, what's on the agenda?" Her Spanish accent is an attention grabber.

"We are discussing the Halloween party." *Again.*

"Did we decide to have a Halloween party?"

Oh, my fucking god.

Sitting in the dark feeling like a bomb went off, two hours painfully wasted, I'm ungrounded, anxious, and angry as an email comes in, a reminder I sent an invoice to our client in Arizona that is still unpaid. I set a new reminder to call him tomorrow. *Now is not the time to engage.*

Remy walks out with a glass of wine and a beer, one in each hand, and my black cashmere shawl draped over his shoulder. Placing the pinot grigio in front of me, he covers my bare shoulders and clicks the new, overhead, party lights on. After a long sip, I wrap my legs over his, my head on his shoulder.

"Thank you, Steph," he says sincerely after a short silence.

"For what?"

"For taking such good care of Imogene."

Looking into his eyes, the color of a perfect day, I remind him, "I love her, Rem, you know that."

"I know. I know." He kisses me, like a warm breeze, wet and languid, my whole body ignites as strands of love cling to our mouths before he gently tags me on the forehead. "How did your meeting go?"

"We finally settled on the party. We'll host it at our house on Hallows Eve, which happens to be a Friday night."

"How did CruDelia take that?"

I snort. "She just kept going on and on about it not being safe and not being good for Gerry, that he has too much homework to catch up on. Seriously, her idea of helping him not stress out about school is keeping him from a party that happens to be the only social function these kids have had access to for over six months.

Finally, I said, "Don't come! The rest of us are planning the party for the kids. They deserve a break and a celebration." Revisiting the conversation causes me to recoil. "Once she was uninvited, she wanted to come. It was classic. And did you know FEMA is tracking us with 5G, and they're going to round us up and put us in cages?"

My spouse blinks back at me.

"Yeah, that's what Holly actually believes."

He shakes his head. "And Gabriella?" he asks, pretending not to be caught up in the drama.

"The meeting was two hours long, and she talked for a good hour and a half about how busy she is at work and how she doesn't have time to make a costume or make food for the party because she has back-to-back meetings and that Al is so behind on his school work, she doesn't know how long he can stay. Oh, and, her tanning bed is broken. She has to fly a guy in from L.A. to fix it. A tanning bed in New Mexico! And I had to remind her for the hundredth time, that we've been discussing this party for over a month. It's fucking mayhem."

"I bet Costa Rica is looking really good right now?"

My spouse's answer to all our problems is escaping to the tropics. "Don't even."

He laughs, his whole chest flexing, then he turns serious for a moment, "Did you know a woman named Evangeline from the charter school?"

"Yes, she's a tutor there. What do you mean, did?"

"She's dead. During lockdown, they found her body. She died from exposure."

"She froze to death? Here?"

"Strange, right? Remember those sub-zero nights we had when everyone's pipes burst before lockdown? It happened then. It took them a while to find her."

"Seriously? That's creepy." *And that makes two.*

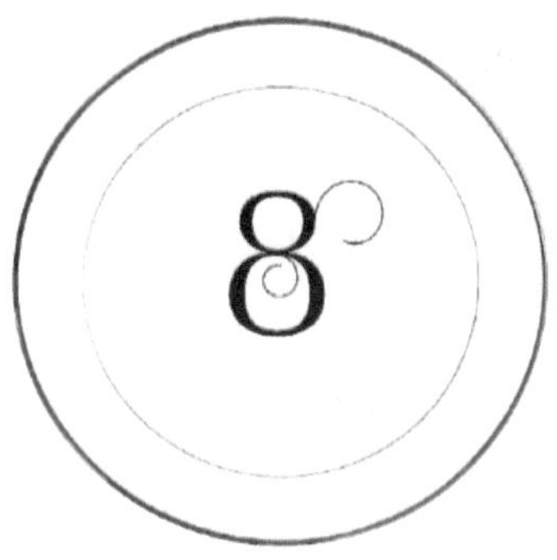

The galaxy

"I'm not sure we can continue to manufacture your products anymore."

The emotionless face stuffed into a collar and tie in front of me continues propounding, "The cost of purchasing your packaging and raw ingredients is not working in our algorithm. It would be cheaper for us to buy the ingredients directly from one of our vendors. If not, we may have to adjust costs or cancel your contract."

"I'm sorry. What's your name again?" I ask twenty-something on the screen in front of me. *Like I need to see what he looks like. Knowing full well the newest controller for our New Hampshire licensee is Aaron, but he's the fourth controller*

I've spoken to in the last six months that doesn't know who we are or what we do, and frankly, I don't like his tone.

"My name is Aaron."

"Well, Aaron," *with two A's and a business degree*, "we haven't raised the pricing for your packaging, coffee, or tea blends since we signed our license agreement." *And this conversation is the direct result of implementing that price increase. I get it- we're negotiating.* "That means you've been paying the same price for goods for seven years. Can you name one product in the food industry that hasn't increased in price in the past seven years? Never mind the supply chain issues with the pandemic."

"Well, no," he responds flustered. "They're coffees and teas? I thought you made mocktails?"

Come on, guy, it's called Mad Hatter Coffee and Tea. "We make both."

"I can show you the numbers," he continues a smidge more humbled. "Our gummies and our tinctures are nowhere near your COGs."

That's because they're gummies and tinctures, and there's no middle man. We're talking sugar and suspension liquid. "Most of our products have over thirteen organic ingredients in them, including hand-harvested roots that can't be cultivated." *My distaste for accountants grows with every word I utter.*

"Hand harvested, what?"

Oh my god. "There's no middle man between you and your sugar and food-colored gummies. There's also no branding and no promotion either. Our organic and sustainable: ingredients, packaging, branding, marketing, and promotion, plus our full line of complicated recipes and IP, can't compare to your in-house cost of goods for gummies, it's apples and oranges, and that's what's bundled into the price."

"If you just let us buy the ingredients directly from our vendors, we're sure we can get the price down."

"Aaron, there is no way you can buy our raw ingredients cheaper than we can. We purchase coffee and tea by the palette, hundreds of pounds at a time. We service six other states, including California and Nevada. Our sales on one holiday weekend in one of those territories is more than you sell in half a year in New Hampshire."

Danielle drops a note on my desk while I'm assailing this guy.

Call Delia!

Taking his silence as a white flag, I end his suffering, "Aaron, I have to take another call. Can we re-schedule?"

"Sure. I'll get back to you," he adds a trifle dejected.

"Great. Thanks." I dial Delia.

The first ring she picks up, "We have a problem." She's exasperated.

"OK. What's the problem?"

"During lunch break today," she states, taking a long, growling, dramatic breath, "Imogene played our group of youngsters a very disturbing video."

Disturbing to you, maybe. "What was it?"

"Oh, she'll play it for you when she gets home. In the meantime, I've confiscated her phone."

What? "You did what?"

"I can't risk her playing anything else that might negatively influence our group." Her low, gruff voice is eerie and petulant.

"Listen, Delia, you're not the school monitor. We hired teachers to interact with our kids, and we pay them to do so. Under no circumstances are you to take Imogene's phone or anything else away from her. Do I make myself clear?" My voice becomes unrecognizable. Remy, now standing in my office door, looks concerned as I continue, "In fact, put Imogene on the phone right now!"

There's a clanging sound, and then I hear. "Aunt Steph?"

"Are you OK?"

"Yup."

"Do you want me to come get you?"

"Nope."

"Delia will be giving you your phone back in case you need to reach me. Call me if you change your mind. I love you."

"I love you too."

"Put Delia back on, sweetie." I stand up dropping into a pace until I hear Delia's voice.

"This is my home, Stephanie. I have the right to say what goes on here."

"Delia, you are hosting four children from four other families with different beliefs and customs than you. It's your job as an adult to ensure each child feels safe and is welcome, and that's it! If you can't handle that, we'll find a different host family and go online until we do." I'm verging on tirade, avoiding Remy's terrifying gaze.

"I'll be taking this up at the meeting," she retaliates.

"So will I." Hanging up, Remy is now in my chair. The nefarious look on his face is volatile, "Bring it down," I say gently. "I can't handle another argument. I've got it under control. Imogene is fine. Besides, she can think circles around Delia."

With an eyebrow raised, he returns to his office.

Being a principal of a school must be hell. A notification comes through on my desktop that Chatura has released a new vlog; at the same instant, she emails me; ***Yoga session in an hour?***

Oh, thank god. Our outdoor guerilla yoga sessions are a lifeline. Impromptu, but consistently three times a week. **Yes**, I respond, **Same bat time,**

same bat place.

Scrambling to close my day up early, I run through my emails, and see the reminder for the invoice I sent to our licensee in Arizona, still unpaid, seven weeks later. The blackout of the pandemic lockdown almost a vague memory. I was hoping things would change. The news of Venice canals returning to crystal clear waters with fish in them, and pollution levels lowering historically, combined with families reconnecting with each other and nature, it all gives me so much hope that the world can change. People can change. Now that the hamster wheel has stopped, they can get off. We can get off! I send another text out to the Arizona CEO;

Hi Devon, hope all is well, and you and your family are safe. I sent an invoice over via email several weeks ago. The order can't be processed until payment is made. Please let me know if you have any questions. Thanks, Stephanie.

This invoice will give us the cushion we need to get through these uncertain times. Two words come to mind, eggs, and basket, but that sixty thousand will make all the difference in the world. Clicking "send" I run downstairs to change; we'll have exactly an hour for Yoga before I need to pick Imogene up. Soter's very excited and lets me know Chatura's already here; I meet her outside.

"What a beautiful day. Have you had a chance to see my vlog?" She asks, tossing her matt down under the cottonwood trees in my backyard, squeezing in a selfie with a beautiful smile.

Her skin is literally glowing. It's shimmering in the light. "No. I did get the notification though. It's been a crazy day." I can't tear my eyes away from her skin and decide not to bring up Delia. Starting off with a sun salutation and a series of twists, *I need to detox.* The stress sheds as we take turns leading one another, five moves for me and five moves for Chatura. Fifteen minutes later, I've got a real sweat, my breath regulating my uneasiness. I focus on the opposing energy coursing through my body, linking the sky and the ground through me like a conduit. Time goes by in the blink of an eye. Before I know it, I'm centered and resting in corpse pose literally winded, staring up into a matrix of branches against the clear blue sky, and it strikes me how very few people are truly connected to our network now. The handful of people we really care about is shockingly small. The rest move in and out like a mechanism of their own. They either call back, or they don't, and now more than ever, the phone's quiet. *It does feel safe not to be so spread out and exposed.*

"That was exactly what I needed," Chatura breaks in, mask-free, outside.

"Me too." I take one more deep breath while rooted to the mat. Opening my eyes, Chatura is smiling at me in lotus pose. "Do you need me to pick up Satara for you today?" I ask, rolling over on my side, making my way to a seated position, knowing how busy she is. Driving Satara around with us and grocery shopping for both houses is Imogene's favorite part of the day. I split up the grocery list and set the girls loose on the store. *They love it.*

"No, we're grabbing take-out in town tonight, but thanks. It's so important to support the local restaurants," she says, shaking out her mat. "I really think you'd benefit from my new vlog. It focuses on empathy. You should check it out." Recalculating her Fitbit, she walks to her car like that's not a bomb. Then with a cat-like stretch, she slides into the driver seat in one graceful movement and closes the door, abandoning me in the driveway, the dust from her departure a psychological mist. After several seconds of wonder, Soter licks my leg, shaking me from a standing slumber. On autopilot I climb into our Subaru, and he jumps in too; *he is, after all, an emotional support animal.* "What's with all the self-help suggestions? Are people trying to tell me something?" I ask him as he sits in the passenger seat, watching the road ahead. *He's no help at all.*

The drive to Delia's on the north side of town is chock full of imaginary conversations, none of them ending well. Waiting for the security guard to check me in and open the gate to the walled, exclusive neighborhood. The apparent computation of housewife and middle school math teacher doesn't add up to this address. The views alone are worth well over a million dollars, never mind the vast, faux adobe mansions dotting the gateway to the Santa Fe National Forest. We drive up here every weekend to ski in the winter; it's never dawned on me before, but I'm sure Grandma Josephine has something to do with this, *and it's none of my business.*

Pulling up to the sprawling one-story ranch-style home complete with a life size, bronze bison in the center of the circular driveway, dotted with an American flag drooping from a fifty foot pole, I take a deep breath. Avoiding confrontation at pick-up is my only tactic at this point until I get the whole story. I text Imogene; ***I'm out front.*** It looks like I'm the first to arrive. I wait anxiously as a response from Devon in Arizona pops up.

Stephanie, I never received an invoice. Please resend.

OK. It takes me three seconds to resend the invoice to the email thread of his original order from February. *This is the fifth time I've sent it. So much for this order being a cushion.*

I resent it, Devon. Let me know if you have any questions. As I'm texting, one eye watches Imogene as she walks out to the car; I can tell she's distressed. Soter gives her a warm, wet welcome then returns to the passenger seat like he's got somewhere to go.

"Hey, there, sweetie."

"Hi."

"Are you OK?"

"Yup."

"So, honey, what happened today?" I ask as she climbs in the back and buckles up.

"I don't know, Aunt Steph. It was bizarre. We were at lunch, and I was just sharing a video that Satara and I made last week." She becomes noticeably upset.

"You made a video?" I ask gently, glancing back in the rear-view mirror encouragingly as we head back down the mountain.

"Yes, in performing arts class, for school." Breathing hard, I can tell she's holding back tears.

"What's the video about?" I ask gently, attempting to gain perspective on our hour-long drive home.

"We were just singing the Galaxy Song."

"The Galaxy Song?"

"Yeah, you know the one in the Monty Python movie." Her hands are overly animated. "It's funny," she explains.

"I'd love to see it when we get home." I give her a smile. "How about some snacks?"

"YES!" Perking up immediately, I've hit her sweet spot.

Stopping at a convenience store on the way, we fill the counter with Arizona Tea and Smart Pop Corn, grins on our faces. Knowing most of the remote areas she's lived with her mom, they don't have packaged food, so it's a big deal. She grabs the bag, and I wrap my arm around her shoulder on the way out. Once we're back in the car, Imogene confesses vulnerably but a little more at ease, "You know Aunt Steph, I really don't know why Gerry's mom was so upset with us. She was more upset with Satara than me. But when she took my phone, I was frightened."

"I am so sorry, honey. That will never happen again." Gripping the wheel suppressing rage inside, a million conversations are going on in my head, none of them good.

Remy's in the driveway waiting for us as we pull up. Imogene gets out and locks her arms around his waist, as Soter circles them. He eyes me with a look I don't think I've ever seen before. "You, OK?" he asks.

"Yup." She drops her bag and heads for the zip line.

"What happened with the video?" He turns to me picking up her bag.

"I don't know yet." We watch quietly as she burns off some steam. Ten minutes later, she runs towards us, "What's for dinner, Aunt Steph?"

"Sliders and homemade fries."

"Yum."

All three of us make dinner together. Imogene in charge of making the meat patties; she pats them gently between her hands, carefully making them all the same size, her oversized hoodie bunched at the elbows while Remy's on salad after turning on the grill. Frying up potato wedges in bacon fat and olive oil I sprinkle them with Old Bay spice. The kitchen is full of love, and so is our food. *Columbo* on the flat screen over the sink is the perfect decompression. My favorite episode where the food critic poisons the restauranteur, is a time capsule of 1970's food, white and ornate, and every time Columbo interviews someone, Imogene yells, "He did it!" and we laugh.

Thirty minutes later, staring at empty plates, Remy begins, "So, what happened today?"

"OK. Satara and I made a video last week for a project in performing arts class. I showed it to everyone at lunch. It's just funny. It's a funny song about science." She hops up and retrieves her phone, then sits on Remy's lap to show him.

Standing behind them, I watch as two adorable twelve-year-old girls with caps, and sticks they use as canes, strike a pose.

"I really wanted to wear pink, like his pink suit in the movie, but I forgot to bring my bag the day we filmed it."

On the screen in front of us, Imogene turns to Satara, and in a toff, English accent, she begins, "Whenever life gets you down, Mrs. Brown, and things seem hard or tough. And people are stupid, obnoxious, or daft. And you feel that you've had quite enough." (Lots of giggles) Then they both sing as a backing track comes in.

"Just remember that you're standing on a planet that's evolving and revolving at nine hundred miles an hour.
That's orbiting at nineteen miles a second, so it's reckoned. A sun that is the source of all our power." (They continue to sing, giggling, walking up and down the length of the courtyard, swinging their sticks in syncopation to the backing track.)
"The sun, you, me, and everything that we can see, is revolving at a million miles a day.
In an outer spiral arm, at forty thousand miles an hour, in a galaxy we call the milky way…" (they dance and tip their hats to each other.)
"Our galaxy itself contains a hundred billion stars. It's a hundred thousand light-years side to side." (They wave their sticks left to right in unison.) Then, (both of them turn sideways, sticking out their tummies, laughing and singing), "It bulges in the middle, sixteen thousand light-years thick. But out by us it's just three thousand light-years wide."

The song continues for another minute or so, the girls faking a tap dance during a bridge; is absolutely adorable. Imogene is actually happy and having fun for the first time in a long time. I remember this song from Monty

Python's, *Meaning of Life.* When it's over, Remy and I both exclaim, "That was amazing!" applauding wildly.

"Do you like it?" She asks wide eyed.

"I loved it!"

"Do you like it, Uncle Rem?"

"Sweetie, I loved it! What's not to love?"

"Well, Gerry's mom didn't. She burst into the room, snatched my phone and yelled at Satara. She told her she should know better."

Sitting down in the chair next to them, both Remy and Imogene turn towards me anxiously, "Imogene, listen to me. You have met so many diverse people with different beliefs and ideas about the world and their lives on your travels. Delia is just one more person on that list. I don't know her well enough to understand why this was offensive to her, but it has nothing to do with you. Nothing."

"And don't let her dictate what's right or wrong," Remy adds on the verge of an explosion.

"OK, but this happens, like, all the time."

"What do you mean? What happens all the time?"

"Gerry's mom always interrupts class. Especially Miss Mays, the English teacher, during her block."

"What does she say?"

"I don't know, she takes her aside and talks to her. But I've seen Miss Mays roll her eyes."

"Are you still reading Maya Angelou?"

"Yes."

"Good."

"You stand by your own ideas. We've got your back," Remy consigns, holding a torrent of expletives back for Imogene's sake. "We'll take care of Delia." His steel blue eyes lock on to mine.

She smiles, gives him a kiss, then runs off to her room with Soter.

After a dangerous silence, I clearly state to my spouse, "I'm not talking to you until you lower your eyebrows."

"Who are these people?" he whispers. "What have we gotten ourselves into? A song about the fucking universe is offensive?! What is this woman? A flat earther? A racist?! An anti-science, Christian, racist? Some Christian!"

"I don't know. Her husband is a science teacher. I mean, I just don't get it."

"I don't care what they are!" His volume rises. "This woman can't dictate what's right or wrong for our niece, period!"

"I agree. This is a make it or break it issue."

"Talk to these women."

Grabbing my phone, I text the mom group; ***Hi, Ladies, I have an important issue I'd like to discuss with you all. If you have a moment tonight, that would be great. Please let me know.***

Instantly Gabriella gets back to me. ***We've already spoken to Delia.***

My back goes rigid. *What the hell does that mean*? Before overreacting, I take a breath; ***Please let me know when you are all available for a call.***

My phone rings immediately. It's Chatura, "Stephanie?"

"Hi."

"I don't know what happened today, but Delia is threatening to leave the group if you don't apologize. And I am so mad at Adriana the performing arts teacher!"

"I'm not apologizing to Delia. By the way, her name is Adriane, and why are you mad at her?"

A text from Holly comes in on the home school thread; ***For the record, Delia, Stephanie does not speak for all of us.***

Coward.

Chatura continues rambling, "I can't believe Adriana instructed Satara to record herself!"

"Adriane. Why? What's the problem?"

"Well, I believe that children are better creating their own sense of self, something they hold in their minds only."

Wait. "What are you saying?"

Showing them pictures or video of themselves is detrimental to that true self-image. Adriana went against my wishes as a parent, and filmed my daughter."

"Hold on. You don't take pictures of your daughters or video their childhood?"

"No!"

"Ever?"

"That's right! Never. It was a real contention with their father."

I bet it was! "But wait. You're a vlogger."

"Yes. But that has nothing to do with my girls."

"Doesn't Satara have a phone?"

"Yes, of course, she has the latest iPhone."

Shaking my head, I ask, "Did you tell Adriane any of this?"

"No. But Satara should have."

Oh, my god, I think I'm losing my mind! "You're going to have to take that up with Adriane yourself. You might want to look at the syllabus I forwarded at the beginning of the year; it's structured towards social media. That's why I hired her- to give the kids skills they can use." Desperately trying to weigh the unique predicament my new friend has found herself in, I lose sight of my argument. I'm reminded of my Great-Aunt Elena. She purposefully cultivated poison ivy and thorny briar outside the windows of all five of her children's windows. It looked like a fairytale fortress gone awry. She had been so traumatized by the stories of the Lindbergh kidnapping in her youth, she was determined to deter any possibility of it happening to her children. *But like most things you covet, instead of keeping people out, she only managed to keep her children in, an irony too sad to explore. Making a mental note that defense mechanisms are a double-edged sword. I concede to my friend's demands.* "Adriane will have to create a different lesson plan for Satara." There's an uneasy silence before I'm back on track. "That aside, are you OK with a family dictating their non-science beliefs on your daughter at school?"

"No. Absolutely not."

"I didn't think you would."

"But I also don't think anyone should be belittled or bullied for their beliefs either."

"Who was belittled and bullied other than the girls?"

"Well, Delia said you threatened her."

What? "I did not threaten her. I told her if she couldn't handle creating a safe space for our kids without her dogma attached, we would host the classes somewhere else. Imogene was frightened when Delia took her phone away."

"She took her phone away?" she pauses a moment. "That's not right. She didn't tell me that. Well, where exactly would we host the school if they can't be at Delia's? I can't have them here."

"My house is safe."

She sighs, "I hope you're not using this as an excuse to get the classes back at your house again Stephanie. I mean, it would be great for me as it's so much closer than Delia's, but the other gals, just aren't comfortable with it."

"And why is that exactly?"

"I don't know."

I say nothing.

"We have our first field trip coming up," she offers like a carrot.

Yeah, that I planned and talked everyone into for weeks.

"And we have the Halloween party that everyone is *so* excited about."

That I'm hosting after fighting for its life.

"Think of the kids."

My eyes turn towards the ceiling before I heave a sigh, "In the real world, Delia should apologize to both Imogene and Satara for her erratic behavior."

"There is no real-world anymore, Stephanie. It's a pandemic."

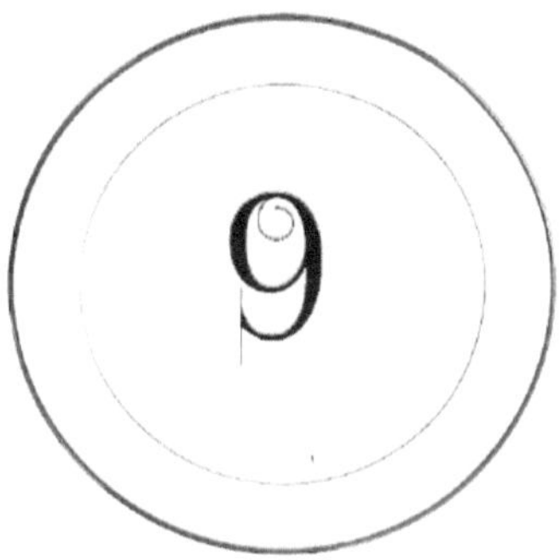

Give me a pig foot

Thirty seconds till the parent Schloom meeting begins, and I'm the first to log in. Sitting in my Covid nesting chair outside at six o'clock on this Sunday evening, adjusting my hair in the screen reflection, I have a micro-dosed cannabis tea in a mug as an unabashed crutch, the perfect suggestion from my husband. After a long sip, the ping of attendees begins, Chatura smiling, as usual, her camera at the most optimal angle for her features and the lighting perfectly accentuating her shimmering skin, looks calm and collected. Holly clicks in with her consistent glum and exhausted aura, her mic muted before Delia chimes in with her camera off. *That's new.* My composure is straightforward and pleasant but business like. *I will not let them get the best of me.*

Adjusting my smile, I hear the inevitable robotic voice state on cue, "Gabriella Cecilia Garcia Fernández del Olmo, mother of Alejandro Juan Carlos Garcia Fernández Del Olmo Lopez," followed by Gabriella's Spanish laced accent. "Ladies, what's on the agenda?" her corporate voice on.

The agenda has, of course, been attached to the call. As usual, we can all see it. Item number one is workload for kids. *I say nothing as this has been talked about ad nauseum, and absolutely no one, is listening to me.*

Holly actually speaks, "The workload for this home school curriculum is too much for Seraphine," her monotone voice drones. "We spend four hours a day on homework after school. It's too much," she claims, her face tortured by a constant state of anguish.

"Yes, Alejandro Juan Carlos, is terribly behind. He will be spending all this weekend catching up." Her phone goes off, Taylor Swift's song "You Need to Calm Down" is the ringer. "Ladies, excuse me. This is a work call. I have to take it." She turns off her camera and mutes herself.

"This curriculum is terrible," Delia confirms, her dulcet voice, low and definitive.

Of course, I chose the curriculum. "Ladies, you do realize that this is a home school?"

"What does that mean exactly, Stephanie?" Chatura asks, her bright smile glowing against her teak, bedroom headboard.

"It means, it can be altered and redefined for the group and for each individual student."

Silence.

I continue recounting, "When we purchased our curriculum, the dean of the school told us that all of the subjects we chose weren't designed to be taught all together. They were designed for kids that are either working, training, or traveling. He said, 'Three subjects, tops,' otherwise it would be too much work. Does anyone remember that?" I ask as patiently as possible, slurping my cup.

Again silence.

"We've customized Imogene's workload. She is only required to complete one-third of all math problems instead of half, and half of the requirements for each science lesson. And because the English workbook is mostly busy work for her, she chooses only the most interesting assignments but does them immersion-style, same with history. You can ask the teachers we hired for their feedback. I have at length. They have a much better handle on this than we do, and they love the curriculum. Plus keep in mind, each of our kids is different with different needs, which is why an adaptable structure is such a good fit."

"I'm not going to lie to Gerry's teachers," Delia steps in full throttle, "who happen to be my husband's colleagues, and tell them next year that he's completed this year's work if he didn't! It's as simple as that!" She takes over the screen share with a copy of the New Mexico Home School requirements, "According to the New Mexico Department of Education, they have to have 120 days of instruction." She circles 120 days on the sheet about 129 times, "No more and no less."

Taking a deep breath, *I need to move carefully*, "I think you're missing the point, Delia."

Her camera turns off.

"No one is lying." I continue, "The curriculum is designed to be personalized. They're not meant to complete every question of every lesson. And most importantly, it shouldn't be based on how much time they put in. It should be based on how thoroughly they understand the work they complete. Not all kids are the same. They work differently, they learn differently, and the beauty of home-schooling is it compensates for each child's needs. This is one of the reasons public schools are such a mess; learning shouldn't be timed."

"How can you say that? My husband has worked for the public school system for twenty years!"

"Alejandro needs to get on track," Gabriella steamrolls back into the conversation, officiating her CEO title with every syllable enunciated. "I don't have time to sit with him, and the work isn't getting done," she interlopes, having missed the entire conversation, her accent deliberate, and heavy.

Delia turns her camera back on, "My husband Brock said he could work with the kids on the weekends," she offers, readjusting her attitude. Near desperate eyes continue, "To catch up on math and science."

Like a drone, Holly responds, "That would be great," her voice devoid of any inflection is a marvel.

"Wonderful, Delia, thank you so much," Chatura agrees with a flourish, then adds, "Can the kids sleep over, so I don't have to drive out there twice a day?"

"Sure. The boys can sleep in the basement, and the girls can sleep in the guest and living rooms," Delia answers with her camera still on. "I'll leave the windows open. Grandma Josephine says she'll cater the study group."

So much for pandemic safety. I say nothing as the scales tip away, *again.*

"Of course, we'll have to cancel the camping, field trip. There just isn't any time for that until they catch up," Delia exalts comfortably with the majority behind her.

What? "Wait a minute."

Everyone agrees, except me.

"Can I just say," I rebound. Delia's camera turning off again, "that I think these kids need this field trip. They need to be outside playing. They need a break.

They need to be kids! They're overloaded, they're stressed out, they're depressed. Nature would be good for them."

Camera back on, "Well, if they can catch up with their work, they'll have the Halloween party. But there's a lot of wood to chop. Which reminds me, I think we should alter the school calendar."

"Wait. The Halloween party?" I break-in. "That's in two weeks?"

Delia turns her camera infuriatingly back off.

"That they're all looking forward to and making costumes for? Isn't concrete?" I ask astounded.

Camera on she pontificates, "Not if they don't catch up. Actually, at the rate Gerry's going, we'll have to adjust Thanksgiving and Christmas break as well. They're too long. The kids need the extra days of school."

What?

"Now that we've straightened that out," Delia, now fully weaponized, continues, "what do we do about French?"

"What's wrong with the French class?" I grip my chair.

"It's just too much. It's not necessary. I mean, how many languages does a kid need?"

"I don't know," I say as she turns her camera off again, "Imogene speaks four languages, and she still wants to take French."

Camera back on, "Well, not everyone can travel the world, Stephanie. I think it's a waste of money. They don't even need a second language yet." She oozes snark.

"We should have chosen Mandarin; we're wasting our time with French," Holly actually speaks, and as usual, I'm dumbfounded. Gabriella's phone goes off again, and this time the ringer is Fleetwood Mac's, *You can go your own way*, which is almost lost in the clamor of personal agendas.

"It's my ex," she states with a grimace, "I have to take this."

And off Gabriella goes again! Staying the course, I remind them, "We all voted on French because that's what the kids wanted. Remember? And no, not everyone can travel the world," I say, remembering how last week Delia complained about having to cancel their yearly missionary trip to Mexico because the only member of her parish that speaks Spanish is hospitalized with Covid, before I continue, "But everyone should." Re-grouping for a moment, I add, "You know what?" Gritting my teeth, while her camera turns off again, "We started this home school so our kids would be around other kids during the pandemic, so they wouldn't have to suffer online isolation. But that is exactly what *you're* creating. The worst-case scenario, too much work and no play! And the crazy thing is, we have a choice! We don't have to subject our kids to hours of looking at a screen, sitting in a room alone. You're actually creating the worst public school system in the country!"

"What's wrong with the public school system?!" Delia explodes like I'm insulting her husband again, who's been a teacher for twenty years. *Which she doesn't have to remind me because she's told the group a couple of hundred times!*

"How long have you got, Delia? You know what? You all do what you need to do. If your kids don't want French, then drop out! We'll continue with the French teacher on our own for Imogene. But as for tutoring math and science on the weekends? We do other things on the weekends that are more important to our family than busy work." With that, I turn my camera off, my finger hovering over the end call button.

There's a deliberating silence, a long, deliberating silence. I take it as an opportunity, "I also want to say that if our kids don't feel safe at school, we're doing something seriously wrong."

Gabriella pops back in.

"Exactly!" Delia blurts, her camera intact and in full swing, "Which is why phones should not be allowed! They should leave them at home!" She says, as if wounded and breathless.

"Absolutely not! Imogene needs her phone in case there's an emergency. It's not negotiable. And while we are on the topic, politics and religion need to stay out of the curriculum. I don't care what you believe or who you voted for, but everyone in this group needs to keep their agendas out of the school room, or we are **OUT**!"

"Agreed," solidly confirming my point, Chatura concurs with a hearty nod that gives me hope.

"I agree," Holly throws in, but like I'm twisting her arm.

Wait for it.

"I'm not so sure politics or religion should be ignored or can be ignored, Stephanie. These are crazy times. I mean, look what happened to Columbus Day?" Gabriella interjects like she's on Mars.

"What? Gabriella, their world is upside down." Feeling the pull of a diminutive sisterhood finally behind me, I add, "They need to know more than ever, that someone has their backs."

"I don't know. What do you think, Delia?" Gabriella commiserates.

Here it comes.

"Stephanie is acting like I interrupted the school day with my beliefs. And that is simply not true." Camera off.

"Actually, Delia, you stopped the class with drama about a video for a class project. A song about the universe! You pointedly shamed the girls and punished them by taking their phones because it was a song about science. Known facts about our galaxy that offended ***you***! I won't stand for it. You should apologize to both girls. And if you can't keep your beliefs to yourself, classes will be moved to my house." *I rest my case.*

Conspiratorially quiet, I wait but there's no response. *She's texting the group. I need to go.* "Ladies, I have to go. I have another call. Have a great rest of your weekend." I push the end call button like it's oxygen itself.

Mother popcorn

The frenetic roar of the popcorn popper momentarily fills the kitchen with aggression as Imogene and I slip our I Can't Believe It's Not Butter covered hands into a large bowl, quickly tossing the popcorn in hot corn syrup, before patting them into balls and laying them out on wax paper to congeal.

"This stuff is so goopy!" she squeals, spreading her hands with Karo webbing between her fingers. "I'm so glad I didn't have to go to school today. What's next?"

"Mummy cookies."

"Mummy cookies," nodding her head involuntarily, she repeats in a sugar trance before jolting up, "I'll be right back! Gotta go." In a whirl, she takes off for the bathroom, Soter barely beating her to the door as Remy walks in for his post-mid, pre-afternoon coffee.

"It smells good in here. Watcha got goin' on?" He plants a soft kiss on my neck before instinctively moving towards the coffee pot, loyally followed by Danielle, of course.

"This is the first Halloween Imogene has experienced here in the U.S. We're going for it! We picked out a dozen or so recipes of what she calls, "ghoulish party food" that both meat-eaters and vegans can eat. I have to say it's been tricky." Questioning the flavor profiles, I nod my head involuntarily, "But it's a potluck, so, hopefully, everyone will bring something. We adapted every recipe: vegan cornbread without bacon." I eye Danielle, who raises her eyebrows in response and continue, "Stuffed mushrooms with olive eyeballs, black bean hummus dip, vegan split pea soup, homemade broomstick pretzel sticks, guacamole that will spew out of the mouth of a small pumpkin that you and Imogene will carve later, bread and chips because they're safe. Oh, and a boat load of candy and enough cupcakes to cover the entire kitchen table that will create a Chuck Close inspired pixelated Frankenstein when you put them all together."

"Wow! That's impressive!" Danielle lights up, genuinely excited, her golden eyes surveying the kitchen table with delight.

"So, you think Chatura will bring over that coveted solar oven stew?" Remy chortles.

My eyebrows purse just thinking about it. *The poor brown muck suffering who knows how many hours of uncontrollable solar oven temperatures in her yard. The odds are good she will bring it because that all she's been vlogging about for the last week.*

"You're going to an awful lot of trouble for a group of women who don't care."

"It's for the kids, Rem. They deserve this."

"Sweetie, just don't get your hopes up." He takes his brew and disappears.

"You need any help?" Danielle asks, surveying the party loot. "I love Halloween."

"I am so sorry you can't come to the party," I confess, "These women are Covid Nazis."

Danielle laughs, her smile bright, beautiful, and easy. "It's all good," she throws Remy's favorite line out there as Imogene returns, hopping up on her chair.

"Hi, Danielle."

"Hey, girlie." She picks up a breadstick, "Tell me, what do mermaids use to wash their tails?"

"That's easy. Tide."

"You got me, again! How do you do it?"

Imogene cackles, pleased with herself.

"What are you going to be for Halloween?" Danielle asks.

"Anubis, the God of Death."

"Awesome! Take pictures. I'd love to see your costume." She turns to me, "Well, let me know if you need anything." She loops the table again, lingering.

"Thanks, Danielle. This is the last of it."

"Ok. Have fun." Halfheartedly, she follows Remy upstairs.

Maybe I should have invited her to help? I was mortified when I had to uninvite her to the party. She took it like a pro, her only reply when I painstakingly had to explain Delia's unyielding condition that only family Covid bubbles were allowed at school events was, "The cau-dacity." We both laughed, but I knew it hurt.

"Aunt Steph?"

"Yes, honey."

"Your phone is buzzing."

The non-sensical imbalance of the other women weighs in like a hammer as I reach for my phone.

Stephanie, I still haven't received the invoice you say you sent over. We are running low on packaging. Can you send over the new order in the meantime? Devon.

Hmmm. I'm Giving him the benefit of the doubt, but this is beginning to look like a payment, procrastination ploy.

Hi Devon, Have you checked your junk mail? Because I sent it over five times to this email. I'm sorry, but all invoices must be paid in full before the orders are shipped. But your order is ready to go once we receive payment. Stephanie

Resending the invoice as an attachment and as an invoice directly from my point-of-sale app, I'm crossing my fingers, this doesn't turn into a pissing match, but my phone dings immediately with Devon's response.

There is nothing wrong with my email. I receive over 2000 emails a day! Something's wrong on your end. Please advise.

OK, here we go. Sending a test email with an attachment to my Mad Hatter account and my personal account, they both come in immediately. *It's definitely not on my end, but the customer is always right.*

Devon, it must be something on my end. My apologies. I resent the invoice from our POS system as well this time, just in case. You will not be able to pay through the invoice as they don't allow cannabis companies to do that, but you should see the invoice shortly. Please let me know if you don't receive it. Thanks for your patience, Stephanie.

This economical slow down only emphasizes the cat and mouse game of sales. I get it. I just don't like it.

"Something wrong, Aunt Steph?"

My face must be quite the picture. "No, sweetie, everything's fine."

After taking the last of the dozens of mummy cookies out of the oven to cool, we're both simultaneously tired and pumped. Cary Grant's *Arsenic and Old Lace* is playing on the kitchen monitor over the sink and has us both transfixed watching his aunts happily bop up and down through a house of murderers and dead bodies.

"Do you think we've hung the proper, excessive amount of spider webbing?" I ask, her eyes full of darling excitement.

"Do we have more?"

"Yes! And I have an idea."

Outside we spin a monstrous web encasing the entrance to the area you have to walk through to get to the fire pit and food table we set up outside. Once it's pulled between the two colossal sister cottonwood trees in the backyard next to the zip line, we throw purple and orange lights on it, hoping for the best in the austere afternoon light.

"Aunt Steph?"

"Yes, honey."

"Do you think anyone will come?"

My heart stops. *Facing her, what can I say?* "Of course, they'll come. What did the kids say at school?" *She's been working so hard on her Anubis costume. If these moms don't bring their kids, she will be crushed. Rethinking my actions with the mom group, I should have just swallowed my pride. If I've turned these parents off and they take it out on Imogene? I can only blame myself.*

"They're all really excited about it. They were all making costumes. But it's not up to them, is it?"

"No," I say as gently as possible, "But no matter what happens or who comes, we're going to have a party tonight. Right?"

"Right."

I put a spell on you

Just before sunset, Remy lights the fire, flames rising into an auburn sky, an ancient incantation against the purple and orange glow of oncoming twilight. Two owls fly overhead on their evening tour of the village, silhouettes as Imogene creeps out the back door with Soter. Her black Anubis papier mâché mask and costume are a prophecy waiting to happen. The ears are at least ten inches tall; she painted the inside of them and around the Egyptian eye holes white, then painstakingly painted gold and blue lapis arm, wrist, and ankle cuffs on her brown body suit, topped off with a beaded necklace she made from old beads she found at the thrifty store. I sewed a white skirt with a gold see-through, over-layer she bound with a matching beaded belt. A large ankh tattoo on her back is impressive as she moves from tree to tree stealthily, only Soter giving her away.

Remy pretends not to see her, knowing she's sneaking up on him as he tends the fire. When she is just three feet away, he turns around quickly, "Whoa ah ah ha haha!" he yells, arms up, his Horus, falcon head mask dramatized in the firelight. Imogene screams, and they both laugh with delight, Soter galloping around them with the excitement of a puppy. *A great start to an uncertain evening.*

Looking down at my costume Imogene deliberately designed for me reminds me of how much this party means to her. She attached a life-size pair of blue, pleated, shimmer wings to a gold lame´ dress I've had in my closet for years, then spray painted a small round mirror gold that sits on my head, on top of a golden headdress, the symbol of the throne. *It's a bit heavy, but the winged strap around my chin should help keep it on if I don't bend over or walk too fast.*

Isis is no stranger to me. Last year, facing my worst fear, the Goddess of protection, healing, and magic guided me to the strength I needed. *I hope she'll be able to help me again tonight.*

Standing by the fire, watching the last of twilight diminish to absolute black, Remy turns the music on, and Imogene and I dance to "The Monster Mash." But my anxiety, that no one will show, is upon me like a noose. Attempting to dance it off, Remy joins us in his can-can style that's hilarious while I'm trying to convince myself that it doesn't matter. *This party doesn't matter.*

Thanks to chunks of dry ice we strategically placed all over the food table, it's smoldering beautifully as we head over to refresh ourselves with cranberry punch.

"Aunt Steph, what do you get when you cross a bear and a lion?"

Distracted by our lack of guests, my mind's a blank. I look to Remy for help but he's at a loss. "A lion and a bear, I don't know," he says in defeat.

"Killed! You get killed!" She swirls around laughing, murderously dancing, absorbing her character with the nuances of the night, her imagination taking hold, transporting her far, far away. *I'm glad she's so unaffected by our lack of guests.* I watch her spin, and my heart lightens.

An hour and a half into the playlist, I've entirely given up on anyone showing. We're head banging to "Highway to Hell," my body releasing tension into the atmosphere that's been bottled up like a time bomb. *Imogene's having fun, so who cares?*

"Good thing we uninvited Danielle," Remy remarks in my ear, his eyebrows dangerously elevated, before they're flooded by light for an instant.

It's Gabriella. Instantly happy and mad at the same time, I walk over to the spider web entrance and force a peace offering once she makes her way to the table, "Gabriella, thanks for coming."

"Alejandro Juan Carlos has been looking forward to this," she responds, her accent implying she's slightly annoyed as Al walks up in full, actual armor, clanging with each step.

"Wow, Alejandro Juan Carlos, that is an amazing costume! You both look amazing!" I lighten up. Gabriella is dressed as a queen. I'm not sure which one, but definitely Spanish; her jewelry catching in the firelight, is mesmerizing.

"Thank you, Stephanie." With a less guarded tone, she seems almost relaxed as she manages awkwardly in heels through our woodchipped paths.

"Come on, Al!" Imogene grabs him by the arm and drags him straight to the zip line.

Good luck.

Gabriella unloads what must be two hundred or so chicken wings, each box with a different flavor printed on them.

"Chicken wings! What a great idea, thank you." Then she unpacks about twenty pounds of BBQ ribs from a butcher in town, "Is that from Mitchell's Butcher? I've been dying to try them." My mouth involuntarily salivates.

"They are the best ribs in town! They use our meat!"

"I had no idea. How wonderful!"

"I love barbeque. Any time of the year!" she exclaims excitedly, "There's chipotle-sage rub, honey-juniper rub, Thai-basil rub, garlic and herb, honey-bar b que, ginger-pecan rub, and my favorite, hot n' bitchin." She laughs, surveying the platters with an adoring, kittenish look as they now take over every empty space on the table. "And I brought this for spritzers. It's my favorite Halloween cocktail!" She pulls out a bottle of Campari, the red liquid glowing ominously, two six-packs of club soda, and two bottles of prosecco.

"Ooh, I'll have one of those." Suddenly, I feel a bridge has been crossed.

"Atta girl, I think we all need to decompress." She mixes me a glass of the villainously, red cocktail, and we chink as Chatura pulls up.

"Thank god," I whisper. "Which queen are you, by the way?" I ask, feeling happier by the moment with each sip. "That is such a beautiful dress, and your jewelry looks real."

"They are. They're real! They're heirlooms from my family. From Spain!" Her accent, somewhat thicker than I remember, combined with perhaps hundreds of thousands of dollars' worth of jewels, sets me back. I'm flabbergasted, "Wow, I knew you were from Spain. But I didn't know…."

"Make way!" Chatura interrupts, "Hot dish coming through." Cutting between us in long, flowing, white silk robes, her hands are grappling with a giant bowl. "Solar stew for everyone!" she announces, strategically placing the dish in the center of the table, stacking several bowls of wings on top of each other and even off the table, much to Soter's surprise.

This is going to be a battle of the fittest. I smile. I'm not sure she's in a costume, but she looks great as usual. "Thank you, Chatura, that's very thoughtful," I say, catching Gabriella's eye roll.

"Wow! That's a lot of meat," our vegan friend states soberly.

"There are carrots and celery sticks in each of the wing boxes," Gabriella notes with a grin, "Just wipe the chicken juice off with a napkin."

"Thanks." Chatura turns her attention. *Always the diplomat.*

"I love your costumes, Stephanie."

"They were Imogene's idea. We had a lot of fun making them. As long as it stays warm, I'll be OK."

"You are so handy. I wish I had the time to make the girls costumes, but my vlog posting timetable doubles during the holidays, so it's just not possible. I literally have to have outlines for all my posts through New Year's now to make it work." Her girls run by dressed in matching, store-bought witch costumes with different colored fluorescent wigs under their pointed caps.

"The girls look great! By the way, everything else on the table is vegan."

Remy joins us, *and it's like I'm not even here.*

"Remy, would you like a Campari Spritz?" Gabriella proffers her voice silky.

"Thanks, I'm good with a beer. How is everyone tonight, ladies?" He eyes our guests, piling a plate high with everything but stew, definitely taking stock of our guests.

"I'll have one of those." Chatura nods towards my drink. "What a great color – very vampiric!"

Gabriella quickly whisks together a cocktail for her as headlights run up the drive. *It's Holly.*

Remy feeling my anxiety level drop, gives me a smile. Chatura catches our moment and turns away towards the fire, the light capturing her eyes.

Seraphine is the first one out of the car, black ponytails trailing behind her Wednesday Addams costume. She speeds by us with just enough time to grab a handful of chicken wings and mummy cookies, followed by Holly dressed as a very pretty witch and her husband Nate the surgeon, dressed… *as a surgeon.* They plop a container of bakery mini cupcakes on the table, and even though we all know each other, because we never see each other in person, it makes for uncomfortable re-introductions. Nate grabs a beer, and Holly falls in line with a Campari spritz.

"Everything but the chicken and ribs is vegan, Holly."

She nods, lifting her eyebrows.

"And it's non-GMO," I add.

With a curious smile, she picks up a pretzel broom stick, then asks, "Do you think Delia will come?" she asks out of the gate, scrunching her nose at the tonnage of barbeque.

"I have no idea." *And I don't, because absolutely no one RSVP'd! Is that just an east coast thing or what? Standing here, I feel like I'm two people; on the outside, a calm and collected hostess with everything under control, while the other, is having a fucking heart attack!*

"I put a spell on you because you're mine…" Screaming J. Hawkins croons over the blue tooth speakers and Remy throws me a glance as he and Nate move towards the firepit with plates full of meat. *Everything's going to be just fine, just breathe.*

"Who are you, Gabriella?" Holly asks one hand on her waist, notably animated tonight.

"I'm Queen Isabella the first, of course," disgruntled, she responds like there could only be one.

"Who was she?"

"Ferdinand the second's, wife." Her accent is so thick right now, she might as well be speaking Spanish.

Our blank expressions, say it all.

"My god, you live in New Mexico! They united Spain as one country."

Again, we're lost, nodding our heads.

"They funded Christopher Columbus!"

"Oh!" We both respond.

Wait. "Wasn't that the beginning of the Spanish Inquisition?" I inquire.

"Yes. And?"

"Well, you look great," Holly intervenes as I hide a
choke, "Those jewels are incredible. They look real."

"They are real!" Yelling now, Gabriella throws both hands up in the air, exasperated. "My family in Spain were in the royal court prior to The Glorious Revolution." She puts her glass down heavily, rolling R's all over the place, waiting for a response that doesn't come. "I can date our family bloodline back to the 1200s. Our ranch here in the U.S. would be the largest in the country if we included our grants in Mexico. We own over half a million acres in New Mexico and Texas alone, all land grants from the King himself."

I'm not the only one speechless for a moment. "That's a ton of land."

"All for cattle?" Holly is not impressed. I notice her glass is drained before she continues, "Did you know ranching displaces small community farmers that would be more regenerative and sustainable for the land? Goats are a better choice."

I don't even recognize Holly; this is the most I've heard her speak, ever!

"Well, no one eats goats." Gabriella waves her hand away, "And we haven't displaced anyone. So, relax. We've owned the land for over three hundred years. Can I get you another drink?"

"Yes." Commandeering the floor, Holly continues, "Did you know the Oxford definition of a cow is a ruminant or even-toed ungulate mammal that chews the cud regurgitated from its own rumen."

Laughing, I reply, "I didn't understand a single word you just said."

"Exactly. Does that sound like something you should eat?" Her large doe eyes focus on the pyramid of meat weighing down the table. "Besides, cattle farming is one of the largest contributors to greenhouse gases. I watched a broadcast that showed how goats eat a lot less than cows because, well, they're smaller, of course, and they eat noxious weeds."

"This would be a great vlog," Chatura murmurs in between hungry spoonsful of stew. "Ruinous Ruminants!"

"I'll have to remember that." Gabriella's teeth clench with an eye roll.

But Holly's on point, "Wait, wouldn't there have been Native American Indians on the land here before you?"

Gabriella shakes her head, glaring in a don't go there stance, that closes Holly off. *Maybe for the night. We all feel the energy.* Soter barks, clearing the air and a brand-new, black Cadillac pulls up, that I don't recognize. My spine's rigid, thinking it's Delia. *What's wrong with me? Why am I letting this woman get to me?*

The car stops. An armed soldier in full combat gear jumps out! Remy's next to me in seconds. I look for Imogene, who's tucked behind the house on the trampoline. Noticing our change of stance, Gabriella turns around, "Oh good. Delia's here." Oblivious, she looks back at us like we're causing trouble as Gerry, the commando runs by. But once I see Delia in a medieval princess dress, that seems appropriate, I submit to Defcon two. I've never met her husband, Brock, so there's no way I would recognize him in an inflatable dinosaur suit. *Ironic.*

More awkward introductions are made, and I feel the other moms watching me intently as Delia unloads gorgeous candy apples and numerous pies from her car. *Like this was the plan all along.*

"These are from Grandma Josephine," she announces, her deep voice an odd contradiction to the velvet princess attire. Placing a tray of life-sized sugar skulls, one for each kid, on a second table Remy is setting up for the overflow, much to Soter's disappointment. Delia surveys the food tables with a look of absolute triumph.

"Those are amazing," I say as gracefully as possible. *They are! Intricately sculpted in different colored patterns, they literally look 3D. No doubt some indigenous tribe in Mexico made them.* "Thanks for coming."

"Gerry said he wouldn't talk to me if I didn't let him come," she shares with the group like it's adorable.

Remy runs a block and turns to Brock, "Can I get you a soda or some cider?" His helpfulness is not unappreciated as he acknowledges Brock is permanently on the wagon.

"Cider would be nice. Thanks."

Brock is a tall but slight man with almost nugatory, brown eyes glaring out of the mouth of the inflated costume that surrounds his head.

"Delia? How about a Campari spritz?" Gabriella shakes her tumbler in the air.

"Yes!"

Brock shoots her a glance and she readjusts her shoulders, "Just a little one," she restates then quickly diverts the topic, "Are any of you going to Evangeline's memorial?"

"The tutor?" I ask.

"Yes." Nodding she continues, "She worked at the school for over ten years. Gerry worked with her on English. Actually, I think all the kids were working with her except Imogene. What a shock!"

"She was odd." Holly adds quietly, almost to herself. "Even her house was odd. All those tires for walls. There was something… not right about her."

"They're called Earth ships, Holly, and they're a sustainable alternative to post and beam homes," Chatura clarifies, "I just posted about this. I sent you all a link. Didn't any of you watch it? Are you all getting my notifications?"

"Well, she was odd then," Holly re-emphasizes ignoring Chatura, finding newfound courage in the spritz. "Do you remember her collection of mice?" She asks, tucking her chin into her chest with disgust.

"I do!" Chatura whispers with a gasp.

"She collected mice?" I respond. "As pets?"

"No." Holly spells out slowly, "In-her-freezer."

Wait, what? "Why?"

"Her house was infested. The tire walls were up against the dirt, and the rats and mice burrowed in constantly," she adds, nodding as though I should know what she's talking about, her face all scrunched up again. "Not a very good house design."

"So, how did they wind up in her freezer?"

"She used, glue traps."

"OK."

Chatura intervenes, "She didn't have the heart to kill them, so she stuck them in her freezer, to die."

"*Wait.* Remy told me she died of exposure."

"Yeah. Talk about karma," Holly adds, ladling out split pea soup, "This looks good. Is it organic?"

Eh Cumpari

Between the crackle of the fire and Nick Cave moaning about where the wild roses grow, the third round of spritzes are pouring freely. I hold off but noticeably sense the routine tension I've grown accustomed to with this group, dissipating. I feel relaxed around these women for the very first time, and it feels good.

Everyone safely distanced around the firepit with plates of food, our masks pulled down around our chins. *It actually feels like we're all having a good time. Finally, we're making a connection. It's liberating!* The theme from Harry Potter eerily breaks through like the soundtrack to my life, dramatizing the firelight with Wagnerian hues cast upon our guests' faces, *or maybe it's just my tea kicking in?*

"It's a perfect night," I offer, entranced by an inky black curtain pulled around us, "I love Halloween."

"Has anyone tried my solar stew?" Chatura inquires. Her face caught in the firelight, looks much younger than her years, clearly showing disappointed in the lack of response from the group. But the answer is evident as multiple eyes jolt around, the bowl standing as full as it was when she arrived. That however, does not deter her, "It's amazing how easy it is to make, you know?" She repeats for the third time. "You literally just put everything in a pot and set it out in the sun. That's it! That's all there is to it! I don't know why anyone would have a regular oven; they're such a waste of resources, especially here in New Mexico. Someone should teach people how to make these on a mass scale. It could save the world!"

Catching Holly's raised eyebrows, I quickly confirm, no one is eating the stew. Delia, secretly on her fourth spritz, has become increasingly more talkative and friendly, she's actually smiling. I take this rare, calm moment to ask an honest question, "Has anyone else noticed their kids depressed? Because Imogene has been terribly upset lately. The kid's group chat is blowing up. I thought it would be a helpful tool during isolation, but it's backfiring; she's miserable." Without name dropping I offer, "The kids seem to be taking their anxieties out on each other."

"Boys are much easier than girls, but of course, you wouldn't know." Delia morphs back into herself.

"They're saying that this whole thing, all this isolation is just a big smokescreen for 5G control. It's causing the virus to spread using an electromagnetic spectrum from 5G output. They're already starting to track us," Holly rambles self-consciously.

"They do that now." Gabriella waves her phone in the air.

"I know. I told Nate he should never take his phone when he leaves the house."

Ok, that makes no sense at all. Jokingly, I ask, "What are you, a bank robber? I mean, who would care what you're doing? Unless you're up to no good?" Flashbacks of our old cannabis days stream through my mind. *If they only knew. Wait, of course they know! That's precisely why they don't like me or want school at our house!*

From behind me, I hear, "Oh, my goodness!"

Everyone turns towards Chatura, her face anchored in pain, "Look at all these disgusting bones." She points to the mountain of stripped rib and wing carcasses now towering in the middle of the table.

I quickly cover them with a couple of napkins.

"You know, chicken farming is one the most inhumane industries worldwide," Holly states, shaking her head from side to side, almost in a trance.

"Gabriella, do you really have a tanning bed?" Delia changes the subject, amused and a bit tipsy.

"Yes." She nods her head. "It's top of the line, but finicky." Sounding more like Selma Hayek now, she commands the floor, "I have had to fly *three* technicians in from California to have it repaired!" Like an umpire, she raises her fingers in the air. "Three! The first was a complete moron; he knew nothing! I knew more than he did. The second technician, same thing! A moron!" She waves her hand like swatting a fly. "Now the third guy is finally ordering parts, but with this ridiculous pandemic, who knows how long it will take to get them in. Anyway, since I started using it, I have never once had to apply foundation; it tans so evenly. Look for yourself. It's perfection!"

"Perfection? That's the name of my new CBD brand. You are all going to love it!" Chatura confirms to herself.

"You do look good," Holly replies, back on track, with just a touch of envy, "My skin is so unpredictable. Asians are supposed to have great skin, but not me. I'm still getting pimples. And I don't tan at all. It's just not fair." Sloshing her cup towards Gabriella, she's on a roll, "You don't even need a tan. What a waste." Reaching involuntarily for a chicken wing, she catches herself.

I pretend not to see.

"What's in these drinks anyway?" Delia asks. "They're so good."

This is the first time I've seen her happy, her masculine features softened by the dress and crown, she looks pretty and sweet. It's quite a transformation from the hard-lined personality I've been at odds with for so long.

Brock joins us, the fan from his dinosaur costume humming over the crackle of the fire. I notice he's taken his wife's elbow firmly. "Campari is made from the cochineal beetle."

Umm, what?

"In fact, they're native to the Americas. They eat prickly pear cactus, the little buggers. That's what makes them so red. I believe they've dated their harvesting back to the Aztecs. Of course, it would take thousands of them to color the Campari due to the fact that they're smaller than a ladybug. I read somewhere that Starduds uses cochineal juice for their strawberry flavoring in Frappuccino's too!" He ratifies, quite pleased with this horrid bit of obscurity.

"Seriously? A beetle?"

"You've been feeding me bugs**?**" Gagging, Holly throws her cup on the ground.

"You know I'm vegan." Chatura levels Gabriella.

"I'm drinking bug juice?!" Clearly unraveled, Holly dry heaves exclaiming, "How could you?" This condemning radical new person in front of me looks at both of us, "What's wrong with you**?**"

"I'm sure this is just a misunderstanding," I offer, not knowing what to say, "Gabriella couldn't have known. Who would know that?" I'm waiting for Gabriella to jump in, but she doesn't. In fact, she says absolutely nothing, and is just shy of a smirk.

Chatura, in one swift motion, puts her glass down and grabs her pot of stew, "We're leaving! Girls! Time to go!" The ducklings pile into her car without a word and they exit in a whirl of dust.

"Let's go!" Holly yells. I've never heard her voice angry or loud, she morphs in front of my eyes. "Nate! Seraphine! We're going!"

Confused, her husband, who had been standing slightly outside the firelight, doesn't know what tactic to take as he watches his wife face off with Gabriella, "I trusted you." Are her final words before they climb into their car.

Moving swiftly, Brock takes this opportunity to gather Delia up, which is no small feat. Arms flailing, she giggles, "Were there really bugs in those drinks? I didn't see any bugs," she asks incoherently, as he steers her towards their SUV. Brock's face, noticeably dark while he bundles the princess up unsuccessfully for the second time before finally managing to close the door. They leave without a word.

Gabriella and I are left standing there like a couple of cartoon characters.

"Well, that's one way to clear a party," I state, purposefully not making eye contact, collecting a couple of bowls to carry back into the kitchen because *the party is over.*

Silently, Gabriella follows me with only her glass rattling in her hand and nothing else. Once we're inside, without any prodding, she confesses, "OK, I knew."

I say nothing, placing four bowls on the counter, standing directly across from her at the kitchen table, waiting.

"I'm so tired of her bad-mouthing ranching and meat-eaters! Did you hear her? Goats? Seriously? Who the hell eats goats? And the other one, with that damn solar oven! Is she kidding me? It's not even edible! Am I crazy or what? It's like brown muck with garbanzo beans! Right? I mean, no one eats it! And she just goes on and on and on about global warming and sustainability like a parrot, and yeah, she drives a Tesla. But it has leather seats!" Without any accent at all, the diatribe continues, "Holly's no different. They're both such hypocrites. I can't help myself, Stephanie! Every time there's an opportunity, I add meat to my dishes. Seriously. And you know what? They love it!"

Mortified, I'm speechless for a moment, my body shivering with anxiety, as I rub my eyes in disbelief, "Well, you got caught tonight."

"I was hoping you would understand."

"Oh, I understand. Believe me. It's a lot! You're all a lot! In fact, three months into this home school has been a bigger personal challenge for me than a decade in the cannabis industry, and that's saying something! But tonight, was supposed to be for the kids, Gabriella, and again it got caboshed by personal drama from a group of women running around without filters, like teenagers!" My hands fly up in the air.

Thankfully, her mouth closes.

Looking at the table full of uneaten cupcakes, I nod my head in defeat, "You know what? Except for the cupcakes, every dish Imogene and I made tonight was vegan and it was a pain in the ass, but I wanted to be inclusive. I don't know what I was thinking. I guess I was trying to redeem myself."

"What do you mean?"

"The first time I invited Chatura and Holly over, I accidentally lined a pan with bacon fat for the cornbread."

"Ha! You're kidding?"

"No." Shaking my head, I look her in the eyes. "I'm not proud of this, Gabriella."

"No. No, of course not. Did you tell her?"

"No, I did not."

"Well, obviously, I won't say anything." She grabs a cupcake and moves towards the door. Her round features, notably marked by something I can't quite put my finger on, as she proclaims, "Well, they'll get over it."

Part Three

Everybody eats when they come to my house

The morning light presses through our black-out drapes like paper on fire.

We've slept in, it feels good, but I'm hungover. Remy's on the edge of the bed, my legs wrapped around his, keeping him tethered. Nuzzling my face into the back of his warm neck, I inch closer, filling all the space between us.

"You know if you get any closer, I'll be on the floor," he mumbles into his pillow, then faces me with a grin.

"I was just… cuddling."

"Um-hmm."

"Really, I was following you."

"Across the bed?" He pulls me towards him, amused. "You know, there's a difference between following and pushing?"

"What about leading?" I ask, backing up.

"Exactly." Hazel blue eyes move above me like a beacon, drawing me in. Lifting my nightie off, he tosses it across the room, caressing my neck, his lips so warm, each kiss is a timeless fuse. Working his way down slowly, playfully kissing each of my breasts, a sigh escapes. Pressing up against his leg, the warmth of his tongue etching a line in my tummy, the touch of his long hair tickles my sides, pitching my breath. Grasping the pillow behind me like an anchor, he spreads my legs, lifting them up and over his shoulders before diving in. Sweet deliverance instantly overcomes me. The pressure building again and again, his tongue transitioning from slow, long strokes to fast, pulsating rhythms opens at will, and I'm taken to a whole new world, no walls, people, or anything familiar except the ecstasy as my entire being, overcome by a tremendous non-abeyant source of pleasure. Moving faster and harder, his strong hands pull my pelvis close in one grasp, sealing us finitely together as glorious waves wash over me, resetting my entire being, born anew.

Licking my thighs, his heavily lidded eyes lock with purpose as he crawls up the bed on his fists and knees, arms blistering with strength, pushing my thighs over his shoulders until we're face to face. Kissing his nose, running my hands down the sides of his firm jawline, he smiles almost imperceivably, before entering.

"Yes," slips from my lips into his ear. Bearing himself against the wall above the headboard, both arms firmly embedded, I cling to them, greedily meeting thrust after thrust, every nerve in my body, tingling awake, thriving. The melody of our breath co-mingles, it's the only sound I hear, an overwhelming force of its own, until I'm lost again in glorious euphoria. With one final burst, Remy arrives deeper, his arms enveloping me in our dual climax. Frozen in the moment, my legs finally slip down to the bed, his voice hoarse and primordial, before he collapses on top of me.

Sensitive to the touch, the warmth between us is combustible. Rocking my body back and forth, caressing his head and back dripping with sweat, my legs wrapped around him, toes touching each other like a circle, we hold one another; our unity reinforced, our bond stronger.

"My little acrobat," he murmurs in my ear.

"It's the yoga." We both laugh, and he rolls off to the side, his hand on my tummy.

"You can lead me anywhere," he says, guiding a hair out of my eyes, "I love you, Steph."

"I love you."

"How are you? That was some crazy party last night?"

I sigh, "I don't know, honestly. What a mess. I was so nervous about Delia; I was completely blindsided by Gabriella." The three seconds I take to think about the party, diminishes the pleasure we just shared instantaneously.

"Yeah. She stepped over the line." Pulling himself up against the pillows, he offers, "But I understand her frustration."

"It was deceptive and intentionally cruel, Rem."

"I know. I know. But hang on Jersey, vegans and vegetarians can be a pain in the ass. Have you ever had a vegetarian make you a meat dish? Or a vegan cook you something with dairy or even something vaguely edible for that matter? It's rare to even be invited over to their house. They don't cook! Most of the vegans I know, don't even actually eat. I mean, they eat all day long like birds with nuts, but they're not food centric at all. It's like eating is a function more than a ceremony. There's nothing sensual or sensory about it for them."

Chewing on that for a moment, it's as accurate as it is ridiculous. "Still, I respect their choice for not eating meat due to animal suffering and karma."

"Yeah. So, you go out and buy a Tesla with leather seats?" He shakes his head, "Look, sweetie, if karma actually exists, and I come back as a cow because I ate a hamburger, it's out of my control. I'll live life as a cow, and someone will eat me. Life is out of our control. You know this."

His statement reminds me of the countless times we've learned this lesson. Lost in thought for a moment, I mumble, "I'm not that selfless. When we we're in the tropics, I was happy with fruit and fish; it's too hot for anything else. But my body craves protein from red meat," I confess, "It's almost as if they're missing a taste bud." Knowing I'm missing the big picture, I snap out of it. "None of this justifies what Gabriella did, though."

Conspiratorially silent for a moment, Remy moves closer, "Obviously, no one should eat animals that suffer. There are sustainable meat farms everywhere now. But when someone uses dogma as a means to elevate their social or spiritual status, they're missing the fucking point! The haters are the new bourgeoisie, and it isn't about Rococo frames or pastoral frescoes. It's about idle time, sitting around judging people while they're projecting a perfect self-image on social media." He pauses, tilts his head away for a moment, then asks, "Why did you alter your party menu for them?"

Caught off guard, I draw a blank, "I don't know." I look around the room for an answer, "I guess because I wanted everyone to be able to eat what I presented."

"OK. But it was a potluck; they could have just brought their own dishes. The kids would have eaten anything."

"I don't know, Rem."

"Don't you?" He looks down at his hands contemplating.

I'm used to my husband playing Devil's advocate, but at this moment, I'm not comfortable with him aiming it at me. "I suppose, I was hoping to find a friend in this group. I mean, Chatura's not as crazy as the others."

"Did you just hear yourself? That's your gauge? Not as crazy as the others?"

"I don't know what I'm saying."

"Don't you?" He leans in, "Sweetie, you deserve better." Holding my face in his hands, I'm lost in hazel as he continues gently, "The world is spinning at nine hundred miles an hour. Don't pay attention to it." With a kiss, he's up and off to the shower, leaving me to my thoughts.

Coaxing myself out of bed, I wander through the house untethered, the birds outside distracting me as a woodpecker ungovernably hops inverted down a tree trunk. "Let's hope this is a lesson from the gods, that's not humility," I say to Soter.

He just stares back.

Ultimately, I find the laden shower steam a respite from the dry desert air, my mind a fog. Sitting on the edge of the claw foot tub, gripping the sides, the shower curtain pulled around me for a brief guilty moment, my head is clamoring with ideas and intentions, garbling my compass. *What am I doing? Am I so desperate for friends that I'm willing to endure this level of dysfunction and crazy? Am I accepting bad behavior subconsciously? Are we just feeding off each other? Am I the reason this group is so hostile? Are they just reacting to me? Is this what society has become?*

Anxiety, literally racing through my pores like a breeze sends a chill through my spine as Imogene calls through the shower curtain, "Aunt Steph, someone's at the door."

"OK, sweetie." *Shit.* I turn off the water, wrap a towel, then my robe around me, slipper-less, my feet leave a wet path through the house to the front foyer, where Soter is sitting silently. Strapping on a mask, I open the door. "Hey Brock, this is a surprise. Did you leave something behind last night?"

"No, I didn't leave anything behind," he says mask-less, cynically disheveled.

"OK. Would you like to come in? I just got out of the shower. Just give me a min…."

"Whatever. I don't have time for this. I know what *you did.*"

Bar b que

Detective Chavez removes her hat with a groan and places it on the empty passenger seat of her unmarked cruiser, the same seat her partner of six years used to occupy until a month ago. As a first responder on the scene, the early morning song of birds is nothing but a contradiction. She takes a deep breath walking towards another stranger's front door she will never meet, that opens magically on its own, before a middle-aged woman, clearly distraught, runs out.

"¡Entra, ella está aquí! ¡Ayúdame! Senora, ella esta muerta!" She screams like the officer is deaf. Chavez follows her silently, knowing there's nothing she can say that will help while entering an enormous great room with thirty-foot ceilings, the furniture dark and formidable against adobe beige walls, are a premonition.

"Me desperté a las seis y me fui a trabajar, tengo la tarde libre. Me empieza a el otro lado de la casa, para no despertarla la señora. ¡Desayuna a las siete y media todos los días! Cuando no bajo, subí para ver cómo estaba. ¡Y ahí fue cuando la encontré!" Utterly prostrate, the woman recounts at hyper-speed.

"Ma'am, what's your name?" Chavez stops her mid-stride, thinking if she speaks English, she may calm down.

"Marisol."

"Marisol. I need you to be calm." Making a mental note, Chavez continues towards the front door. The almost fifty-year-old woman in front of her, is short, fit, and no-nonsense. Her hair is pulled back into a tight, almost elegant ballet bun. Chavez notices, she wears no make-up and her clothes are simple but clean, pressed black slacks and an extra-long, button-up, collared shirt with a gentle abstract print on it are a comfortable uniform. Her shoes are new black leather clogs. Nodding her head involuntarily, from side to side, she wipes her face, silently, then leads the detective through two huge iron and glass French doors with nothing else to say as tears track down her weathered cheeks.

The hall and bedroom are noticeably cold. Chavez shivers as she enters a master suite as large as an Olympic-sized swimming pool. The king-sized, wooden bed is ornately carved and unslept. New Berber carpet topped with vintage, Ganado, Navajo rugs in black and dark umber, the rarest colors, are spotless, if not imprinted with vacuum marks. A treadmill and stair-stepper are contained within a glass room affixed to numerous French doors that span a good twenty feet of wall opening to an enormous flagstone patio with a gurgling, Spanish fountain. One door is wide open with a cow doorstop in front of it. Opposite the bed a large, red- leather couch with brass tacking and a stone coffee table, sits across from an 80-inch TV monitor hanging above one of three kiva fireplaces.

To the left a barrage of straight-back, antique, Spanish, Inquisition-style chairs with leather seats, line the walls between each of the French doors and a hand-carved wooden chaise upholstered in Kilim rugs sits at the bottom of the bed. An expensive leather purse is tipped over on the chaise, and it is the only noticeably disheveled item in the entire room.

"Have you touched anything in here? Opened the door? Tidied?"

"No! Nothing. I touch nothing." "Did you turn any of these lights on?" She asks as both bedside table lamps, all five standing lamps, and four iron chandeliers are on.

"No! I touch nothing."

The room, cold and emotionless, feels like a hotel lobby, no personal touches, no photographs, only one painting behind the bed, a pastel landscape on a smooth diamond-finished wall. *It's hard to believe someone lived here.* Moving beyond two incredibly old hand-carved doors guarded by life-sized suits of armor, Marisol leads her into a dressing room of sorts. There are several headless, full-scale mannequins fitted with costumes and work clothes, multiple custom closets, and cupboards full to the brim with every imaginable accessory, and an entire wall of shoes. It looks like a department store, and it's twice the size of Chavez's bedroom.

"What did she do? What was her occupation?"

"I don know."

Straight ahead, a limestone bathroom gleams in an overhead skylight. The mountain view is a portrait in plate glass, again everything spotless; the sunken tub, walk-in glass shower, and private toilet closet nestled between them, look as though they've never been used. To the left of the bathroom door is a sauna that's on, but Marisol opens the door to the right and the familiar smell of freshly cut grass mixed with acetone, ammonia, and feces wafts out immediately. The room is uncomfortably hot. A large, leather, winged back chair sits empty next to a small table with a cell phone on it, behind that is a thick bathrobe hanging from one of two hooks. Like an exercise in tolerance, between her mask, the heat and a grating low buzzing sound, the hairs on her arms and neck stand rigid with electricity. The discordant sound, that commands the room reminds Chavez of a fluorescent light waiting to combust.

The sound emanates from a tanning bed that monopolizes the windowless room, filling the intimate space to capacity. Lid down, the unit is glowing with a woman's lifeless arm hanging out the side.

Chocolate Jesus

"Brock, what are you talking about?"

"My Wife! That's what I'm talking about! You think I don't know what you've done?"

I'm confused.

"Gabriella fed the vegetarians meat, and you got us all high!" He screams, "You and your marijuana bull shit! I told Delia you were no good! What was it? Some sort of sick Pagan ritual you were both in on? How dare you!" Brock attempts another step towards me and Soter bares his teeth. *The only warning Brock will receive.* I give him the signal to stand down at attention as the diatribe continues. "You, in your hippie house with your naked photographs everywhere and your fancy dog. Paying cash for all the teachers! You think you're so smart! But you're just low life, ***drug dealers***!" Spit flies out of his mouth in slow motion onto my cheek, and I feel Remy next to me.

"What's the problem?"

Obviously out of his league and element, Brock's lanky, elongated body takes on the appearance of a shadow against the sun in a bulky overcoat, uselessly puffing up his shoulders. But I notice his left hand hasn't strayed from his pocket during his irrational display. *That's a concern.*

"What's the problem? The problem is you dosed my wife, you asshole!

"We did not dose Delia," I respond to deaf prostration.

"Don't lie to me! I just spent the night at the emergency room, she had twelve stitches, and she was high!"

Remy and I are silent.

"She passed out! Hit her head on the sink last night when we got home from this… your debauchery! You did this to HER!" he screams his arms madly waving all over the place.

"We did not dose your wife," I repeat, "If she was stoned, it was on her own accord. You may want to ask her how many Campari spritzes she had. I counted four." In response mode, I know exactly which Hapkido move to initiate should he attack.

"You filthy liars. How dare you!" venomously unrestrained, he continues, "She doesn't drink! And she doesn't *DO DRUGS*!"

Remy moves forward, "This sounds like a domestic issue. I suggest you take it up with your wife."

Without moving his feet, Brock leans into Remy's face. "You. Filthy. Liar."

"Brock, you have five seconds to leave."

"Or what? You gonna hit me? You gonna hit me, *DRUG DEALER*?" The saliva around his mouth froths.

"No." Remy smiles, nodding in my direction, "But she might." He closes the door firmly.

I'm shaking, hair dripping on the floor, feet numb, in shock.

"What an asshole!" My spouse, partly amused, states before surveying my rigid body. "Hey you, come here." Bundling me into his arms, he kisses my forehead. "That guy's an asshole, Steph. This is who we're really dealing with! It's not COVID. It's not isolation. It's people showing their true colors. Now we know. No more pretenses. This is what he really thinks of us. It's why Delia and Gabriella don't want school at our house." His anger rises to a pitch, "It's why Delia and Holly will never be your friends! The righteous have no middle ground! It's black or white! There's no reasoning!" His amusement gone, his temper awaiting take off, he's on a roll, "It's an actual medical condition Steph, proven by case studies on fucking terrorists! Their moronic, dogmatic beliefs are stronger than facts!"

I haven't seen this alarming side of my spouse since last year. I need to tread carefully as a relapse is not an option for us. But everything he says makes sense. It hurts, but it's the truth, and like walking through a door, I'm on the other side of something; but feel forsaken instead of liberated. "I reached out to these women knowing we were all different but hoping we had our kids' welfare in common. I really thought we could go beyond our differences." My head shakes with disappointment, "What a waste of time." Looking up, taking a deep, unsteady breath, I pledge, "I'm out. I can't do this anymore. I'll talk to the teachers directly for Imogene's sake, but I won't interact with any of these people anymore."

"Yeah, well, it's not over yet. So, brace yourself," he states with agitation but calmer, pulling me into a hug before walking off through the living room, attempting control.

Soter follows me into our bedroom, my mind in kaos. Unable to tackle getting dressed or anything else, I sit down on the rocker across from our bed, "Why is it so difficult for humans to get along?" I ask, and he turns his lovely head sideways in an attempt to understand. Flashes of the news, hordes of obdurate social media feeds from family and acquaintances surround me like nameless Chaldean demons, their only purpose to cause discourse. *I've never known a world so at odds with itself. Everyone is so angry. I am so angry. This pandemic is making it worse. It's in the air, like waiting for lightning.*

As a child, I grew up unknowingly poor in elementary school, and coarsely entitled in high school. I saw and felt both sides of economic and social status, and somehow, it pulled the curtains open for me, or at least I thought it had. *Am I being unsympathetic? Am I subconsciously judging these people because they're rich, Christian, or environmentally sensitive, and they're just reacting to me? Am I getting what I'm giving? Has what's happened to Remy and me in the past three years with H.S. and the normalization of our world's discontent deprived me of empathy?* My heart heavy, I reach for my phone. Dialing the number, I don't even know what I'm going to say, but I know I need to say something.

"Hello?"

"Hi, Chatura."

"Oh, hi."

"I just wanted to call and say how sorry I am about last night. I had no idea."

"Thanks," her voice is dry and short.

"Really, I am so sorry."

"Well, I appreciate that. But I find it hard to believe you had no idea what Gabriella was up to?"

"What do you mean?"

"The cornbread, Stephanie? Can you explain that?"

16

Sausage and eggs

"What's her name?" Chavez asks, squeezing her own noticeably swollen fingers into nitrile gloves.

"Gabriella Cecilia Garcia Fernández del Olmo Lopez," Marisol cries, unable to look at her employer. "I make her favorite breakfast for her, chorizo and eggs, but she no come to the kitchen. I thought maybe she fall asleep. Sometimes she wears the earbuds when she tans. But she no wake up! She's dead!" Sobbing, she suddenly backs out of the room, like death is contagious.

The sunbed lamps glow blindingly as the detective carefully opens the lid. The naked woman is tiny compared to the unit and the stain of feces she's lying in. A large contusion on her forehead matches a smear on the glass of the lid. Chavez doesn't need to check for a pulse as mortis stain has already collected on the victim's shoulder blades, calves, and buttocks. Observing how hot the body is, much hotter than if she were alive, is noticeably strange and her lips are retracted and severely chapped. "Don't these units turn off? Isn't there a timer or a fan?" She asks over her shoulder feeling the sweat collecting in her arm pits.

"Yes, it broke. The fan, the timer, they no work," She mumbles almost incoherently, covering her nose. "Men were fixing it."

"Men? What men?" Turning with one last glance, the detective escorts Marisol back to the great room.

"This week, they try to fix it. Repair men from the company, from California. They come to fix that thing, but it no work."

"The deceased knew it was broken?"

"Yes."

She gently leads Marisol, distraught and whimpering back through the labyrinth of clothes and shoes. "You've had a terrible shock." *And I need to lock down the crime scene.* Chavez knows that when a death is called in, no one's in a particular rush to get there, and this gated home barely inside the Santa Fe City limits is more than a commute. The driveway alone to the estate is well over two miles. "Was anyone else in the house last night?"

"No."

"Did she live alone? Was she married?" She continues in a calm voice.

"No! Poor mijo! Alejandro Juan Carlos, her son, he live with her on the week! Gracias a Dios, she drop him at his Papa's house on the way home last night! He doesn't know his momma is dead!"

Leading Marisol back through the frigid bedroom, Chavez asks, "To the best of your knowledge, did the deceased get along with her ex-husband?

"Sometimes, they get along. Sometimes, they fight."

"Do you know if she took drugs or drank alcohol excessively?"

"No. No, I don't think so. I never see any bad drugs here. She drink, but not crazy."

"Was she on any prescription drugs?"

"Yes, they're in the bathroom. I don know what for."

"How long have you worked for her?"

"Fifteen years."

"And you lived here the whole time?"

"Yes, since before Alejandro Juan Carlos was born. He like my son."

"When was the last time you saw Ms.," she looks down at her pad, "Fernandez del Olmo?" her Spanish accent clearly a soothing factor for Marisol.

"Last night. She dress up for a Halloween party. I help her dress." Her body shudders against the leather couch.

"What time was that?"

"A las seis."

"And when did she leave?"

"After seven." She wipes her face.

"What time did she come home?"

"I don't know. My room it's downstairs."

"How did she seem to you when she left? Was she happy? Afraid? Stressed?"

"She was happy. She was so happy." Marisol wrings the bottom of her blouse. "She was wearing family jewelry; it make her happy."

Wiping away tears on her sleeve, her posture crumples with grief, "She look so pretty."

"Family jewelry? Was it valuable? Do you know where it is? Where she keeps it?"

"Very valuable, very old. She has a safe in her closet. I don know how to open it."

Chavez stands, "Can you show me the costume she wore last night?"

Marisol nods her head yes, in defeat.

"Do you know where Ms. Fernandez Del Olmo went last night?" Chavez asks as two state troopers walk through the front door.

They nod, "Anything we can do?" Their demeanor is prickly. She recognizes both of them and their attitudes.

"Don't let anyone in but the coroner and the team."

"Yes, Ma'am," they reply, dripping condescension.

Marisol is instantly sobered by the officers in their intimidating uniforms. Unrattled, chavez continues, "Do you know where Ms. Fernandez Del Olmo went last night?"

Staring blankly, afraid to say anything else, Marisol freezes.

"Where was the party?" Chavez repeats.

She looks back at the officers, "Marisol!" Chavez raises her voice, "Do you know where the deceased went last night?"

"Yes," she replies, nodding her head back and forth, before finally offering, "She went to Stephanie Beroe's Halloween party."

"The Beroes?" Officer Dean interrupts, "We know the Beroes."

Ain't no rest for the wicked

Driving south on the Turquoise Trail towards the small village that sits at the bottom of the Cerrillos Hills, Detective Chavez runs over the most disturbing details of the case, while huge golden cottonwoods dapple the autumn, juniper landscape dashing by like jewels on a map. The high desert can be a strange and barren place on any given day, especially with another death hovering over her head. The pandemic has brought an endemic of violent crime and murder this little town has never seen the likes of; her partner predicted it, but she didn't believe him. He predicted a lot of things, none of them good; for hours, they would sit and talk at the diner just outside of Santa Fe. He loved diners and always complained there weren't enough greasy spoons in the small western town.

Every morning, they met at Momma's Pantry over hashbrowns burnt to a crisp, just the way he liked them, and black coffee.

Dom was from the 22nd ward in Chicago, known as Little Italy, but he knew it as Little Hell. His parents immigrated from Sicily in 1962, and he was born a year later. He saw it all, the depths of it, a street urchin, hawking papers on the corner instead of going to school. He wore the grime of the city streets like a tattoo, never to be removed. His father was a baker and raised his son with delusional tales of the American dream that "Little Dominic" grew up to resent. After serving in the army in wars no one cared about, he returned and was a cop a week later. Homicide in a filthy city with lots of dirty little secrets, was a wake-up call. He finally moved out west for "the simple life, simple crime, simple time," he used to say. They were a dynamic duo; twenty years older than Chavez, he was the most decorated detective on the force. Revered and feared for his straightforward, if not brutally honest opinions given at will. He used to tell her with his rough gangster accent, "Cayatena, we need to stick together. Everyone else is a stunad." She was inexperienced and green as can be when they met, but he liked her name and told her it meant someone from Gaeta, a beautiful Roman city on the coast of Italy. It made her feel romanticized but not in a sexual way, in an adoring way. They were two peas in a pod; they thought alike, and their instincts were in sync. He taught her how to use them and to trust herself. He was a father, a brother, and an irreplaceable figure that she has lost forever.

An early morning call brought them to a homicide scene in Albuquerque at 1:00 a.m., they drove separately. It was medieval. A woman from Santa Fe had been abducted from her home; very little was left of her. Not the first victim in a stream of brutal homicidal deliverances; the FBI was all over it. There was blood everywhere, splattered all over family photos of track meets and football games, pools of it on the kitchen floor like a sinister moat guarding unopened cases of water and Gatorade stacked in the corner by the back door. The perp commandeered the track house while the family was on vacation; like poking a finger into a bag of water, he was breaking into a moral fabric to see what would happen. It was a tableau from a Netflix show, pieces of her body strewn through each room; her torso, split open from collarbone to pelvis, had been liberated of its organs on the dining room table. It was inhuman.

They did a walk-through since the victim was from Santa Fe, but they wouldn't be able to put any pieces together until the FBI Special Unit shared profiling and background information. It was a night for a diner, but he hated Denny's. "Ain't no rest for the wicked," he said, getting into his car, and waving good night. Dom never made it home. A drunk, on Interstate I-25 rearended him at ninety miles an hour, sending his car through the guard rail and off the end of seventy-foot cliff.

She might never be ready for a new partner. Living with her memories and the stories Dom shared with her over eggs, made her thankful to live in Santa Fe. But her hometown is slowly becoming estranged, especially with Dom gone. She's never felt so alone.

"The victim's contusion," she dictates into her phone, "obviously blanched due to livor mortis, could have been made by the lid of the unit. The hinges were loose, maybe too loose," She states in her car. "The mortis staining was difficult to read due to the heat of the unit, but the coroner approximated she was killed where she lay, eight to ten hours before she was found, placing the death between ten p.m. to a little before midnight." Comfortable in the isolation of her patrol car, she continues, "The crime scene was so clean, it's as if a cleaning crew came in to sweep."

Understanding how people live in their surroundings is key to fitting pieces of a puzzle like this together. She understands this but is seriously bothered by the scenario.

"We confirmed no jewelry was missing, so robbery is not on the table. Marisol Gilberto, the house keeper, stated the victim was very tidy, and it wasn't unusual for her to put all of her things away at the end of the day." But not even a shoe out of place? Or a washcloth? And who sleeps with the door wide open in October?" *Something's not right.* Officer Dean's words come to mind, "*We questioned the Beroes last year about a homicide. Witnesses saw the deceased- a local man, put a gun to Stephanie Beroe's husband's head at a party. A couple of days later, the guy was found dead in a ditch not far from their home. A week later, the Feds were looking for Mr. Beroe in connection with those nuclear tanker explosions. No charges were ever brought against him. He's a cool cucumber, that one. You want us to pick him up?*"

Knowing Dean is a cool cucumber himself, she's reluctant to be coerced. He's quick to judge, not inherently bright, and no investigator. Dean and his sidekick like to play the intimidation card, using their uniforms, their height, and side arms as scare tactics, unlike Chavez, who wears her holster on the back of her pant waist, so it's not the first thing a witness sees, and she purposely wears disarming light colors. She's never found intimidation to be a conversation opener. Her old partner taught her that too. He was a cop from another time when police grew up on their beats and knew everyone in their neighborhood. *It's hard being a cop today, even a detective. The world hates you.*

Checking herself in the mirror, her eyes are tired. With a heavy sigh, she nudges the blinker and turns right into the village. A church steeple peers out among hundred-year-old trees and adobe homes embraced by the colorful display of the Galisteo River Basin; it's deceivingly welcoming. Hard to believe this territorial town was once the capital of New Mexico at one point, if only for twenty-four hours; it's so sleepy.

To her surprise, this afternoon, the saloon on the corner is bustling with patio diners, and the shop at the end of town has live music; cars line both sides of the dirt intersection of First Street and Main.

Crossing over the railroad tracks, the Beroe house stands alone and formidable against the hills behind it, giving Chavez a strange, unnerving feeling as it looms over the village.

The sound of the cattle guard under her tires and the trail of dust they generate is a reminder she's not in Santa Fe. Things are different out here. People are different. It wasn't too long ago that there were stories of hippies and Viet Nam Vets shooting at sheriffs as they rolled through town. The area's reputation as a marijuana hotbed precedes itself. Mostly, these little dog patches have been left to themselves. Unincorporated, the water co-ops are the only real organizations. She reminds herself that people are out here for a reason- to be left alone, and Santa Fe has been happy to oblige.

Parking in front of the impressive two-story, she grabs her coat, neatly folded on her partner's seat, and puts it on with another sigh. Walking up the drive she adjusts her mask, the adobe home is both imposing and welcoming, if that makes sense. A German Shepherd stops in front of her, followed by a young girl.

"Come here, Soter," the girl calls out. The dog turns on a dime sitting at the child's leg.

"Hi, I'm Officer Chavez." She shows her badge with a congenial smile, "I'm looking for Stephanie Beroe."

"I'm Imogene. We're in the back. We had a Halloween party last night. I've never met a lady police officer," she leads the way around the house, chirping like a little bird.

"Actually, I'm a detective."

"Wow, really?"

At least I can still impress the kiddos.

The Cerrillos Hills rise dramatically behind a well-cared-for xanthous orchard. Sixty-foot cottonwood trees dominate the estate, their shocking yellow leaves against a bluebird sky, is surreal in contrast to the party cobwebs strewn everywhere; it's wholesome. A fit, beautiful, dark-haired woman in workout clothes with a trash bag in one hand spins around curiously before she smiles.

"Aunt Steph!" The young girl announces with glee, "The police are here!"

Pour some sugar on me

Now what? Desperately, grasping the abalone pendant around my neck I was hoping would act as a healing talisman after Brock; it's clear the desert is harboring me to my shells today. The unassuming woman in her thirties with dark eyes and black hair pulled to a painfully, tight ponytail is discerning. "Hi, what can I do for you?" I yank my mask out of my back pocket and string it onto my ears.

"I'm Detective Chavez. Is there somewhere we can talk? Privately?" She flashes her badge, eyeing Imogene.

"Sure. What's this all about?" I ask, leading her over to the picnic table near the back door, knowing this must have something to do with Brock and Delia. "Imogene, would you go in and make us some tea, please?"

"OK." She runs inside.

As I sit at the end of the picnic table on an old tree trunk, Soter positions himself between me and the lady detective. I discreetly give him the hand signal for rest, and he lies down as Remy walks out the back door, catching my eye, and joining us.

"Mr. Beroe?"

"Yes."

"I'm Detective Chavez. You may want to sit down. I have some bad news."

We're dumbstruck. I hear every word she says but can't, for whatever reason, register any of it. An all too familiar déjà vu strikes me. Looking to Remy with my thoughts, he squeezes my hand.

"Can you tell me who else was at your party last night?"

I give her everyone's names and contact info, silent tears running down my cheek.

"How well did you know the deceased?"

Deceased! Oh my god. I wipe my eyes. "Our niece goes to school with her son; we created a micro- home school so they wouldn't be online during COVID lockdown this year. I met her in August while we were planning all this; we saw her a couple of times at potlucks and, of course, last night," I ramble.

She nods, turning towards my husband, "And you, sir? How well did you know Ms. Fernandez Del Olmo?"

"Not enough to know her last name," he replies.

Raising her eyebrows, she nods, dashing a note down on her pad, "Can either of you tell me what she was wearing last night?"

"She was Queen Isabella," I reply, "Her costume, it must have been custom made. It was black taffeta and red velvet with gold beading. She wore a gold tiara with several red stones that looked like rubies and long pearls that were pinned to the front of her dress by two golden brooches, and she had a gold choker with rubies. She told me all her jewelry were heirlooms from her family in Spain."

"Was anyone particularly interested in her jewelry?"

"We were all impressed. It was over the top."

"Was there anything unusual about her behavior? Did she seem depressed or estranged in any way?"

"She wasn't depressed," Remy and I mumble through our masks in unison.

Readjusting her bottom on the picnic bench, the detective continues, "What was your relationship with Gabriella Fernandez Del Olmo like?"

"We weren't close if that's what you mean."

"In a few words. Were you friendly? Did you lunch together?" She pinches the nose bar on her mask, her large, dark eyes, tired but deliberate.

"We were friendly," I respond, not completely believing my words. "I didn't see her socially unless it was about school. We have weekly Schloom calls, all the moms, every Sunday. That's the extent of our relationship."

"Did you like Gabriella Fernandez Del Olmo?"

Finding myself mute, Remy intervenes, "Is my wife a suspect?"

"What do you both do for a living?"

That's a change of tactic. "We own a cannabis infusion company."

"And you make products here in New Mexico?"

"We have contracted state-licensed producers that manufacture our products in several states, including New Mexico," Remy states rotely.

Imogene interrupts with tea and cookies on a tray. We're all silent while she serves.

"Thank you, Imogene. Sweetie, would you mind taking the party decorations down in the kitchen for me? The ladder is in the hallway. Please be careful," I suggest, giving her a coaxing smile.

"Sure." Grabbing a cookie, she knows something's up as she looks back, going through the door. I signal Soter to follow her and notice Detective Chavez watching every move I make.

"Mrs. Beroe, where were you between 10 p.m. and 1 a.m. last night?"

"She was here with me. The entire night," Remy affirms.

Nodding her head again, making another note to herself, she then asks, "Are you aware there was a formal complaint filed against you this morning, Mrs. Beroe?"

I feel Remy's grip tighten around my hand.

"No. For what?" I reply, already knowing the answer to my question.

"For illegally dosing Delia Garner with medical-grade cannabis."

"I did not dose Delia."

She picks up her tea cup and takes a sip calmly, "Uh-huh. Well, you may want to consult with your attorney because the medical examiner found high levels of THC in Gabriella Fernandez Del Olmo's bloodstream as well."

Crawfish

Death is an obscurity, and when it strikes close, it sends you into hiding; it's never satisfied. But I have bigger problems today; *I'm literally suspected of murder.* Thankfully, awash in Remy after the detective leaves, I almost believe this will all go away.

"I need to clean up the lab," he states gently, relieving himself from the couch, "so when they come back with a search warrant, we're squeaky clean."

"This is no coincidence, Rem. No way!" I jump up. "Both Delia and Gabriella are high or hospitalized? Dead? I mean, don't get me wrong. I don't like any of them, but I would never!"

"I know."

"We're getting set up again."

He shakes his head, "I don't know."

"That wasn't a question."

"I find it hard to believe H.S. would try anything after we… re-programmed him last year."

"He's not the only one on our watch list."

"You mean Jameson? Yeah, I need to make a couple of calls." He heads upstairs, and the further away he walks, the more alone I become, the weight of isolation bearing down more intensely than lockdown. *My world is tiny. It's a problem.* I feel my breath stutter.

John Jameson, one of the world's latest trillionaires, was a ring leader at the park where we had been interned against our will. *In fact, he owned the damn island!*

Literally, fighting the worst of the one percent for our lives, it seems like it was both yesterday and a decade ago but no less sinister. Then last year, H.S. staged the world news to believe Remy was a terrorist! *Of course, he was the mad man behind it all, murdering thousands of innocent people, destroying whole communities, and terrorizing our nation! And for what?! For military contracts! For fucking money!*

It almost ruined us! Remy barely made it back and his anger, changed him forever. In the end, it took a serious intervention for him to see the value of a higher path. And here we are again. Were we wrong? Is the higher path just a bunch of crap?! The group effort it took to round H.S. up and give him a dose of his own medicine, liberally laced with ours, is enviable today. I need help. Reaching for my phone, I dial.

"Chatura?"

"Stephanie." Her voice is dry but less hostile.

"Have you heard about Gabriella?" I ask.

"No."

I bite my lip, "She's dead."

"What! Dead? Oh, my god! You're not serious."

"Yes, I'm serious! The police think she was murdered."

"What? What happened? How can this be?"

"I don't know all the details yet."

She stutters, "What does that mean?"

"Do you know her maid, Marisol? I heard her talk about her a couple of times."

"Yes, of course." She states, holding back tears.

"Do you have any plans tomorrow morning?"

"No."

"I know this sounds crazy, but would you come with me to her house, Gabriella's house?"

"Why?" Blowing her nose, she's confused.

"I need to ask Marisol some questions, and it would be better to have someone she knows there."

"That's crazy! What's going on, Stephanie? Is this some ploy to make up for the cornbread?"

"Chatura, I did not intentionally taint the cornbread. As I said before, I went out of my way to make the dish vegan for you. It was an accident."

There's silence before she finally replies, "I know. You're not Gabriella. Oh my god, Gabriella! This is so tragic! I can't believe she's dead! This is really scary, Stephanie! Poor Alejandro Juan Carlos. Seriously, murdered? Why? Who? When?"

Holding my breath, I spill it, "The police think I may have had something to do with it."

Her silence is worrisome.

"Chatura, I did not kill Gabriella."

"I didn't say you did." She pauses and an awkward silence ensues before she responds, "Of course, you didn't. OK, how can I help? I'm in."

Relieved that my only friend has faith in me, I hang up, formulating a strategy for tomorrow, cursing myself for not getting to know Gabriella. I don't know who she hung out with, what she did for fun, or even what she did for a living other than cattle ranching. Suddenly struck, *I've never bothered to get to know any of the women in our micro-school except Chatura. How callous am I? OK, so they pissed me off. So, I don't agree with their education decisions, political alignment, or their religious values. Should that make us enemies to the point they would blame me for dosing or killing them? I would never! Wait. Hold on. Who am I kidding? That's not true, is it? I have dosed my enemy- twice.*

I'm wishing

Ⓗ I'm frightened. We trusted her with our children! She is a sociopath!

Ⓓ She is! She dosed me, and she killed Gabriella. I think she was trying to kill me too! We don't know her niece either. Where did she come from? Her mom could be part of a terrorist cell. Maybe she can't come back? Maybe she's wanted? We should at least agree that Imogene, or whatever her name is, is not welcome in class with our kids on Monday.

Ⓗ Delia, what if she's in danger too?

Ⓓ That's the next call I'm going to make. What kind of a Christian would I be if I didn't call Child Protective Services on a murderer? Besides, look at what she's exposing that child to.

My heart in my throat, fingers hovering over the keys to my phone, knowing exactly what I'd like to say but finding it more informative to hear what they have to say, I wait with tears in my eyes. Two minutes go by, and there's nothing. *They must have finally realized I was on the text thread.*

Remy and Danielle, walk into the living room and sit down quietly facing me. *Not a good sign.* I wipe my eyes clear. *I'm not sure I can take any more bad news.*

"Horace has put us in touch with an exceptionally good attorney. She's making some calls to the police now to see how we can cooperate. I agree with her that our best defense is a good offense," Remy states calmly, but there's obvious, unspoken agitation in his face.

"Rem, the group chat is exploding! Delia and Holly are plotting to call CPS! I'm worried about Imogene."

"We're leaving early in the morning. I'm taking her to Celeste's, so she'll be safe and far away from all of this."

Nodding my head in defeat, I know she'll be well cared for by Remy's other sister.

"Danielle will stay here with you. You have a call with Jean, the attorney, tomorrow at two."

Looking to my spouse in disbelief, "This is all happening so fast." I take a big breath.

"Hey," he moves over to my side, "It's just preliminary. We've been here before."

Staring down at our hands on the couch, I feel his strength.

"Sweetie, we've been here before and much worse. Everything's going to work out. Steph?" He claims my attention, "Everything's going to be fine."

"What about all those calls you made? Did you find out anything on H.S. or Jameson?"

"We're still digging," Danielle replies.

Imogene walks in with Soter. She looks at us for a moment, registering the anxiety in the air, "Does anyone want to jump on the tramp with me?"

"Let's do it!" Remy gives me a nudge, hopping off the couch, we all follow her outside.

While walking down the path to the trampoline, I easily realize the sun will be gone in an hour. Taking off my shoes I climb up the ladder. *I'm glad to see this day go, and I'm also terrified of what tomorrow may bring. But for now, at this moment, jumping and laughing with a sweet little girl as Remy and Danielle throw yellow leaves on us, I'm not going to think about it.*

After dinner, we escape to a binge-worthy show; Danielle squishes all six feet of herself into a bean bag chair next to the couch in our small TV room with a huge bowl of popcorn she absolutely won't share. Cuddled up, a cozy fire crackling, all three of us under a giant blanket on the couch, I'm suddenly frightened. *This may be the last happy moment of my life!*

Remy catches my eye and gives my leg a squeeze. *He knows what I'm thinking.* I blink the tears back as Nicole Byer from *Nailed It,* tries to make something salvageable out of a real hot mess. *I can relate.*

Three episodes later, Remy's got Imogene packing an overnight bag for their departure in the wee hours of the morning. Tossing her favorite stuffy, he announces, "For the next contestant, Mr. Biggles will be performing a double back, bacon flip with a twist!"

Imogene cackles as it hits her in the head, "Good one, Uncle Rem."

"OK, kiddo, listen, I'll see you soon." Danielle squats down and hugs her, "Don't let your aunt talk you into a body piercing, anywhere you may regret." She smiles.

"Clearly, you've never met Aunt Celeste. I don't even think she has a belly button."

With a bright smile, Danielle gives Imogene a kiss on the head and a hug, "Good night, everyone."

"Good night, Danielle."

"Keep me posted," Remy implores as if she wouldn't. I've never met anyone so loyal. Danielle is one of a kind. She comes from a strict upbringing. Her mother is old fashioned and tough, but very loving. Danielle on the other hand is very modern, and independent, and she never makes excuses for her actions because they're always so well thought out. She is all that and more. That's why a year ago, I genuinely believed she was a serious threat.

Soter walks her to the door and returns with one of my slippers in his mouth and drops it in Imogene's bag.

"Aww, he wants to come. Can he come with us on the road trip, Uncle Rem?"

"No, sweetie. Soter needs to stay here." Remy eyes me, and with those words, I'm right back where I was two hours ago, but I've got a happy face on for our girl.

After loading her bag in the car, Remy says goodnight and leaves the two of us alone. Tucking her blankets under her chin, I sit down on the bed next to her. *She is so sweet, so pure, and innocent; I will never forgive myself if anything happens to her.*

"Aunt Steph, what happened to Al's mom?"

Taking a long, deep breath, *I knew this was coming,* "I think she may have been robbed," I reply, "Do you remember her costume? Those were real jewels."

"Someone would kill Al's mom for jewelry?" She starts to cry.

"Come here, sweetie. Sweet girl, I'm so sorry. I really don't know what happened to her." Wiping her eyes, I find my strength, "But I promise, I'm going to find out. Now, let's wipe our tears and think about Al. He's going to need a good friend."

"Yes. Yes, he is." She sniffles. "Aunt Steph, do you think Momma's safe? You know she's not like you and me." She starts to cry again. "We have Uncle Remy, and he would never let anything happen to us… But Momma? She's all alone. What if something happens to her? What if she gets sick? Do you think she's in danger?" Her fear rolls out unabandoned, triggered by our local tragedy.

"Honey, your mother is one of the strongest, smartest people I know. She's safe. I promise."

"Aunt Steph, do you think whoever killed Al's mom was at our party?" Her eyes wide with worry, she asks an honest question.

Taking a moment to squeeze myself into her bed as a distraction, I reply, "No. Now scoot over. I'm coming in." Hanging off the single bed, I wrap my arms around her, snuggling my head on hers.

"I'm afraid," she whispers.

"Don't be afraid. Nothing's going to happen to us," I whisper back, "Uncle Remy's going to take you to Aunt Celeste's house tomorrow. She's already planning a bake a thon like you've never seen!" I say, giving her a kiss on the forehead, smoothing her hair back gently.

"Aunt Steph, are you ever afraid?"

Visions of standing on the beach in the park, an oar in my hand, H.S. behind me, his words, "Remy's dead. I killed him. I told you I would," slice my soul even to this day. I felt it. I was terrified. Then last year in Egypt, on Tyler's dahabeeyah seeing the change in my husband, seeing how H.S.'s actions transformed him into a stranger, a terrifying stranger, scared me to death. All of our friends, Horace, Tyler, Laure, Aalin, and Danielle, watched me knock some sense into him. He was ready to kill. Determined to kill H.S., and he would have, having killed before. But those are not bedtime stories for little girls. "I remember when I was your age, I was frightened by thunderstorms."

Of course, I was left alone most of my childhood and had to confront those fears by myself, but that's another tale. "I remember being so scared one night in our big house all alone, watching the blinding, light flash through our giant windows after knocking out all the electricity in our neighborhood, I hid under a table between two couches for hours," I admit.

"Really? You were afraid of lightning?" she asks, her spirits lifted, heightened by a new bravado.

"Oh, yes. I hid watching the shadows from naked tree branches as they crawled around on the floor like they were looking for me. I was petrified."

"Oh, no. Is that true? You were really scared they would come get you?" She asks, now amused I could be afraid of lightning.

"Yes, I was sure of it," I answer, glad she's forgotten her own fear.

"What happened?" She asks, curled under my chin, looking at the glow-in-the-dark constellations on the ceiling above her bed.

Settling in, our faces almost touching, the smell of her endearing, I respond honestly, "I sang to myself."

"Which songs?"

Clearing my throat, I'm eleven years old again and sing, "I'm wishing, I'm wishing. For the one I love. To find me.

("To find me,") she sings along.

"Today."

("Today.")

"I'm hoping."

("I'm hoping.")

"And I'm dreaming of, the nice things."

("The nice things.")

"He'll say."

("He'll say.")

She smiles.

"And then, I fell asleep and woke up to my mom calling me. She was so upset. She hadn't been able to find me for hours."

Laughing, a tired laugh, Imogene yawns.

"You know, my mom used to say this to me at night when she tucked me in, 'Sweet dreams, sweetheart. I love you. See you in the morning.' It was like a spell- she cast her magic around me, and I was comforted and safe... from everything."

"Would you say that to me?"

"Sweet dreams, sweetheart, I love you. See you in the morning." Turning out the light, I feel the ease in her breath as she falls asleep, her grasp around my shoulders loosening.

The darkness of her room emphasizes the anxiety we are all akin to. I swallow at the enormity of the promises I just made, knowing I can't let her down. Crawling out of her room, literally on my hands and knees as quietly as possible, I head upstairs to my office. Remy's light is on to my right, I pop my head in. Danielle stands up quickly as I open the door. *I'm not surprised.*

"I was just leaving, good night, Stephanie."

"Goodnight, Danielle."

She closes the door quietly behind her.

"Come here, you."

I walk over behind his big, stainless steel doctor's desk, and he pulls me onto his lap, the chair swivels, squeaking in protest, but there's nothing to say. Nothing needs to be said. We just hold one another, knowing our thoughts and fears. *And for a brief moment everything's just fine.*

Several moments later, Remy's phone sounds out the crash of a wave. Responding slowly with a sigh, he reluctantly releases my grasp and picks up the call, "Hey, Miles, thanks for calling back so late."

I leave him to it. Crossing the hall to my office, I'm captured for a brief moment by lamplight in the far corner of the unfinished second story. *Remy must have left it on while he was looking for something.* The diffused light between the unfinished lathe walls is creepy in a supernatural way. The walls suddenly feel haunted, as though a subconscious signal is lurking in the space within the spaces. My nerves on edge, I pull my office door tightly and quickly behind me.

Peaches and cream

Waving goodbye as the tail lights diminish down the drive into the blackest hour of darkness, my heart relinquishes itself. *I will miss that little girl; her light and love have made me stronger.* But there's no time for tears or self- pity; *I have promises to keep.* After I make a few phone calls, Soter follows me into the kitchen where we share two pieces of bacon and some avocado toast. The morning light finally settling on the almost barren trees in the river basin is warm and glowing, but gives me no solace. I'm nervous and unfocused; an omen has cast its shadow, pacing incoherently, I force myself through a couple of sun salutations.

The yoga settles my mind putting a whole new face on the day, and at nine o'clock on the dot, Chatura is at the front door.

"Hey Chatura. Thank you for coming," I say honestly.

"Of course. I must admit, I'm a little tantalized by all of this, Stephanie. I mean it's absolutely horrible. But I'm intrigued at the same time." She flashes her bright smile. "And this will make a great vlog."

I guess this would be tantalizing to me too, if my life weren't at stake. I give her a hug, and grab my coat, Soter heads out behind us. The sky, already mottled by huge autumn clouds, is moody and mysterious against the golden grass covered hills. *It would be beautiful, any other day.*

Looking over her shoulder, Chatura asks, "Are we taking my car?"

I shrug.

"No dogs, Stephanie. I don't want to scratch the interior."

"Sure. Soter, stay."

He immediately stops on my command and watches us climb into her Tesla.

The last time I was in a Tesla, it was the beginning of the end. I exhale maybe a little too heavy.

"Are you OK?"

Taking a deep breath, I answer, "Yes."

"By the way, I was totally against banning Imogene."

"What?"

"The group chat this morning, barring Imogene from class tomorrow."

My look says it all.

"Oh, my god, you don't know!" She gasps. "You didn't read the text this morning?"

"No. I didn't read the texts." *I don't need to.* Boiling, I restrain myself. "No one else needs to know this, Chatura, but Remy's driving Imogene to his sister's.

"Got it. Where does she live?"

"Arizona."

"Good idea. So, what's the plan?" she asks, artfully changing the subject.

"I want to look around. Get the maid's take on this."

"I hope you speak Spanish because her English is not good."

"I do. Good to know." Turning out of our driveway, I prod, "So, how well did you know Gabriella?"

"Our kids were in class together before lockdown. You know, birthday parties and such. We met through the PTA. I saw her at the monthly committee meetings. I've been to her house a couple of times." She elaborates, her blue fiber coat and matching hat remind me of a woman on her way to church in the '50s.

"What did she do for a living?"

"You know, I have no idea. Ranching but she never discussed it. It's a mystery, really." She whips a pack of gum out of her pocket, "Gum?"

"No, thanks."

"It's vegan."

"What makes gum not vegan exactly?"

"Lanolin."

"They put lanolin in gum? I thought it was for hand cream and moisturizer."

"It is. It keeps your hands soft. But do we really need to collect the sweat of sheep to keep gum soft?"

Eww. "No, thanks."

"Did you know they use beaver urine in vanilla ice cream?"

"Get out! That's not true. That's disgusting!"

She laughs, "It's true! I did a vlog on it last year!" Smiling, amused she grossed me out, she continues, "That series is full of wonderful information, but I didn't have my lighting down. I'll text you the link. You'll get a kick out of it." Sticking the Juicy Juice gum in her mouth, she recalibrates, "I know Gabriella owned cattle." Shaking her head like it's the first time she's thought about it, her voice rhythmic and singsong, like a kindergarten teacher, she presses on, "I don't like to speak ill of the dead, but I found her a bit narcissistic." She looks at me, "Right? I mean, she never seemed that interested in anyone else." Chewing distractedly loud, she adds, "I don't think she ever watched one of my vlogs. All she ever talked about was her tanning bed. And did you notice she had different ring tones for everyone that called her?"

"Yeah. I did."

"Who does that? It's like a teenage move." She pauses, "What do you think my ring tone was?"

I raise my eyebrows at a loss, *but "She Drives Me Crazy" by the Fine Young Cannibals comes to mind.*

"Stephanie, three women have died in this little town." Her eyes wide, she looks me over in silent deliberation.

"Yes." I snap out of it. 'It's more than a coincidence. But I had nothing to do with it, Chatura. I didn't even know those other women."

"No. I know. I'm sorry. It's just a lot to take in. I mean Gabriella was murdered and here we are driving to her house!"

I say nothing, aware of an uneasy feeling in my stomach as we drive through old town, Santa Fe, "The City Different." It's easy to forget this time capsule of the southwestern frontier is surrounded by big boxes and fast-food pit stops. The unassuming single-story adobes bordering the narrow Old Santa Fe Trail and downtown area are an attestation to the arid and volatile history that "civilized" this territory. "It's strange that Gabriella never talked about her family. Don't you think?"

"Oh, my god. Stephanie. She talked about her cattle ranching family all the time! It drove us all nuts!"

Nodding my head, I agree, "Yeah, but she never mentioned her mother, or her father, or any siblings. Not once! I don't even know if they're alive. Don't you find that odd?"

"You know, you're right." She mulls that over for a moment, "I bet she was an only child."

"Maybe."

"I'm sure her ex-husband could tell us more."

"Good thinking. Do you know him?"

"No. I don't even know his name. Besides, I don't think *your* asking questions about his ex who was just killed would be appropriate."

"No. It would not." Memories of Detective Brennan come to mind while Remy was missing. I had thought I'd be the obvious lead suspect at the time in his disappearance, until Brennan informed me that women account for 82 percent of victims killed by their partners or ex-partners. *That's something to think about.*

Heading out of town towards Tesuque, I can't help but notice the Veterans Cemetery on the right, a bleak reminder of murder. Thousands of identical gravestones line up in dizzying patterns; it's sobering. George Carlin's quote, "fighting for peace is like screwing for virginity," comes to mind. *Our world is off kilter.* Chatura makes a quick right on a street I didn't even know existed, and we start heading up into the foothills of the Northern Santa Fe Mountains. About two miles on the left is an enormous stone wall with an open gate. We drive through as a van with Crime Scene Unit written on the side passes us, on its way out. My stomach drops.

"That is creepy, Stephanie!" Chatura pulls over to the side of the drive, "Are you sure we should be her?"

"Chatura, I'm not sure of anything anymore. We just need to stay calm."

"OK." Finding her courage, we continue.

The driveway goes on forever. We're both uncomfortably quiet when finally, we see an enormous house in front of us, surrounded by large pinon and juniper. The adobe mansion looks like it's been here forever, one story and sprawling, a territorial flat roof is set off by a bright white trimmed portale against light, sand-colored facia. *Very impressive.*

There are no other cars in the U-driveway, and as we pull up, the front door opens, and a woman runs out. Chatura comes to a halting stop and gets out of the car without delay, dashing over to who, I'm guessing, is Gabriella's maid.

Drying her tears with a cloth knotted in her hands, the devasted woman offers, "Thank you for coming. I here all by myself."

"Marisol, I am so sorry for your loss. How is Al, I mean Juan Carlos?"

"He a mess. His mama is dead! I want to comfort him, mi hijo, but there no room at his poppa's house for me. I don't know what I gonna do." She looks over.

I smile gently.

"Oh, Marisol, this is Stephanie Beroe."

"Con mucho gusto. Beroe? They at your house for the party the night she die?" She looks at me oddly with tears in her eyes.

"Si. ¿Podemos pasar, por favor?"

"Of course, come in. The police just finish. They clean everything." She leads us into the palatial home, and Chatura and I take a seat opposite her on one of two immense leather sofas. "I no sure what's going to happen to me. I live here fifteen years. I have no family, no papers. Without Ms. Gabriella here to protect me, I afraid they deport me!"

Chatura jumps up and sits beside her, taking her hand, "Marisol, don't worry about that now. I'm sure Gabriella's family will take care of you."

"No. She have no family. Just Juan Carlos," the forty-something-year-old states, her dark hair a mirror to her emotions, scattered with fly-aways, as bloodshot eyes turn to me.

"¿Quieres una taza de té o café?" I offer.

Wiping her face on the rag, obviously exhausted, she responds with a slump, "Si, té gracias. La cocina esta a la izquierda." She nods her head over her left shoulder.

Always go left. Wandering through an enormous hall that leads to a Gordon Ramsay-sized kitchen, I can't help but notice the house is immaculate. *Not one thing is out of place.* And unlike my home, curated with mountains of curious objects, Gabriella was a minimalist. One object per table seemed to be her rule. *But it's too tidy. Cold even. Like a hotel, and it's pretty obvious that between Marisol's superhuman house cleaning skills and the Crime Unit cleaning crew… there's nothing left to see.* I fix a cup of Earl Grey from the cupboard above the coffee station the size of my closet and return to the living room.

"Aquí, tienes para usted."

"Gracias."

"So, then what happened?" Chatura asks, eyeing me proudly.

"I go to her room to tidy, but everything is put away, bed made already. She always very clean, but the door outside was open. It strange, but I leave it, even though it was cold."

"What time was that?" I ask.

"A las siete, a la mañana."

"Then what?"

"I make breakfast. When she not come, I find her." Lowering her voice she whispers, "Inside the machine."

"What machine?"

"The tanning machine. Dead!"

One meatball

"Did you find anything?" Chatura asks, navigating Santa Fe traffic before jumping on the bypass.

"While I was making tea? No. The kitchen was HAZMAT clean."

"Marisol wasn't very helpful. Poor dear."

"Chatura, Gabriella was found dead in her tanning bed!"

"Yeah."

"That was helpful!"

"How?"

"How many people have you ever heard of dying in their tanning bed? Or hot tub, for that matter?"

"I see what you mean. How about Evangeline?"

"Exactly."

"OK, so what's next?"

"Would you mind calling Gabriella's ex-husband and see what you can get out of him?"

She looks me over for a minute.

I think I've lost her.

"Sure, no problem."

Thankful Marisol was so generous with his contacts, I move on. "Can you also call Holly and see how she's doing? And check in on Delia?"

"Of course. Done."

Consumed by thoughts, the rest of the ride home for me is quiet. I'm glad to see Soter romping in the driveway as we pull up; his excitement makes me smile.

"I'll make some calls and let you know what I find out. I think we're making real progress here. Don't you, Stephanie?" She touches my shoulder empathetically, "Remember, no matter how dark it seems, there's no corner of this world light cannot penetrate."

That's not entirely true, but her enthusiasm is endearing. "Thank you, Chatura."

Walking up the driveway to my house, pleasantly echoing with laughter and the life it contains, I realize how cold and vacant Gabriella's was. It's almost as if it knew she was gone and decided not to hold space for her anymore. Shivering through our back door, I'm startled by the roosters in our coop crowing to get my attention. For a moment, I become alarmed and scared but it has nothing to do with my surroundings, it's all in my head, and as I close the back door, I feel the literal shelter of our home protecting me.

Pouring a cup of tea, my mind races through a flow chart of information, the deaths of all three women line up as Danielle appears out of nowhere; like a mind reader, she hands me printouts of articles outlining both Gabby Menckawitz's and Evangeline Burrows' deaths.

"You read my mind."

"Uh, huh," she coaxes, finishing off a peanut butter sandwich.

PTA President found dead - Gabby Menckawitz, 39 years old, was found dead at her home in Santa Fe at 7 am on February 20, 2020. David Menckawitz, the spouse of the deceased, called 911 after discovering her unresponsive in the family hot tub. The cause of death is drowning, but still under investigation. Gabby Menckawitz was the President of the PTA for a local charter school and had been a resident of Santa Fe for over 20 years. She is survived by her two sons, Robert and William, and her husband.

Death by exposure - The death of Evangeline Burrows, a 40- year- old tutor for a local charter school, has neighbors in an uproar over the lack of cellular coverage on Route 59A, the road to the Galisteo area. A neighbor found her body an estimated two weeks after she presumably died due to exposure during record low temperatures of negative 28 degrees Fahrenheit. "Burrows, was a single woman who lived alone, and led a solitary life," says Regina Patterson, a neighbor who noticed an excessive activity of blackbirds from her quiet neighbor's property. Patterson reached out by phone and social media to burrows, unsuccessfully. After receiving no response, Patterson's husband Dean visited Burrow's home to check in on her and found hundreds of blackbirds perched on the deceased's roof and property. "It was like something out of a movie," he stated. Then, after detecting an abnormal odor from the garage, he drove home and called 911. "I was not going in that garage. I could smell death."

Investigators believe that Burrows was locked out of her house during the extreme and unusually low temperatures late at night. Without cell coverage or

WIFI due to brown outs, she decided to shelter in her garage for the night and never woke up.

Settling into my chair facing the bird feeder outside alight with wings and feathers, I realize something. *I've been here before.*

Danielle waits for me quietly, also mesmerized by the doves.

"This is no coincidence. Three women die in unusual circumstances, and they're all directly related to the same charter school? No way."

"How well do you know these women?" She asks, her golden eyes steady, perfectly composed, "Your home school moms? How well do you know them?"

I shake my head, "I don't. I don't know them at all."

That cat is high

"Are you or have you ever been in possession of medical-grade marijuana, Mrs. Beroe?"

Umm. "Yes. I own a cannabis company," I reply. All five windows of strangers in front of me on my computer nod their heads fervently, writing notes. *It's infuriating.* Re-adjusting my laptop on my desk, I take a sip of infused tea to make my point. *If this is the line of questioning my new swarm of lawyers is going to take, I can see this is the first in a parade of Schloom calls.*

"How long have you owned a cannabis company?"

"Long enough to know better than to dose someone."

The severe forty-something, blonde counselor waits patiently.

She doesn't appreciate my frankness. "Fifteen years," I acquiesce.

"Stephanie, these are the questions the police will ask you. It's in your best interest to answer honestly but to keep it short and to the point. Don't be glib. It'll sink you."

I Straighten my back. *I'm not sure I like Jean Penderstone from Penderstone, Snodman, and Blatt. And what's with lawyers and their names? Are they predetermined at birth for indoctrination into law firms?*

"Do you hold a license to sell, manufacture, or grow cannabis products in the United States?"

"No."

"But you own a cannabis company. Who makes your products?"

"Yes, we own company that sells packaging, raw- uninfused coffee and tea blends and the intellectual property for infusing our products with THC. But our licensee's make our products."

"Doesn't your husband run a cannabis lab in Santa Fe that he works out of?"

"Yes, but I am not my husband."

"That's good. Keep it short just like that," she instructs, framed in a little box, the room behind her blurred, her almost black eyes never leaving the notes in front of her.

"Is there cannabis in this said lab you would have access to?"

Trick question. "No. I don't work in the lab."

"Do you have cannabis in your home?"

Umm. "Yes. I have a prescription."

"Perfect. Team, we can all agree that Mrs. Beroe's condition for a prescription is inconsequential and irrelevant."

Everyone nods yes as affirming comments and suggested citings scroll down the right side of my screen, like a telethon.

"How much cannabis would you say you have in your home at any given moment?"

Enough to take down a herd of elephants or a small sociopathic billionaire. "Umm. I don't know."

"That's great. OK, Stephanie, can you confirm you presently have a reasonable amount of cannabis in your possession, off the record? Because they will be coming with a search warrant."

My stomach wrenches at the word warrant, but knowing Remy returned everything he was working on and anything he deemed unreasonable, I answer, "Yes."

"Perfect. Let's turn to…" she filters through a horde of notes, "relationship questions with the victim." After a massive shuffling of paperwork, a young man walks into the room and whispers in Jean's ear while placing a document in front of her. "Hang on a minute, everyone, please." Taking a moment to review the document, she nods her head to herself, the paper sound exacerbated by her laptop mic, "The coroner has just confirmed that the deceased had over 10,000 milligrams of THC in her bloodstream. To be clear, it did not kill her. She was asphyxiated."

"Oh, my god. That's unbelievable," I respond.

"Stephanie, is that a lot of cannabis? What is a typical dose?"

"Well, for recreational- twenty-one and over, the prescribed dose is ***ten*** milligrams of THC per serving for edibles. For medical purposes, the typical dose is between 150 mg, to 250 mg, but I've seen some patients with severe chronic pain, end-of-life conditions, or drug addiction programs go as high as 2000 milligrams per day. 10,000 mg is intentional. Do you know how it was administered? I mean, you couldn't drink ten thousand milligrams of THC without really noticing what was going on. It would smell. You would smell the dope. You would taste it. It would be gross."

"That's good to know. Marc, please note that, and find a lab technician to support this information on the stand if necessary." Jean navigates her underlings with a supple hand.

"Maybe it was injected, or it was a tincture," I contemplate verbally. "But who would let someone dope them up with a tincture like that?" *Knowing the answer to this, I close my mouth immediately because I've done it. I have dosed someone! Twice! And, for a moment, they all know. At least, I think they know. What is this? Some kind of karma? Am I being morally punished because I dosed a sociopath last year? God damn it!*

"Stephanie, the investigators are fortunately sharing information as it comes in, but you understand they're only sharing because they're creating a case against you. You haven't been formally charged, but that is their intent, and my guess, is that the arrest warrant will be served within 48 hours, maybe less."

Great.

"You're going to need cash for bail."

Well, at least that's not a problem. I nod.

"Shall we continue?" she asks, straightening her blouse that definitely came off an REI rack.

I like it, like my attorney its sensible and tough.

"Let's go through the relationship questions. How long did you know the deceased?"

"I met Gabriella over the phone in July, and we met in person in August of this year. So, four months give or take."

"How many times have you seen the deceased in person?" Jean continues briskly.

"We've met four times for our micro-school group, including our Halloween party."

"And how often have you spoken over the phone or via computer? Roughly."

"Thirty or so phone calls, Schloom meetings, and probably ten thousand texts, maybe more."

"Marc, we will need phone records from the deceased and Stephanie's phone providers. Now, Stephanie, you stated you didn't know this woman, but you've communicated a great deal by your account?"

"They were group calls, group Schloom meetings, and group chats. Delia usually does most of the talking."

"Delia?" More paper shuffling, "Is she the mom that filed the complaint against you?"

All eyes on me. *Ah.* "Yes."

Stephanie, stay on task. See how that answer led to a strike against you? Don't offer any other information but the direct response to the question."

"OK, sorry." Squirming, I finish off my tea.

"During any of these calls, did you ever have an argument or disagreement with the deceased?"

If walls could talk. "No, we never argued." I pause, "But yes, we did disagree."

"What did you disagree about? Please, describe your disagreement."

Where do you want me to start? I take a deep breath, "Well, we didn't agree about politics, religion, history, human rights, natural resources, education, masking or Covid. Or the treatment of vegetarians."

The group laughs. *At least I know they're awake.*

"Did you like the deceased?"

Oh boy. I don't know how to answer this. NO, is obvious but definitely not the correct answer. Yes, however, is an outright lie. I mean, I didn't hate her. Hate is such a strong word, but would I be friends with her if not for this home school? Absolutely not.

"Stephanie, we need an answer; your responses must be natural and succinct."

"Gabriella had several good traits, and at the same time, she could be hard to get along with."

"That's not quite right, Stephanie. It's best to stick with yes or no. If that's not conscionable, try to weigh the pros and cons evenly. Let's come back to this."

The paper shuffling and scrolling notes continue for two more hours. Slugging it out, responding to the prompts as uninformatively as possible. For kicks, I scroll through our home school group chat from July, as my legal team confers. *It's a revelation. Strange, I didn't think to do this sooner, or even a month ago. Because if I had, I would have checked out then. The dysfunction is literally a red flag waving in a blue sky. Between Delia's control tactics and Holly with her one-word answers jammed between a horde of vlog invitations from Chatura with topics like "Jihad vegans." Is that even a thing? And "Vegan Carnage – The future of BBQ." These tasty bits were riding right alongside several dozen texts of Gabriella complaining about her tanning bed and how we need to reschedule meetings because of her work schedule and conference calls, it screams dysfunction! Not to mention the diatribe from Delia attempting to refocus the group away from thought-provoking literature and critical race theory.*

One thread alone is over a thousand words, an attack on The Handmaid's Tale, and that was the first of three others just like it. The argument she made against the English teacher's choice of material is an obvious, twisted, right-wing attempt at countering actual culture; it's shameless. And Gabriella backed her up every time, like Mrs. Magoo. There's a sprinkling of one-word replies from Holly, usually pried out by Chatura, who, all things considered, seems to be the only other voice of reason. This is like prepping for taxes; I feel every expense through the receipt, virtually. Closing my laptop, glad to finally be off the conference call, my phone buzzes with a text notification from Remy.

Hey, sweetie. How was the call?

I feel like I just left a Senate hearing.

Hang in there. Jean comes highly recommended. Any news from the police?

No news other than a warrant for my arrest is forthcoming.

Steph, don't focus on that. We will get through this. It's really windy here. I'm going to catch a couple of hours of sleep and then head home. I'll let you know when I leave. I love you.

Be careful. I love you too. *Those three words are my new mantra. Eat your heart out, Jimmy.*

Red beans and rice

"Hello?"

"Hey, Chatura, it's Stephanie."

"Stephanie, how's the rest of your day going?"

"Terrific."

"Really?"

"Ah, no. Did you have a chance to talk with Holly?"

"Yes." She pauses.

"And?"

"Well, she was really upset. Almost uncontrollable. I mean, I've seen Holly upset before. You know how quiet- people are." Chatura pauses, "They explode! But this was different. She was so angry."

"Like how?"

"I don't know, I think it was her voice. It was… different. I barely recognized her. It was weird."

"What were you talking about?"

"Um. You."

"What the hell?"

"I tried to calm her down. Between the beetle juice and Gabriella, it was just too much. She went ballistic!"

"Seriously? Don't we have bigger problems than bug scales?"

Catching her breath, I hear a tinge of annoyance as she adds, "I did manage to talk some sense into her. She's coming over. She should be here in about forty minutes."

"Do you think that's smart?"

"What do you mean?"

"Chatura, three women from the charter school are dead! What if Holly isn't who we think she is?"

"Come on, Stephanie. You can't be serious. Holly, a murderess?" Chatura laughs, "That's a good one! Seems a bit far-fetched, don't you think? I mean, Holly is one of the most passive women I've ever known. She couldn't hurt a fly. She's a vegetarian, for god's sakes!"

"Maybe. Listen, I'm coming over. I don't think you should meet her alone."

"Fine by me, but she'll be pissed when she sees you."

"Yeah, well, she'll get over it. See you in twenty minutes." Ending the call, I pour a cup of sober tea in the kitchen and notice a pan of cornbread

Danielle must have made, sitting on the stove. It smells delicious. Sharing a piece with Soter, I head upstairs thinking about Gabriella's response to me after being caught literally red handed at the Halloween party, "They'll get over it." she said. *She didn't care. She had no empathy, like a sociopath. How long had she been baiting them with meat?*

Working my way to the top of the stairs, lo and behold, I find a cricket before Soter does, "Hello there. Let's find a place for you." She crawls on my hand like she was expecting me, and I drop her off in the geranium in my office window. Danielle is in her office, which consists of two large, plum colored, winged-backed velvet chairs and a round white tiled coffee table over a cream flokati rug. The windows behind her mask everything in diffused light through the sheers; it's very inviting.

Looking up as I enter, she's beaming. "Stephanie, I've sent all the info we have on the deceased women to your old friend, Detective Brennan in San Francisco. He's going to look over everything and get back to us. Also, I've sent the names and addresses of all your home school moms to Galax and Horace. He's going to run them through the FBI database just in case, and you should know Galax is boarding a plane in an hour. She's coming as back up, and she won't take no for an answer."

"I love that." Giggling, I smile, basking in the thought that I have people in my life who are willing to go out on a limb for me; again. *I'm profoundly grateful.* Horace runs several global media outlets; without him last year, Remy and I would not be alive today. His partner Galax, who was also captive on the island, gave me a chance at freedom when I was abducted two years ago, simply because it was the right thing to do. The unlikely couple are trusted friends of ours now. Then there's Detective Brennan, he was a life raft for me when Remy disappeared. He gave me confidence to believe in my instincts. *We wouldn't be alive today if they all hadn't gotten involved. But what's most surprising and not surprising at all, is that Danielle thought to reach out to them. Remarkably, I hadn't even thought of it.*

"Thank you, Danielle." I curl up in the vacant chair across from her, tucking my knees to my chest, watching her multi-task, "You are such a good friend." My confession catches her off guard, her golden eyes lit by the sun behind me. *She's many things, but emotional is not one of them, at least not outwardly. That's probably why she survived the park as long as she did. She is superhero tough.* "I am so sorry," I begin. "I haven't been…." I can't finish my sentence; it's too long, there are too many words and too many reasons. Tears well in my eyes.

"Stephanie," she puts her laptop aside, "We are family. This is how it is. We take care of each other."

Collecting myself with a big inhale, I concede, "You're right. We are family." Suddenly I feel empowered.

"Now, what's next?"

"I'm going over to Chatura's." Wiping my eyes, I explain, "Holly's on her way there now. Chatura told me she's angry, strangely angry- at me."

"Do you think Holly killed Gabriella?" She cuts right to the meat.

"I don't know." I stand up, "But someone did, and you know as well as I do, people aren't always who they seem." Distracted by a car in our driveway, I pull the curtains back slightly. "Shit."

"What?" Danielle jumps up.

"It's Detective Chavez." We head downstairs, Soter leading us both on cue through the kitchen. I smell the cornbread before I see it this time. *Cornbread.*

Opening the door, my team beside me, I have the confidence of a mediocre white guy.

"Mrs. Beroe, may I come in?"

Holding the door open wider, Danielle stands directly in her path.

"This is Danielle, my husband's assistant, and family friend," I offer.

She gives Danielle the once over, "Nice to meet you." Raising her eyebrows, she maneuvers past.

I can't imagine why? Don't all men have gorgeous, six-foot-tall women working for them? Amused, I point, and all three of us sit at the living room table. Briefly hypnotized by a flock of small, electric-blue birds gathering at the feeder outside the window, I watch the micro-mobile army cover the tree like a wave. *It gives me an idea.*

Chavez unbuttons her jacket slowly, then gets to the point, her eyes intent, "Mrs. Beroe, I'd like to know why you were at the victim's house today?"

"Gabriella's?" Silent for a moment, I respond honestly, "Because I made a promise."

"Excuse me?"

"I promised my niece I would find out what happened to Gabriella."

With a discernable look, her eyes flit back and forth between Danielle and me, "You realize the DA has enough evidence to file criminal charges against you, today?"

Ouch, I do now. Holding my ground, I inquire, "If that's the case, then why are you here? What brings you out here on a Sunday if it's an open and shut case?"

Studying both of us, like she's deciphering something, she clears her throat, "That's exactly why I am here. My partner used to say, 'Just because it's easy doesn't mean it's right'"

That is the story of my life.

"I spoke with a Detective Brennan today. I won't lie. He said all the right things about you. But I have three dead women."

"Three? Not just Gabriella?"

"That's right. Gabby Menckawitz the PTA President at the charter school, and Evangeline Burrows a tutor from the same school your niece attends, were both found with questionable amounts of cannabis in their blood stream."

"I had nothing to do with any of this! I didn't even know the other two women."

Reaching inside her jacket pocket, she pulls out a very official-looking, folded document, then slides it across the table towards me without removing her unmanicured hand, "Tell me something, I don't know."

My eyes move up from the document to hers. *OK.* I take a deep breath, "Do you eat meat?"

"Excuse me?"

"Are you a vegetarian, or do you eat meat?"

Confused, she responds, "No, I eat meat." Then squares her shoulders with the back of her chair defensively.

"Do you have any vegetarian friends?"

"Yes."

"Do they ever invite you over for dinner?"

"Umm." She looks up to the ceiling almost amused and responds, "No. No, they don't."

"Do they eat at your house?"

"Yes. Where is this going, Mrs. Beroe?"

"Please, call me Stephanie. Do you cook them meat?"

She laughs, "No. Of course not."

"I know," I reply. "That would be- unthinkable."

"Yes."

"Did you know that Gabby Menckawitz, the President of the PTA, was big on meat stews?"

"I'm sorry, I don't see how this is…."

I hold a finger up, "She served them, at every PTA potluck. Gabby owned dozens of crock pots and filled them with meaty stews and hearty soups."

"She was found dead in her hot tub."

My head nods to a rhythm.

Staring, her eyes narrow.

"Did you also know that Evangeline Burrows, the tutor, froze mice in her freezer that she caught in traps to humanely dispose of them?"

Shaking her head, she answers, "No. No, I didn't." Then laughs, "What's next? Ms. Alfonso Del Olmo Lopez was big on paninis?"

Danielle smirks.

"No. But she was overly fond of Bar-b-que."

I put my finger in the air again, as she shakes her head, "And she was secretly dosing a vegetarian with meat for over a year." *That gets her attention.* "Let me ask you something? How did you know I was at Gabriella's today?"

"Holly Lipstein informed me. She was genuinely concerned."

"Was she? Interesting. Did she tell you Gabriella was caught red handed at our party feeding Holly, a professed vegetarian, juice made from bug scales, intentionally?"

Eyebrows pursing with a disgusted look, she responds, "No. No, she did not."

"Gabriella told me she had been secretly feeding Holly meat every chance she got, for years."

Chavez literally moils this over for a moment before responding, "I don't know where to go with this. Do you have any proof? Because at this point, the DA has to choose between someone dosing people with meat and someone dosing people with cannabis. And there are no laws against feeding people meat."

Ouch. I regroup, "Have you ever had something happen that is so far-fetched, you have no choice but to believe it?"

"Uhh, pandemic!" Danielle retorts.

"Exactly."

Sitting back in her chair, looking out the window for a silent moment, Chavez pulls her hand back slowly, and places the document back in her pocket, "You have twenty-four hours."

Gunning for the Buddha

Purring up Gold Mine Road in our 1971, VW van Trixie, pretending she was made for dirt roads, the red and white paint job is a dead giveaway. *They'll see me coming; but I have a plan.*

Danielle, is following me through a satellite GPS tracker attached to my hat on her phone, a lovely gift from my husband Remy last year before all hell broke loose. It has a built-in panic button. *I hope I won't need.* Plus, I'm excited about a brand-new gadget I've never used, a micro droid that records video and sound. *Giving a whole new meaning to the term bug.* Practically silent, it cruises at a frequency humans can't hear. Remy buys most of these things from a mercenary catalog, which I imagine is why, my mail lady is terrified of me.

Running through my checklist, I also have my Hello Kitty stun ring, a smoke bomb lipstick, my stun gun cell phone, ready and charged, and my new electrified "no-touch" jacket. *Of course, if all this goes wrong, and I'm just delusional about this woman, I'll be in jail. So, no pressure.*

At almost five o'clock long autumn shadows, emphasize the low sun, saturating the world around me in a golden light that's deceivingly beautiful. Behind me, the panorama of the valley below is alienating as our home, indistinguishable in the distance, no longer anchors me. *My palms are sweating.*

Turning right at the third juniper tree past the only decipherable sign halfway up Gold Mine Mountain, Chatura's house, a sprawling one-story with a living roof, and wind turbine, comes into view. Her three-car portales, covered in solar panels, comfortably nestling her Tesla, is snuggled within a stunning, thousand-acre property. The main house, surrounded by an adobe wall with an ancient gate from India that's barely blue, has been left permanently open and inviting. Two huge, hand-carved doors at the end of a flagstone path are guarded by a pair of enormous terracotta pots on either side; taller than me, a towering cactus protrudes out of each of them.

Parking, I gather my thoughts, rolling the passenger's window down. "Soter." I point to a spot next to the sliding door, in the back out of sight, "sit," giving him the hand signal for watch and a pat on the head, his Egyptian eyes are intent with purpose. At full attention, he will not leave the vehicle unless I call or whistle for him. I don't see Holly's car, which is a relief. Activating the micro-drone, it's inaudible to me but curious to Soter while it hovers. Ideally, it will follow the locator in my hat, somehow, guided by sonar by Danielle. If it works, I'll have to remember to thank Horace, Remy's new gadget master, for his monthly selection of classified offerings.

Pulling my tracker cap down over my ears, my pockets full of toys, I slap my cheeks, riling them out of pallid anxiety response, and slip my phone into the back pocket of my jeans. Priming the safety button in the liner of my jacket, in an attack, all I need to do is press the button in the pocket, and kazaam- 150,000 volts to anyone who touches me. *I'm ready, and I'm not fucking around.*

Chatura meets me at the door, "Stephanie, I'm so glad you're here. I was getting nervous." We hug like it's been years, tears in both our eyes. "Please come in." She's shaky but welcoming, her cream-colored, cable knit sweater is comfortably yummy and the black, wide legged, yoga pants reveal her manicured bare feet. "Sit, please. You must be exhausted. I can only imagine how stressful this is for you. I made a relaxing tea from my Chinese doctor; it's valerian, skullcap, and passionfruit. I think you'll like it."

Tea is laid out for three on her Balinese coffee table that is so big, I could use it as a stage, and it's practically on fire from copious aromatherapy candles, she's put to task, cleansing the space.

"Thank you, Chatura." I take a deep breath, lavender, tea tree, and orange settle me before a familiar unpleasant aroma breaks through. Moving closer to the kitchen, the smell of bad fish, is at odds with the surroundings, so clean and fresh, "Your house has such an openness about it. It's really energized."

"Thank you. As you know from my vlog, I've had a virtual Feng Shui master working with me for months pushing energy around, but I think we finally did it. It feels good. Right?" She nods her perfectly coiffed chignon with confidence.

"Definitely." Everything, beige or green, is soft and welcoming, dreamlike even. Two giant, picture windows on either side of the front doors look towards the Santa Fe Mountains, formidable in the background as the entire mountain range to the west transforms into a silhouette against a fading orange sunset; it's sexy and powerful.

Led to an enormous balsa sofa surrounded by hanging basket chairs, I'm disarmed by the low-key- Balinese chic as heated, rammed earth floors warm the space, naturally accentuating stands of exotic plants in every corner. Between the kitchen and living room, an array of different-sized glass bubble planters with air ferns, hang from the ceiling. They create a light and playful wall division, that I remember from her vlog. To the left of the kitchen is the area she has dedicated to her vlogging, tripods with cameras and lighting rigs, face a multitude of chairs and props in disarray.

"So, what's the plan?" She asks nervously, sitting across from me.

"We need to get Holly to talk."

"Ha! That'll be a feat."

"Yeah. It's not going to be easy. Listen, whatever I say, I need you to just go with it. It may get… messy."

"OK. But Stephanie, what if…she really is a murderer?" she asks, her eyes wide, and filled with fear, reminding me of Imogene.

"I'm prepared for anything, Chatura. Don't worry. But keep your phone nearby in case we need back up."

"I hope you know what you're doing." She pours nervously, as Holly pulls up.

Getting out of her car, I watch Holly contemplate Trixie for a moment deliberating through the windows. Chatura opens the front doors as if on cue, "Holly, I'm so glad you're here." She states enthusiastically, collecting her before she can bolt.

At the threshold, Holly stops in her designer clad tracks, "Why is she here?" her monotone is gruesome.

"We need to talk." I pick up my cup, letting her ease in.

Moving awkwardly forward like a mime, she proclaims, "Nate doesn't want me talking to you," without engaging one muscle on her pale face.

Between the unseasonably warm weather and the candle fire- pit in front of me, droplets of sweat are mounting on my eyes and forehead; my jacket and cap forsaking me. I'm afraid to take them off, but worried the perspiration will be misconstrued as a guilty conscience. Ignoring the uncomfortable silence, the need to towel off, and both their stares, I become distinctly aware of the mouth noises I'm making gnawing on a vegan cookie, worried I'm blinking too much. *OK, just breathe.*

"You shouldn't be here," she reiterates, turning to leave.

"No, wait, Holly." I smile gently, "We really should talk."

"Stephanie, there is nothing to say. You're under suspicion of murdering Gabriella, and you tried to kill Delia." She smiles, then whispers, "You're a sociopath." Swinging her Goyard purse at her side, almost playfully, "Of course, it's no surprise to me or anyone else in the group." Her voice, flat and righteous, she's on a roll, "Do you want to know why?" she instigates.

I raise my eyebrows.

"Because you're reckless. Everything you do is counter to society," she seethes.

"I believe the term is counterculture."

Her bag drops dramatically to the floor, "It's all a joke to you, isn't it? I mean, you sell marijuana. Why would anyone take you seriously?"

Wow.

She smirks, egging me on.

"You know what, Holly? That's the most you've said all year. But you're right. My life is reckless, I concede. But not because I sell marijuana." I sip my tea; *it has a calming effect on her.* "I was born reckless, and learned early, never to surrender. It was me against the adult world as a child, like Charlie Brown for god's sake, and now, as an adult, it's me against the conformity of society, just like you said." She moves towards the couch, peeling off her over coat, exposing head to toe Ann Taylor, pleased to be proven right , as I continue, "I'm not like you, Holly. And I never will be. I'm less trusting. I despise routine. I'm hard to please and so much more because I have to be. My life is different. I take risks. Plus, I enjoy feeling alive, really alive, out of my comfort zone."

Narrowing her eyes smugly, she's retreated back to silence.

Time for the attack, "Whereas, at times, it's been hard for me to decipher whether you even have a pulse. You're disengaged, morbid, and entitled."

Rage bottlenecking in her previously unresponsive face, I take it as an invitation, "You've given up. Whatever spark you had, it's gone. Lost to fear and the unknown like you've been stripped of your instincts and senses. You're pathetic."

"Stop!" She hisses.

I stand up, my hand on my chest, "There's a life force inside of me, and I don't take it for granted. Some people create, some people consume; that's the real difference between you and me. I reinforce my beliefs with purpose that I'm not wasting my time on earth. I'm making the world better, through art, music, health care, and even food for my friends." Looking at both of them, I continue, "I'm leading by example to show our kids there's a big world out there that they can be a part of, encouraging them to find their own journey, regardless of where it might take them."

Holly smirks, but Chatura nods her head in agreement.

"You know what I mean, Chatura. You're on a similar path. Look at the dedication you have to your vlog? Sharing all that wonderful information with the world around you, making the world better than you left it. You get it, don't you?"

"Yes, Stephanie. I get it." She smiles, topping off Holly's cup.

It's time to amp this up. "I am reckless, I reiterate. Creating things makes you vulnerable." Turning towards the counter that separates the living room from the kitchen with my cup, I buy time admiring a couple of succulents next to a pile of bills, but I'm looking for my bug as Chatura takes the floor.

"That's right!" She stands up. "I couldn't agree with you more, Stephanie." With tears, she professes, "Being a content creator isn't easy. Everyone makes fun of you. And being, counterculture…" She looks to me, "makes you an outsider and a target. I know you all think I'm nuts with my solar oven and Earth Ships, and Veganism. I know you don't agree with me. But I'm making a difference in my own way. And that's the thing! Just when you think you're doing something amazing, letting people in on something they should know? Someone comes along and tells you, you're crazy! It's thankless!" She throws her hands up in the air and flings herself back on the couch out of frustration.

"I know about being vulnerable," Holly responds, pulling viciously at a button. "You don't know me!" She looks at Chatura. "I don't need to pretend to be a social media superstar." Grimacing, she throws her head in my direction with disgust, "Or make a living selling drugs to justify coping."

"So, it's the marijuana that bothers you? It all comes down to that." I sit down, placing my empty cup on the table like punctuation. *There's only one place to go from here.* "Let me ask you something? If I'm a drug dealer, what's your husband?"

"Nate is a surgeon!" she screams. "He went to school. He helps people!" Mirroring me, she slams her empty cup down. "You don't even have a college degree. You're just nobodies! Dropouts!" She decries with a smirk.

Eyeing both of us, Chatura looks like Tweetie Bird for a moment as I set my gaze on Holly. "At least I don't lie to people. I don't treat symptoms to create long-term patient returns, and I don't charge incoherent prices for natural remedies. There's a statement on our coffee bags, '*Good karma always tastes good.*' It's there for a reason."

"How dare you!"

Pacing back to the large palm next to the fridge, I drive it home, "Really, Holly? You told me yourself you moved here to get away from the HMOs that capped Nate's salary. That came out of your mouth. And you said it like it was OK! You are in denial if you can't see how insurance companies and medical costs kill people. The same medicines in over 35 other countries in the world cost 250 times less than in the U.S.! 250 times! That's a fact. You can look it up." I lick my lips, "Your husband is part of the biggest Ponzi scheme that's ever existed, and you couldn't care less as long as your shopping sprees aren't interrupted and the endless sea of Amagog boxes piling up at your front door arrive in two days. You're a cliché."

"Shut up! SHUT THE FUCK UP!" she bellows.

"You think you're helping animals by not eating them? What do you think you're doing to their habitats shopping online? Where do you think all that cardboard comes from? It'd be ironic if it weren't so sad."

Blistering with anger, she looks to Chatura for backup, but Chatura ignores her, quietly picking up Holly's coat and bag from the floor and placing them on the kitchen counter.

Like a cornered animal, Holly glares, her eyes dilating wildly, "I'm warning you, Stephanie." Pointing an irate finger at me, she claims, "You're just trying to justify what you do by belittling people who are really making a difference." Moving towards me aggressively she adds, "You think you're making the world a better place by opening legal drug stores on every corner? Near schools? Normalizing drug addiction? And what did you say? By making food for friends? Is that why you fed us bacon in the cornbread and beetles in our drinks? You're the one that's delusional! You need to be stopped!"

There it is. "For the record, there are already drug stores on every corner. And with the help of surgeons like your husband, more than ten million Americans a year are now hooked on opioids. Your sacred doctors murder over 128 people a day! Every day Holly! And these people aren't old and dying. They're healthy, 25 to 50-year-olds with families and lives that will never be the same again. The fall of the American Empire is on your husband's head!"

Chatura's eyebrows peak, while Holly plots her next move.

"You claim to be a vegetarian to stop animal suffering?" I hammer the last nail, "What about human suffering? What about all those people whose lives have been decimated for a golf club membership and a condo on the ski mountain? Shame on you! I don't know how you can live with yourself," I say taking a sip before adding, "Maybe you can't? Maybe that's why you're always checked out! Maybe you took all that anxiety out on Gabriella because she fed you bugs?"

Moving inordinately fast around the table towards me, she growls, "You filthy, lying cunt."

I jump up, her eyes darting quickly around the room, looking for something, I don't know what. Raising her hand in the air; she swings at my head!

Without blinking, catching her wrist three inches from my face, my eyes cool and steady, my other hand primes my electric jacket in a stand-off.

Chatura freezes with the tea pot in her hand.

Stopped in her tracks, Holly laughs, "Ha! It won't matter," in a creepy voice as I release her wrist. "You won't matter," she appends, with a frightening shift as she becomes almost giddy, overstimulated.

It's now or never. "You know, of course, Gabriella was dosing you every chance she had?"

Wide eyes say it all. "Oh yes, she confessed to me the night of the party."

"Dosed us with what?" Chatura asks, visually troubled.

"With meat! In every dish she ever made you, for over a year. Intentionally."

Astonished, they're both mute.

"Even before our home school group," I continue. "She told me, you loved it! Did she elaborate on that when she told you about my accidental cornbread?"

"No!" Both of them respond, stunned, digesting every word.

"When did she tell you about the cornbread, Holly?"

"She didn't."

"What do you mean she didn't? How did you find out?"

"Chatura told me. Gabriella was a useless wretch."

I turn to Chatura, waiting.

"I called her the night of the party. I was angry too. I just needed to know why?"

"When was that? On her way home?"

"Yes, on her way home."

"What did she tell you?"

"When I confronted her, she just said, "Why are you so mad at me? Did you know Stephanie fed you bacon fat? Which is worse?"

Uh-huh. I should've known. "And you didn't hold it against me?"

"I did before I realized it wouldn't do any good. Besides, you're not belligerent, Stephanie. I know that."

"Thank you, Chatura."

She nods Namaste as Holly explodes, "Why am I here?" her long arms gesticulate causing her Anne Taylor cuffs to grip her forearms.

"You don't know?" I ask.

"No!"

"I'm trying to decide why you killed Gabriella."

Pass the peas

Danielle stares intently at two screens in front of her, one playing back Stephanie talking to Holly and Chatura in real time and the other a magnified view of the footage leading up to that point in slow-mo. Zooming in on the latter, Holly's purse tipped over on the kitchen counter, the bug literally crawls through it, mail spilling out, hand sanitizer, a vintage Prada wallet, a tortoise hair brush, gum, mints, a prescription. *Wait. What does that say?* Maneuvering the bug closer, she reads the label – Haloperidolt. Taking a screenshot, she moves on as Holly's cell phone lights up, freezing the bug while Holly's hand pulls out the device. Danielle waits as she takes the call with three words, "Hi. Yes. Bye."

For a brief second, Danielle sees a name she doesn't recognize on an envelope in the pile of mail, but Holly collects her things abruptly, her concentration absorbed by Stephanie's brutal verbal attack. The bug crawls out, and she manages to navigate it under a stack of children's drawings before it takes back to the air. Jotting down the time of the footage, Danielle looks up Haloperidolt.

That's interesting. Hitting the print button, an email notification crosses her screen. It's Detective Brennan, his communication is short, and she's stunned by what it says. At the same time, Galax texts her.

On board Horace's Boeing, ETA Albuquerque 3.5 hours, car is waiting to pick me up.

Danielle smiles. Galax is tough. You wouldn't know it by looking at her, doe eyed, and unassuming, but her resilience and fearlessness are astounding. Thinking about the plane sets her back to the park. After a year of fighting for her life, she will never forget the feeling of walking on board a safe space with the real hope of returning to a civilized world. Wiping tears, she rarely sheds, she texts Horace.

Find anything yet?

His reply is immediate. ***No. Still working.***

Hearing the VW van purr up the driveway, she's relieved Stephanie is home safe and once again is reminded of how fragile her new life and family are. Turning back to the screen, she starts the recording at the beginning, determined to find something.

Part Four

Southern fried chicken

A wave of exhaustion washes over me as I follow Soter upstairs. *I'm in the thick of it again.* My statement to Holly about being comfortable outside of my safety zone is biting me in the ass. The most troubling aspect of this afternoon, however, is my disappointment that nothing happened! And that in itself, is a concern! All dressed up for nothing! No attack! No confession! Nothing! I'm no further along now than I was this morning, and the aftertaste of verbally abusing Holly is a bitter stain on my tongue. My behavior at Chatura's was exactly what I detest about our world right now, judgmental, gaslighting rhetoric. Yes, the facts I stated are real, and yes, my opinion of the world around us is quite valid, *to me.*

But negativity and blame never move society forward productively or positively. I know this, and even though I was deliberately riling her, becoming someone, I despise, stings.

At Danielle's office door, I take a deep breath. Her workspace is completely different in twilight with no influence from the New Mexico sunshine; it's something out of a magazine shoot, the furniture taking center stage against stark white sheers. *I should make her some drapes.*

"Hey, Stephanie." She looks up from her laptop with a sincere smile, "I shared the recording with you. I figured two sets of eyes are better than one."

"Good thinking." I sigh, opening my computer. A screenshot of Remy, Imogene, and me on the ski lift with our goggles, and helmets, presses on my chest.

"Are you ok?"

"I don't know. That was a waste of fucking time. I mean, nothing happened!"

"It's not like the movies, Stephanie. You have to be patient," she states, her golden eyes unwavering, "I found something. Have you ever heard of Haloperidolt?"

"No. What is it?"

"It's an antipsychotic used to treat Tourette's Syndrome and Schizophrenia."

"OK."

"I found a prescription for it in Holly's bag."

"Seriously?"

"Yes. It can cause listlessness, expressionless behavior, and lack of engagement unless provoked."

"I'd be hard-pressed to believe she has Tourette's, but Schizophrenia fits."

"Does she drink?"

"Yes."

"That could be something." She turns her screen around, showing me a list too long to contemplate. "Not only shouldn't schizophrenics drink but mixing this medication with alcohol and even simple food items will cause sudden death or completely alter their personalities; they can become dangerous. More than six hundred other drugs, including Benadryl, interact with this drug severely. It's a time bomb waiting to happen."

"Pharmaca at its best, prescribing a volatile product for someone who has no mental or behavioral control." Then I think back, "She was drinking heavily at the Halloween party."

"You need to read this." She hands me her computer.

Schizophrenia disorder may result in a combination of hallucinations, delusions, or disruptive thoughts and behavior that can cause self-harm or be dangerous to others. My head swirling, I respond, "She was right; I don't know her." Talking out loud, I continue, "Living in Santa Fe would have made it easy for Holly to get to Gabriella's by eleven. But how did she get a hold of the cannabis? Jean told me Gabriella had over ten thousand milligrams of THC in her blood stream. That's no small feat."

"Didn't you say they ski in Colorado a lot?" She sits back, her eyes ratified.

"Yes, they do." I hand her laptop back and pace, a million thoughts on my mind. "This is exactly what we're looking for."

"There's something else." With my full attention, she continues, "I don't know how relevant this is, but you should know, Brennan found out that Delia's husband was arrested."

"For what?"

"For beating her unconscious while intoxicated three years ago."

"Oh, my god!"

"She didn't press charges. And their son was the one who called the police."

Speechless, my hand covers my mouth. Closing my eyes, visions of Delia grappling for control over non-sensical minutiae during our meetings races in front of me. *She was fighting back for a reason! Sure, it was misguided and self-serving, but now I see, it was a radical, honest attempt at self-preservation.* Feeling the choke of guilt, that I wasn't more supportive, I whisper, "I had no idea."

"Well, that's not exactly something, someone tells you."

"No, but it puts their extreme Christian values and their behaviors in perspective. They've gone over to the other side for a reason. That's an eye-opener."

"But does it make Gerry a suspect? Or Delia, for that matter? I know first-hand the oppressed can become the oppressors." The bitter tone in her voice, is a slap in the face.

I'm right back on Horace's plane, being airlifted off that island with Remy and Danielle, and all of the other survivors two years ago. The expressions on their faces were undeniable; the innocent full of anguish and relief, while the others were transformed by their own guilt. *They didn't even want to leave; they had become so comfortable in the lap of tyranny they had created. It's a lot to think about.* "We need to start ticking suspects off our list quickly."

"Well, so far, that makes a schizophrenic, an abused woman, a wife-beater, and a narcissist. That's some group."

"Who's the narcissist?"

"Seriously, Stephanie?" Her eyebrows perch over the top of her laptop.

I wait.

"The vlogger," she states like it's common knowledge.

Ouch! That hurts. But…she's right. It's true! I have been chalking personality flags up to idiosyncrasies. "Wait a minute." A thought comes to mind, reprioritizing everything. "You know, Chavez never asked me if I take prescription drugs."

"No." Danielle shakes her head, "But she was all over your cannabis. Seriously, you need your own Me- Too movement."

"Yeah, well, who would care? I bet she doesn't even know about any of this."

"I hope it pans out because everyone else is clean. Horace is still digging, of course. Oh, and Galax will be here by eleven."

"Remy should be back by midnight."

"Looks like a sleepover," she says, trying to lighten the atmosphere, stretching her longs limbs gracefully like a praying mantis.

"Yeah, well, it's going to be my going away party if we don't figure this out." Knowing Danielle has excellent instincts, I ask, "What do you think about all of this?"

She pauses for a moment. "You don't want to know. Let's keep looking. Maybe I missed something. Oh! I almost forgot." Hitting a couple of keys, she shares her screen with me. "Do you know this name?"

In front of me, a magnified view of an envelope pops up with the name Eleanor Grines. I can't read the address, but I can see it's from Tennessee. "No. No, I don't. Where was this?"

"In a pile of mail overflowing from Holly's purse, on Chatura's counter."

"Now, that is something." Instantly sending the name off to Brennan with an apology for being such a nuisance, I also copy Horace. "Was that the only letter with that name on it?"

"Yes, so far."

"Let's keep looking."

We're both hopeful now, meticulously scanning the footage, convinced we'll find something to turn the tide. But an hour later, with nothing more than a headache, I turn to Danielle, my stomach rumbling. "Are you hungry?"

"Yes."

"Let's take a break. I'll make pasta."

"If you don't mind, I'll stay here and sift through these images. You never know."

Walking down the stairs, a cricket that didn't make the winter, blocks the second step. I bend over to pick up its lifeless body, troubled the tiny being won't see spring. *I hope my chills don't confirm this as an omen.*

After an entire glass of water, I turn on *Columbo* as a companion; *he always understands my plight.* "Try and catch Me," with Ruth Gordon starring as the Agatha Christie–ish writer Abigail Mitchell is one of my favorite episodes, even if it's not commercial-free. I know every line and don't need to watch to know what's happening. With a pot of hot water on the burner, I turn the enamel knob and the propane ignites with a deep, familiar whoosh. Chatura's vlog about banning gas stoves comes to mind. *Is there nothing sacred?*

Throwing some bacon fat and bacon in a pan not just for taste but for desperately needed comfort, I chop up a shallot and an onion and wash some kale while the pan sizzles. Once the bacon's halfway, I pour in a healthy amount of olive oil and the rest of the ingredients, stirring until the onions are caramelized before adding the kale. When it's wilted but still green, I turn it off and grate parmesan over the top, leaving it covered, waiting for the noodles. The aroma makes my stomach lurch and probably Danielle's too as she appears, taking a seat at the kitchen table. A commercial for psoriasis interrupts us, making my head itch until the disclaimer states on hyper speed, "Use of this product can cause severe bleeding or death." I look at Danielle with my eyebrows raised.

She shakes her head, "And we can't sell CBD in big box stores?

"Don't get me started."

Thankfully, *Columbo* returns just in time. He's attending a ladies' luncheon for a writer's guild. Ruth Gordon introduces him as an expert on advanced forensic technology. Shocked, he tells the ladies in the crowd, "Someone must be pulling your legs because I don't know anything about it."

Oh, my god! Grabbing my phone, I start texting. Danielle watching my every move, jumps up to rescue the spaghetti pot that's now boiling over.

"I have an idea," I yelp, texting the manager of every recreational dispensary we know on the Colorado border and the handful of dispensary owners I know in New Mexico. *It's a long shot, but it's all I have.*

Plying both bowls with an obscene amount of grated parmesan cheese, Danielle pours us both a glass of Pinot Grigio and grabs a fork for her and fork and spoon for me. *She knows I love to twirl.* The rest of the house feels cold without a fire; I've quarantined us in the kitchen to stay warm. After a couple of bites, my brain starts working again, "You know what bothers me?"

Danielle looks up intently.

"The cornbread."

"What's wrong with my cornbread?" full-mouthed, she responds insulted.

"Nothing. It's delicious. Really!" I laugh, "But I don't understand the sequence of what Gabriella told Chatura."

"What do you mean?"

"Well, I thought Holly had talked to Gabriella first about the cornbread. But it was Chatura who called Gabriella while she was driving home from the party to ask why she had given her beetle juice, and that's when she found out about my bacon-laced cornbread."

"So, what's the problem?"

"I don't know, but last year, when we were all making hard decisions between revenge and retribution, Remy said, 'It takes the perfect conditions to make the perfect wave.' But it's more like a recipe."

Back up in Danielle's office, reviewing the same footage over and over and over again, she involuntarily displays an array of yawns. *I recognize a pasta coma when I see one,* "You know, you don't have to stay. I can do this," stating the obvious, I feel the inevitable tink of vulnerability.

"I'll stay until Galax gets here."

"Don't be ridiculous. Galax won't be here for at least another hour, and you're exhausted."

"I'm not leaving you alone."

"I'm not alone." I pet Soter's head.

"Right. OK. Well, if you need anything, my phone's on." She stands up, towering above me, caught in another yawn.

"Thank you, Danielle."

She smiles, "Good night, Stephanie. I'll be here at five."

Walking her down the stairs, I add, "See you tomorrow." Closing the door behind her. Unfortunately, the comfort I thought I might acquire by solitude is instantly eclipsed. Normally, under these circumstances, I would run a bath or hit the shower, letting the warm water reset my perspective, but I'm not alienating myself from the rest of the house or the sounds of comings and goings.

My phone buzzes. "Stephanie?"

"Chatura?" *Why is she whispering?* "What's wrong?"

"A car drove up to my property. I saw the headlights. They stopped and turned off after that line of juniper just past my parking area." She gasps, "They're just sitting there!"

"Are you sure it was headlights?"

"Yes! I'm sure!"

"Did you call the police?"

"No! What would I tell them? I think I saw headlights?!"

"Are your girls home?"

"No. They're at Delia's for the weekend. I'm all alone! Stephanie, I don't even have a weapon if I need one!"

Well, that's definitely not my problem. "Come here! You're safe here. We'll figure it out," I submit, attempting calm.

"How do I do that? Run? Outside?" She's panic-stricken.

"Yes. Listen to me. Chatura, you run as quickly as you can, but you need to stay focused. And lock the doors as soon as you get in your car."

"OK. So. I'm going to run to my car," she resolves, psyching herself up to avoid hyperventilating, "Stephanie, if I'm not at your house in fifteen minutes, call the police!" She hangs up.

Is this really happening? Would Holly kill Chatura? She wasn't happy when Chatura hung her out to dry today. She was mad, crazy mad. But I would have thought she'd come after me first. I don't know what to think anymore. My brain overloaded; I start pacing.

Soter trots to the back door, cutting me off at the bathroom, "You need to go out, boy?" Opening the door with a wary eye, I feel safe he's doing his rounds.

Setting my timer for Chatura, I decide to change my clothes. I can fight exhaustion, but I'm tired of my underwire strangling me. It's an absolute relief once I have a pair of stretchy yoga pants and a cashmere top on with my comfy scarf wrapped around my neck. Sliding on my slippers, I feel a wave of relief coursing through me as I let my hair down and shake it out. The ponytail I wore with my GPS hat was way too tight, reminding me of Detective Chavez. *Only someone desperately attempting to hold themselves together, wears a ponytail that tight.*

Putting the kettle on, I walk to the back door for Soter. I'm startled to see Chatura standing in the window, a look of sheer terror in her eyes!

"Stephanie, for God's sake open the door!" She pushes herself inside desperately, disheveled for the first time I've known her. "There really was someone on the property! I couldn't make out their car, but they were there!" She hurries in, exasperated. "I got out of there as fast as I could. Do you think they followed me? I couldn't tell with all the dust my car was making coming down Gold Mine Road. Should we call the police?"

"Tell me what happened." Squaring her shoulders to keep her from a panic attack, I lock the door ushering her into the kitchen, "Tell me exactly what happened."

"After you left, I took a bath," she begins, her eyes beading around like a rabbit, "Then I filmed my new vlog, Real Concerns about 5G and Covid." Breathing heavy, she's stuttering. I pour her a glass of water. She takes a long drink, then continues, "I ate an avocado on the couch in front of the fire reviewing the footage. Did you get my notification?"

Oh my god. "Stay focused, Chatura. When did you see the car lights?"

"It was right after that. At first, I thought it was a flashlight, but then I realized it was headlights! Coming towards the house! You know as well as I do, Stephanie, people don't just drop by out here!"

"Yes." *That's true.* "Then what?"

"I watched the lights until they went out, about three hundred feet from my house. The junipers blocked the vehicle. Then I called you! I ran to my car as fast as I could, just like you said, and locked the doors. I've never been so frightened in all my life!" she sobs. "Thank God my girls aren't home. Is Holly trying to kill me?" She falls apart. "Why would Holly kill me? You're the one who fed her bugs!"

"I did not…Chatura! OK, listen, you're safe here. Soter is patrolling the property, and I'm well-armed."

Her expression is both relieved and shocked as she flinches, "Stephanie, you have a gun?"

"No. I don't need a gun."

Bobbing her head up and down, trying to connect the dots, she's shaking, her face transformed by fear.

I've seen this face before. "Come on, let me make you some tea."

"I have nowhere else to go, Stephanie. I'm all alone."

The simple suggestion of normalcy does the trick as she sits at the kitchen table. My phone dings multiple times, and I pause midway to the kettle.

"Let me do that." She gets up slowly, trembling, and takes over.

Six of the eight border dispensaries got back to me, literally weeding through them, the first two are both noes. The third won't help me because it's against their policy to divulge seed-to-sale tracking of patient information, *ya da ya da ya da.* But the rest, including one I've known for a decade, are dead ringers. I thank the overburdening cannabis regulations gods for seed-to-sale tracking, wallowing in the irony.

"Stephanie, I think we should call the police." Chatura brings me back to the table, handing me a cup of tea, craning her neck to look out the kitchen window.

"No. You just stay here. I'll be back in a minute." I take my cup with me and head to the back hall. Opening the door, I whistle and wait. Nothing. *That's a concern.* After a second ignored whistle, I close the door in retreat. *That's definitely not a good sign.* Locking it, I change the settings on my phone and return to the kitchen. Picking up my refilled cup, I walk to the window next to the geranium. Chatura is much calmer now, sitting on a wooden stool at the kitchen table, but she's sweating profusely. I recognize the odor from her house, *and it isn't the trash.*

"Have you ever had Botox?" She asks.

"What?"

"Botox?"

"No." *What the hell?*

"I have twelve injections a month. Twelve!" she chatters nervously.

OK. Wow! "Well, it looks very natural, your skin literally glows. It's captivating. But I would have never guessed." Assuaging her, I'm wondering why she's sharing this, at this particular moment.

"It makes me feel good about myself." She pours more tea. "I know it sounds excessive, and I use a dusting powder for the glow." Her voice reduces to a squeak, "But there are worse addictions." Breathing normally, the tea is having an obvious, calming effect on her. She drains her cup and repours for both of us.

"Whatever works for you, Chatura. I wouldn't be comfortable with someone injecting my face with a needle. It's not my thing. But you look great."

Smiling, her flawless skin, creaseless and firm, draws back into her alarmingly, chaotic chignon.

I can't help myself. "Do you know that over forty people a year have fatal reactions to Botox, and they still have no regulations for it? None." I shake my head, trying not to sound like my mother.

"Really? I had no idea. That is something to think about. I'd do a vlog about it, but I don't want to out myself," she winks, "This is delicious tea, by the way. Is it one of your blends?"

"Yup."

"Y'all are so involved with regulations; it makes sense you'd know that." A tinge of a Texas accent erupts.

"Don't get me started. I'm literally an encyclopedia of cannabis regulation. Ask me any question. Go on?" I say, swaying slightly, sitting back down on my stool, welcoming a moment of brevity.

"Well, all right! Let me think." Her twang presents itself confidently. "Ok. What is the legal med-i-cal dose in Col-or-ado?"

Picking up my cup, eyebrows raised, I'm on autopilot, "Well, for edibles, they measure them in milligrams instead of grams like they do for concentrates and flower. Unfortunately, most manufacturers moved their limits to 100 milligrams per package to meet recreational needs on a mass scale to cut costs. But the handful of companies still serving the medical community, like ourselves, sells products up to 2500 milligrams per package. We will even custom-make a product for someone with end-of-life conditions. So, there really is no limit in Colorado for medical use." I lick my lips, my eyelids feeling a little heavy.

"Milligrams, grams… it's all Greek to me!" Chatura squeals, slipping off her stool. We both crack up. Then readjusting herself, she misses the foot peg, and I burst out laughing. "All right, all right," she continues, "How a-bout the recreational cann-abis?" She asks, draining her cup and the pot of tea with a childlike grin, her now heavy accent out in the open.

"That's easy," I say, my hand waving in front of me, "In legal states, one hundred milligrams is the limit per edible purchase for recreational use, and it has to be visually broken down or dispensable in ten milligrams servings, although tinctures are just placed in a vial."

"H-ow do they kno-w you're not just bu-ying 100 milligrams from dozens of stores?"

"Oh, they don't!" I laugh, "It's ridiculous!"

"Oh, my god Stephanie, you are so go-od at this!" she shrieks. "There should be a game sho-w! You would kill it!"

"That would be hysterical! Go on, ask me about another state." My mouth is moving a little slowly, but it doesn't matter.

"OK, ho-w much cann-abis can you sto-re in your ho-use in New Mexico if you have a medical ca-rd?"

"Ooh, that's a good one. Thought you had me on this, didn't you? You're tricky, a tricky, trickster. Eight ounces if you have a license. One ounce of concentrate and up to seventy-two ounces of edibles." Picking up my tea cup, I make my way slowly back over to the geranium in the window and tip the last of my tea. Stretching my back, I brace my hand on the table turning to Chatura, "You know, if I didn't know any better, I'd think we were both stoned."

Tempest

Eyes blurry, holding in a piss, foot pressed against the floor, Remy's anxious he hasn't heard back from Steph; he texted her 20 minutes ago with no response. Pinpointing her phone on the Find Family app, he knows she's home, but she's not replying. "Dammit!" With one finger he dials Danielle's cell. She picks up on one ring.

"Where are you?"

"I'm home. Why?"

"Steph isn't answering her phone, and I'm a good hour away going ninety."

"I'll be there in twelve minutes." She hangs up.

Texting Galax, he's even more frustrated when she doesn't reply. *Maybe she's landing?* He throws his phone down on the passenger seat beside him. It isn't the first time a cell phone has been completely useless. *Shit!* The theories in his head are not good. With each tick of the white line screaming towards him, leading into a seeming abyss, his mood grows darker. Alone in the middle of nowhere, there's no one on the road at this time of night; it's completely abandoned except for the occasional tractor-trailer, like a beacon of light in a black sea.

After years of trying to protect her from fucking crazies, I've left her vulnerable in our own home! The ifs, whys, and what's, close in on him. "Fuck!" Helpless, all he can do is drive.

Hypnotized by the rhythm of the road, he remembers the same feeling of helplessness watching Steph enter the temple in Egypt last year. Even the massive stone walls paled to her presence; everything determinably human became insignificant. Her stride and countenance were unmistakable, like a goddess returning home. Her dark hair tangled into purposeful knots, the profile of her face the work of the millenniums, captivating. Once through the enormous, celestial doorway of Karnak, he felt the same pang he feels now. The fear of losing her. *She is everything.*

As he turned to the monitor in front of him, he could only watch as she offered herself up to H.S. once again. His hands tense, gripping the steering wheel, sweat beading down his forehead, remembering how transfixed he was by her self-control. All he wanted to do, was kill that mother fucker. It took every ounce of restraint he had to stick to the plan, he could smell the blood on his hands while they all waited. Then, for what seemed like an eternal account of inevitable banter, lies, and delusional bullshit, the son of a bitch finally reached his hand out to her with the promises of the literal world and all the riches it contained. Of course, Remy knew what she was thinking, and yet his heart stopped for a brief, painful moment, at the time. Because if she had taken that son of a bitch's hand, his world, their world, *the world*, would've stopped. Bracing the wheel, a deep breath coaxes a smile across his face remembering what happened next.

Steph took H.S. down with one quick move, paralyzing him; like she was born to it. "She's tough," he whispers to himself, wiping his eyes on his sleeve. *She's tougher than I give her credit for.* The phone rings, "Horace?"

"Remy, we have a problem."

Brose and butter

"Stoned? I haven't been stoned since I was in hi-gh scho-ol!"

"Yeah, if I didn't know better." Laughing so hard, I cry, as I sit back down.

Chatura's elbow misses the table, and we both crack up, eyes wide like teenagers, then she squeals, "Steph-anie, that's a go-od one." Her accent thick as molasses, she walks around the table slowly, stumbling slightly, her eyes intensely blue, and places one hand on my shoulder to balance herself and the other in her pocket. "You are such a good friend," she states slurring, "But… you should know better." Her drawl disappears.

Confused, wiping my eyes, my head lolling slightly, I stare back while she pulls out a giant zip tie, grabs both my hands, and secures them.

"Hah!" I burst into laughter. "What are you doing? Chatura?"

"Oh, you're stoned, alright." Deadly serious now, she continues, stone-cold- sober, "In fact, I'm surprised you're still sitting up," she adds with a smile.

Shaking off the heaviness overwhelming me, my hands tied in my lap, sirens firing in my head. My heart breaks. "Chatura?"

"Wow, Stephanie. I gave you so much more credit than you deserved."

My mouth sticks together, "Tell me this isn't about meat."

Looking around the kitchen, she grimaces, "No. It's not *just* about meat." Pulling on latex gloves from her other pocket, she turns to the stove and ignites the burner leaving it on high, with one eye on me. "It's about righting years of wrongs. There's no place in this world for thoughtless people anymore."

Unable to speak, I say nothing, distracted by the heat from the burner next to me.

"And you thought you were so clever, didn't you? With your coveted IP and your fancy design guy? It's not rocket science, Stephanie. I made my own infused tea without your precious secrets. See this?" With a smirk, she pulls out a glass vial from her pocket. "It's called a tincture. All you need to do is squeeze the dropper." Shaking the bottle sarcastically in front of me, I lose focus. "It took me three months to collect all this dope," she continues, gloating, "I don't even know how many milligrams are in here anymore." Her once lovely face, muddled by judgment and anger is unrecognizable as she contemptuously spits, "You're just like the rest of them. I thought you were different. I thought we were friends. But you proved me wrong." She pauses to tighten the pashmina scarf around my neck slowly and uncomfortably, "You don't listen. You don't want to learn or adapt."

Moving to the sink, she grabs the pasta pot off the dry board and fills it with hot water. "How many of my vlogs have you actually watched? Two?" Smug and angry, she waits for the water to fill.

My head collapses against my shoulder in disappointment; I can't lift it.

"You, see? It's all about you!" She says, carrying the pot over to the stove. "You think I'm a nut! Don't you? You don't take anything I say seriously. The solar oven? That was a joke to you. Be honest." She looks at me contemptuously, waiting for a response.

I'm mute, tears in my eyes.

"When I told you about solar power and your stupid gas oven, you just tuned out, like the rest of them." Her animated arms transform her into a doll-like creature as she continues, "Like you're not part of what's happening to the world around you!" Placing the pot over the burner, she throws the lid on with a crash.

"Chatura, what are you doing?" I mumble.

"I'm culling the flock, so to speak." She turns towards me and flicks my forehead. "Isn't that what you do to your chickens?" She whispers in my ear, "Animals that trust you? You cut off their heads and boil them in water to pluck their beautiful feathers? Face it, Stephanie, you're just another person cultivating darkness."

"What happened to no matter how dark the world seems there's no corner light can't penetrate?" I slur, a spittle of drool running down the side of my cheek.

She looks at me and laughs.

"I can't believe you've done this. You killed all those women? I don't understand."

"You can't or you won't believe I could do this? I am not a doormat. I don't eat animals because they deserve a better life. But people? People are just a disappointment."

"Not all people, Chatura."

She turns her head from the hot pot and smirks.

"You know, if you cut off my head, it won't look like an accident."

Completely amused by my statement, she laughs again. "It always looks like an accident, Stephanie. Gabby, Evangeline, Gabriella, my husband. They all looked like accidents. And now you! I can see the headlines.

"Woman Suspect of Murder- Dead!" spreading her hands in the air with a warped smile, she narrates, "After imbibing a lethal amount of marijuana, cannabis company owner Stephanie Beroe, inebriated, knocks over a boiling pot that blows out a pilot light and causes a deadly explosion, killing herself and blowing up her historic house! How does that grab you? Should we add a touch of bacon fat to *elevate* the situation?" Grabbing the molded chicken next to the spaghetti pot, she pours the grease over me, my head swinging in slow motion from shoulder to shoulder, unsuccessfully avoiding the globs. Moving towards the wood stove, she stops in front of me, "You will have left the woodstove door open. That's how it causes the explosion."

"You think of everything," I mumble.

She flashes me a smile.

"You killed your husband?"

"He was the first actually. Yes," she states breaking up kindling, kneeling next to the woodstove like we're having quality time.

"On purpose?"

"Yes and no." She looks at me as if questioning something, "Come on, Stephanie, he only married me because, I'm beautiful."

"Why did you marry him?" I manage, my chin on my chest, eyes straining to watch her every move.

"Because he was rich, of course. I put up with his narcissistic politics and good ole boy's clubs for years, but he was such a pig. I've never seen a human consume so much meat. No one's ever seen a man eat so much meat! Every single night and every morning!" She looks off to the past, air banging her head, "Every – single – night!" repeating like a hammer. "Every day! I could see what he was doing. Anyone with a conscience could. But nobody cared, they were all just like him! He just got bigger and bigger, farting, and stinking up the bathroom and the whole house. The foul smell followed him everywhere he went, like he was tied to the souls of the animals he devoured. Try sleeping with that! No amount of money's worth that! When I tried to make changes, he laughed at me and told me I was crazy. He started introducing me as his crazy vegan wife!" She lowers her head, eyes glowering, "They all laughed at me."

"Great name for a vlog, though."

"Yeah," she answers distractedly, almost morphing into the woman, I know, tears blinking down her cheeks. "When I told him I didn't want him taking pictures of the girls anymore, that it was weird, and it wasn't good for them? He hit me. I saw him for who he was, a controlling monster!" She snarls, tossing the last piece of paper into the fire. Picking up the clicker, she lights it. "Well, he had his last steak. I can te-ll yo-u th-at." She admits with a swager, walking back to the pot to check if it's boiling with a possessed grin, like we're preparing for the holidays. "Tell me, Stephanie, do you have any idea how toxic air fresheners are?" Prodding me with my mother's wooden spoon, her voice malicious and rotten. "No?" she taunts me. "Don't know that little bit of trivia? Aww, too bad. Well, you can take my word for it." She turns back to the pot, "It's lethal. And when you chop it up and blend it with the perfect balance of mashed potatoes and gravy, it's the perfect heart attack!" Tossing the spoon into the sink from across the room, she regals, "He was easy. He was so stupid! Not like Gabby. She put up a fight. Evangeline, not so much; she really was a mouse. Ha!" Laughing to herself, amused, she confesses, "Gabriella? Once the lid hit her on the head, it was all over. But she deserved everything she got! That woman had an evil streak. Even you can't deny that!" Stopping momentarily in thought, she considers out loud, "Dosing me for over a year with meat!" She tremors. "Who did she think she was dealing with?" Turning back towards me, her eyes crazed, she sighs, "But I thought you were different. I thought you were so tough. Fighting against the tyranny of bad moms everywhere. You were an inspiration on those Schloom calls. How you outsmarted Delia, that was priceless. What happened to you?"

Pulling her stool around the table, the legs squealing against the new floor, echo through the entire house until she's in front of me, her knees straddling my legs. Resting her forehead against mine, I smell her peony perfume. Disappointment written all over her face, she looks me dead in the eye, and whispers, "I thought you were tougher than this."

The right side of me

Not stopping to dress, Danielle grabs her keys and stun baton, a gift from Remy last Christmas, then jumps in her car. The twelve-minute drive is more like 720 seconds. It's unbearable with only her headlights in front of her, the rest is no man's land. The few solar malibu's scattered throughout the open landscape of this solar community mimic constellations, obscuring any horizon in the pitch. Gripping the wheel with each turn, ignoring the rocks and potholes, she slows only for a coyote wandering through the night well ahead, and oblivious to her threat.

Four years ago, how could she have pictured herself where she is now? She could never have imagined this future. An urban girl, the city was safe, surrounded by humanity and the predictable workings of daily life; everything was so simple, both the good and the bad. It was what you did. There was safety in numbers, she thought to herself. *What an amazing false sense of security that was.* The pandemic is proving that. Now nature is sacred to her, even this shrubby desert offers her comfort. But among an almost overwhelming, inherent sense of tranquility, a conflict grows within that she can no longer ignore. The constant strain of persecution and futile vendettas that continually surround her new life should have started wearing on her, but they haven't. She's almost embarrassed to admit, it's making her stronger. She's not the same person that she was before the park, that's for sure. Not even close; no longer sheep, she's a predator, *and there's no turning back.*

Her mother's voice comes to mind, the weekly plea, *"I know you like these people, but why do you stay out in the middle of nowhere? With your resume' you can go anywhere! Can't you see that bad things are attracted to these people and what they do? It's like they're cursed! Danielle, use your head!"* She knows better than to rebuttal before the inevitable, *"You were making more than twice the salary they pay you. You're worth more. You're throwing away the best years of your life. How are you going to meet anyone out there? When am I going to have grandchildren? You're not getting any younger."*

The only statement that really bothers her is the constant reminder that the best years of her life are gone, meaning everything from here on out is a downhill slope. *At thirty- two, that's just depressing.* The rest, she's well aware of. The reasoning behind her commitment to Remy is complicated, profound even. "Yeah, I made a hundred and fifty thousand dollars a year working for a prestigious, sleaze bag investment company executive, and where did it get me? Abducted! Raped! Sterilized! What? I'm going to tell her that? She'd have a fucking heart attack!" Wiping a stray, lonesome tear collecting at the corner of her eye she screams, "God, I hate white people!" Then resolves, *no, I choose to stay because Remy and Stephanie are good people. Maybe danger is attracted to them? But it's inescapable for me. I'm a junky now. I'm positively sure Remy understands that; we're both warriors. But Stephanie? She's a conundrum. She's so simple, cooking and nesting and so trusting. I know how fearless she really is, squaring off with H.S, taking her own husband down as a wake-up call last year. Oh yeah, she's in charge of her own fate, but there's a vulnerability about her that defines reasoning for saving mankind.* "These people are my tribe."

Amused that she's talking to herself, she takes the cattle guard slowly and quietly on the final stretch. The dirt road to the Beroe house is tricky without headlights, but if something is going on, she wants to be the element of surprise. Ignoring the right turn into their driveway, she goes straight and hides her car behind a low, bushy juniper tree. Making sure the interior light is off, she gets out and quietly closes the door. Her year in the jungle taught her several things: never let your guard down, anything can be a weapon, and bare feet are stealth; no one can hear you. Taking off into the night like a lion, baton in one hand and her keys threaded through her pointer and middle fingers, in case she needs to blind someone, her eyes adjust to the pitch instantly. Their two- story house, not far in the distance sits below the glow of the milky way, like a vision in a fairy tale. Crouching on her approach, she finds herself lucky the windows are all at eye level, and the curtains are wide open. Making her way towards the living room, peering in, careful not to be caught in the light cast out upon the ground, she sees no one; it's empty, but all the lights are on. Moving to the kitchen, it's easy to hide behind the potted geranium in the window full of crickets Stephanie finds in the house. *Honestly, I've never even seen a cricket on the floor or anywhere else in the house. It must be a Greek thing.* She smiles, thinking to herself before her instincts snap. In the middle of the room, Stephanie is sitting on a stool, her back to the window, her head lolling oddly to her shoulder. The vlogger is cooking something on the stove, facing Stephanie. *There's something very wrong here. And where's Soter?*

The hair on her neck stands straight up she walks quietly to the front of the house careful to stay in the juniper tree line before whistling for Soter quietly. Nothing happens. Walking around the northeast facing side of the house, she carefully hides behind Chatura's car before moving alongside Trixie and whistles again. Something inside the vehicle catches her eye, it's dark out, and hard to decipher.

"Oh no! Soter!" His body, dead still, his name tag catching the reflection from the back door light, stops her heart for a moment. Slowly opening the sliding door as quietly as possible, "No, no, no."

Next to him is a half-eaten steak, inches from his muzzle, she places her hand on top of his tummy. *He's warm! And he's breathing.* His head moves slowly to her touch. Angrily throwing the steak on the roof of the van, out of his reach, she leaves the door open and moves stealthily to the back door of the house. Texting Remy, she puts her phone in silent mode, careful to stay out of view of the small window at the top of the old, paneled back door. She checks the knob, but it's locked. For a moment she debates climbing in the dog door, then decides against it as she slides the house key in as quietly as possible instead, like a surgical procedure, until it clicks. Known to stick, she gives the door a little push with her shoulder to get it open and holds her breath until she's confident no one heard her.

Remaining in a crouch, her back to the swing door of the kitchen hall, she passes through like a cat, silent and methodical, eyes forward, alert for shadows crossing the open archway from the woodstove into the kitchen where she saw Stephanie. Her breath even, she inches towards the opening and waits.

Take me out

Lifting the lid on the pot impatiently, the steam swirls about Chatura's head, delicately.

She thought I was tougher? I've had enough. "You have no idea of what I'm capable of, Eleanor. Can I call you Eleanor? Eleanor Grines, right?" I growl, lifting my eyes and shoulders with vigor, both feet planted firmly on the ground with a bang.

Startled, Chatura turns around at my movement.

"Have I got your attention now?" Our eyes lock, "First of all, there's no lethal dose of cannabis unless you do something stupid like kill yourself while you're high."

She squirms, as I continue, "Confused?" I ask, completely sober. The look on her face, is priceless as she backs away, "That's right, I'm not high. I could smell the dope you squeezed into my tea from New Jersey. I dumped it out in the plant." I nod my head towards the window, "And if you killed my geranium or my crickets, we're going to have a real problem.

Oh, and there actually is an art to infusion. It's called homogenization, and it took us years to perfect." I lick my lips. "What do you take me for? You're in my world now." Unblinking, I stare her down, from my perch, "I don't know why it took me so long to see this, Chatura. Maybe, you're right. Maybe I didn't want to. Maybe, I just wanted to believe there are people out there that still care in this world," I say, staring. "Maybe, I just wanted a friend." I shake my head, "What a fool." A tear falls from my cheek, "Who could be your friend? You are the most selfish person I've ever known, and that's saying something. Oh, you hide it well, behind weaponized spirituality you've perfected down to the hand-woven garments you drape yourself in like a guru, piloting yourself to the world as a savior, but it's all a farce, isn't it? You don't have time for anything or anyone, including your own daughters or their needs because, everything is about *you*." Straightening my back with defiance, everything falls into place, "You're a frightened, righteous, sociopath that's angry the world doesn't think the way you do. It's unfortunate, really, because some of your vlogs were thought-provoking. But it wasn't enough. You're not interested in a dialogue. You're so used to being at the end of a device projecting, you don't know how to compromise anymore. It's your way or the highway, no matter how insane that road is or who you run over! You will never understand, civilization doesn't progress under those constraints; it withers."

She smirks like it's my last confession. *Silly rabbit.*

"Stephanie, I'm going to miss yo-u," she drawls, "You were the clo-sest frie-nd, I've ev-er had. But not too bright." She shakes her head.

Standing up, I break the zip tie in one motion. My hands now inexplicably free, I barrel towards her, "I'm not stupid, and I'm not easy."

Whipping out the smallest pink handled, pocket pistol I've ever seen with a look of triumph, she smirks, "A gi-ft from *my* hus-band."

I stop in front of her shaking my head, "Remember what I said, Chatura? I don't need a gun." Smacking the ridiculous pistol with my right hand into my left, I empty the magazine on to the floor in one fail swoop, before giving it back to her.

Aghast, she drops the empty gun on the floor, desperately reaching for the boiling pot. I close the gap, grab her thumb on her right hand, twisting it painfully away from her body, wrenching it out to her wrist with my left hand and watch her knees buckle in pain, while she screams. With one step, I throw her backwards to the ground, knocking all the air out of her. "For the record, that was easy. Hapkido. Technique number one. How's that for a bit of trivia?"

From the corner of my eye, I see Danielle standing in front of the wood stove watching my display with a smile on her face dressed in pink, silk, camouflage pajamas, barefoot. She beams, "You didn't look like you needed any help." She gives me a wink.

"Nice jammies. Where's Soter?" I smile, grabbing the towel from the sink, and wiping the grease globs off my head.

"He's fine. She dosed him." Flashing Chatura angry eyes, she adds, "I'll find some rope."

There's definitely something comforting about a friend who's willing to tie someone up with you, no questions asked.

Chatura, slowly recovering, is now dying to talk, "Stephanie, you've got this all wrong. I'm the victim here," her sing-song, kindergarten voice returns miraculously, "My husband made me this way! He drove me *crazy*! Think of my kids! You were my friend! I thought you understood my pain!" She works herself into a tantrum from the flat of her back.

Squatting down, my elbows on my knees, I state honestly, "When we first met, Chatura, I admired you. Raising three girls on your own, your positive outlook, your determined, unique values, contrary to mainstream society."

"Counter culture," she murmurs, looking for empathy.

"No." I shake my head, "You gave into hatred, and it turned you into a monster. I've seen it before. Believe me, I've been there. I honestly hope you can get the help you need."

Danielle returns, Soter hobbling shakily after her, wagging his tail.

"Come here, my boy." He sits between my legs facing Chatura, still trying to protect me with a quasi- growl, even though he's vulnerable. I feel a lot of love as I pat his head.

Danielle secures Chatura's hands and feet with her favorite household accessory, duct-tape. Shaking her head, she scolds, "Zip ties? What an amateur."

Chatura begins to cry.

Admiring our handiwork, my chest heavy*; I would have given anything for a different outcome. My heart is truly broken. This world is so out of control, it's making monsters out of us all.*

Suddenly, the back door slams open, and Galax bursts in, crossbow aimed at the ready.

Hurtling herself under the kitchen table Chatura squeals, "What is it with you pe-ople?"

After a moment's pause, I smile at my friends.

"Good to see you." Danielle greets Galax, eyeing her weapon. "That's nice." Stepping over our captive's legs, she asks genuinely curious, "They let you carry that on board?" like there isn't a woman huddled on the floor.

"Private plane. I can take anything I like." Galax smiles, and they hug. A lot of intention moves between them, "We're in this together," she states like a password we all understand.

"Thanks for coming. It means a lot to me." I hug her too, her brown eyes, soft and fierce as an Immortal's, so much power packed into a compact person. I feel sorry for anyone that underestimates Galax, and I know Horace does not.

Soter draws my attention, hobbling as fast as he can towards the back door. Three seconds later, Remy bursts in out of breath. Seeing Chatura on the ground, he relaxes, "What I miss?"

Favorite crime

Driving into Santa, I'm nervous and once again, asking myself how my actions rippled into these horrifying circumstances, *because it always takes two. Horrified by the memories of walking through Gabriella's house with Chatura, now knowing how evil she was, is incomprehensible. The crimes she committed while I was reeling her in for friendship make me question everything. My beliefs, moral compass, integrity, inclusivity, judgment, loyalty, honor; vulnerability, everything's on the table. And after all this time, why am I still the trusting fool? I'll never learn. What hurts the most is knowing I would be living in denial thinking I didn't play a part in this. Like an accomplice, the sad reality is, I never poked my head in to tell anyone what I really felt. I just judged them and let the dysfunction unfold. Can I blame someone for trauma dumping when I allowed it? Maybe I even encouraged it? Maybe it made me feel better about myself? Maybe, I was so desperate for friends, I couldn't see what was in front of me. Either way, there's more than one person to blame here. It's like I took a giant ax and banged it hard on the ice, then wondered why there were so many cracks beneath me.*

Remy squeezes my leg, feeling my anxiety, his other hand firmly on the steering wheel. Wrapped in his touch, I know warmth and confidence once again, as he gives me a wink. I don't know how, but as usual, he knows what I'm thinking.

Horace had sent him a copy of Chatura's driver's license as Eleanor Grines, I can't imagine how panicked he must have felt for miles, knowing how close we were. I was lucky, I got my information from the border first. Now, I feel like the clean-up crew with Danielle and Galax in the backseat of our Subaru. Pulling up to the police station, I can just make out Detective Chavez standing with another officer by the glass doors of the police station, the sun glaring against the faux titanium facia they're leaning up against. Remy parks in the red zone, and I jump out first. Both officers are a little taken aback by our, abruptness.

"I should arrest you," Chavez states walking up to me stiffly. Her arms clearly confined by her suit jacket.

"Yeah, well, you still might," I say honestly, as everyone empties out of the car.

"You're putting me in a tough position. Now, what's this all about?" She straightens her jacket and follows me to the back of the car that is now surrounded by my posse she still hasn't figured out. Popping the hatch, I see her visibly blanche, not knowing what to do with Chatura lying there, hogtied. Giving me the once over, she pulls the gag out, as the officer behind her draws his weapon.

"She attacked me! She's crazy! She's trying to kill me! You must believe me! They're all in on this to save her!"

I stick the gag back in.

Shifting her weight, Chavez shakes her head, "What am I supposed to do with this? I could charge you with kidnapping!"

The officer behind her, unsure which of us is the most dangerous, takes a step back, aiming at all of us in a mad dance. Oddly enough, none of us are reacting to him.

Danielle steps up and throws my phone on top of our bound cargo. "It's a confession," she states sardonically, "Good thing Stephanie knows how to use voice notes. "Oh, and here's a zip drive with footage from her house of her real name, Eleanor Grines. You might want to investigate the whereabouts of her husband too, because he's definitely dead."

Galax chimes in, "And Stephanie tracked the dope Chatura used to dose her victims back to the dispensaries where she purchased it from with her Eleanor Grines I.D. So, I'm thinking a thank you is in order."

"Let's just call it a citizen's arrest," I add.

After an hour or so of statements, Chavez walks us out. "I knew you had it in you." She smiles, watching us from behind the glass door, waving like a school teacher. We climb back in the car, enveloped in my noisy puffer coat, I take a deep breath, knowing I've learned a great deal about myself and the world around me. There's a quiet, satiated silence among us, before Remy suggests, "Burritos?"

Cake by the Ocean

It's been two excruciatingly long weeks since we dropped Chatura off, and I'm still exhausted. But most of the dust has settled. Mad Hatter is running full steam ahead with a little push from all the news on how a cannabis entrepreneur uncovered a serial killer in the midst of rural New Mexico; Horace was granted exclusives, of course. With Imogene back, life is almost normal too, *Covid normal anyway*. A pot of real New Jersey chili is in the crock pot and Danielle's cornbread is on top of the woodstove, we're watching Imogene beat chocolate cake batter with Columbo on the flat screen. The Irish poet/ terrorist marks his bottle of whiskey with his ring, 'This far and no farther,' he says, not knowing that is what does him in.

"He did it!" Imogene yells, and we all laugh, especially Danielle. She really enjoys spending time with her and us.

I am so grateful for our new friendship. My phone dings, and it's Devon from Arizona. *Who still hasn't paid his invoice.*

The money order for our invoice was mailed out today. This has taken so long. When can we expect our order?

There are almost too many ways to answer this. I smile, eyeing Remy as Soter trots to the front door.

"Now what?" Remy asks rhetorically, obviously not in the mood for company. Opening the door, a beautiful blonde woman with hazel eyes walks in. I drop my phone.

"Momma!" Imogene screams, running.

"Ma petite gateau! My darling, I missed you so much!" Esme´ whispers, wrapping her arms around her mini-me, kissing her face and forehead, all of us standing there with tears in our eyes.

Remy's dumbfounded, "Why didn't you tell us you were coming? How did you manage this?"

"I've never seen so much handling in all my life." She picks Imogene up and walks into the living room towards me with a smile that makes my heart alight. "I flew compliments of Mr. and Mrs. Adom. Literally whisked out of Iraq on a private plane and flown here under some diplomatic orders, I never quite got a full story on, that absolutely no one questioned."

"Laure?" Remy looks to me.

I say nothing. But Danielle gives me a nod; she knows.

Esme´ kisses me on both cheeks, pulling me into a deep hug. I feel Imogene's arm around my neck, wet tears on her soft cheek. My smile would break my face if it were bigger. Seeing Imogene so happy, knowing I kept my promises to her, fills me with love I didn't know I was capable of. My tears are happy, and I've learned a lesson. From now on, I'm going to strive to be a better person, more understanding, and less judgmental. Living in a pandemic can have lifelong symptoms that go beyond health and finance. I need to be sure my instincts for protecting the ones I love don't steer me across the line of selfishness because we're all going to need a better world to integrate back into when this is over. Imogene is going to need a better world.

After dinner and delicious cake, Imogene talks us into scrabble, but I think she's reading the room. Everyone is so happy at this moment, no one wants to go to bed or even talk about it. Several rounds later, the board looks like a tarot reading, loaded with words like S-T-E-A-K and V-L-O-G and M-I-C-R-O-S-C-H-O-O-L. *We're obviously still processing.*

Danielle's legs monopolize the entire couch. Imogene, Remy, Esme´ and I are perched on whatever pillows we could scraped up around the house, surrounding the coffee table now filled with scrabble tiles.

"Imogene, honey, it's your turn," Esme´ prompts, giving her a playful nudge as she sits between her legs, and as if the tiles just appeared for her to play them, she places C-O-V-I-D on the board.

"Well played, sweetie," Remy states, eyeing the board like a hawk. Not exactly known for grammatical eloquence, he always looks like he has seven vowels on his slate, taking *forever*. Then, just when you've given up on him, he pops one tile in the middle of an illiterate maze of words. S, he plunks down this time, creating no less than eight words and collects 140 points!

"Unbelievable!" I exclaim. We all roll our eyes as he reconfirms his points three painstaking times.

"Danielle, your turn," I say to get the ball out of Remy's infuriating court.

After another exasperating length of time, Danielle connects V-O-Y-A-G-E to our many-branched tree of words.

"I've been thinking," Remy states nonchalantly as she adds her points to the score card. Everyone raises their eyebrows. "No, really. I've been thinking." He nods his head in silence, as we wait, "We should buy a sailboat."

We all look at each other.

"We could go anywhere. We can all work from anywhere. All of us, anywhere in the world!"

His excitement grows with every spoken word; a manifestation. "We'll see the world! Be one with the ocean. Live off it. Play in it!" He looks at Imogene, "Learn from it!" Nodding his head with the confirmation he's imagining from the rest of us, he continues, "Yup, we should buy a sailboat," he states confidently. "And arm it."

To be continued...

Excerpt from Prytania- A new series by the author

*Stephanie Beroe will return in Book IV presently underway, we will go to the sea, and join the Beroe's on another adventure. In the meantime, here is an excerpt from a new series by the author – Prytania – no spoilers. You have to read it for yourself. J.A. St. Thomas

Prytania

Stepping out into the delicious evening, humidity greeting her as an old friend, her thick, auburn hair, curls instantly and beautifully around a timeless, oval face, dusting delicate shoulders carelessly. Wishing she was wistful, a moment of nostalgia slips by, but wishing is useless because existence is ironic, and her time here will be anything but easy.

Silver clouds above the tree lined streets, drenched in sodium light are heavy and threatening, as they should be. The two laned boulevard in front of The Rathbone Mansions Hotel holds it breath, vacated from the safety of daylight, even the bulbous blooms expressing themselves seem anosmic, like a set for a movie, everything is perfect, bucolic; but not real.

When the letter arrived three days ago, the handwritten address bore a hole in her heart. Each letter connecting the fluidity of time, the words strategically chosen. The two-day train ride, was a perverse type of torture, even the sleeper car was noisy, exposed and a brutal reminder of mortality, as scenic and dismal towns flanked the tinted windows at hyper speed.

Digesting the correspondence, holding the paper in her mercurial hand, knowing he held it too; willfully engaging, was her first step towards an impending doom. There is no turning back now, Prytania reminds herself, turning her head to cross the ghostly street. Rows of two story French Colonial houses surrounding the historic Treme district are a ploy at civility, but there is no law here, and only justice that one brings upon themselves.

It has been years since she even thought about him. Their bound time together had been both exhilarating, and terrifying. She knowingly had been complicit and illicit. And for that, she had locked her feelings up; burying them deeply within the marrow of her bones for fear of expressing them. There could be no link, not even the slightest of recall, but now, none of that matters.

Sweeping the avenue with steely almost black eyes out of habit is truly pointless, because the realm she has entered is already aware of her. There are few foolish enough to wander this time of night, and those who do, never resurface. Walking quickly with purpose, she pulls the light- weight hood over her head, the floor length cape trailing behind ominously.

Years ago, she had worked out the answers to any and all responses she would need to survive him again; forging in her mind methodical replies, to keep her safe, distanced and detached. But the years have withered those responses, and time has only set a wave of intrigue in her path. In the darkest hour of night, she navigates the empty streets from memory, a bouquet of stench leading her in. Moving a stray hair from her face, her hand trembles, stopping her in her tracks. Taking a moment to bear resolve, she knows there is only one choice to make.

Chapter Song List Appendix

The Chapter Song List is my super charger. I rely on these songs; chosen for their energy or title to complete the emotional arch of the chapter it is named for. I might listen to a chapter song over a hundred times to inspire the perfect moment, word, or syllable necessary to achieve the emotional range of a character or plot line. Music is power. It is a power I have divined since I was five years old. It started, as far as I can remember, driving in my mother's, ragtop Cougar pushing the buttons on the radio the minute a commercial came on, and continued with my infatuation with Barbara Streisand, Disney songs, Pat Benatar, Blondie, Elizabeth Frasier, and Kate Bush, through my youth and continues with Olivia Rodriguez, Lana Del Rey, and many more.

Not only is this music powerful, but the words… what they yield with such passion was, and always has been a life line for me. In 1988 I started a band in New York City with Ray Carroll known as The Waterlillies, we were signed to Sire/ Reprise/ Warner Records and my journey as a songstress took flight. I now continue my journey as a wordsmith- Siren, and am systemically covering each of my novels, Chapter Song Lists. The library of my covers can be found on my website and Social Media accounts, www.JAStThomas.com #thesingingauthor #Thoughtsfromthenest for the curious.

My intention is that my readers will divulge in the extra sensory experience that has been meticulously designed for their enjoyment. As a creator that is all anyone can truly hope for. Jill Alikas St Thomas

* Scan the QR code in the Chapter Song List to open my Youtube playlist.

Chapter 1 "What's Inside" written and performed by Sara Bareilles: *Songs from Waitress*

Chapter 2 "Dancing in the Moonlight" written and performed by King Harvest: *Dancing in the Moonlight*

Chapter 3 "Accentuate the Positive" written by Mercer & Arlen performed by Johnny Mercer & The Pied Pipers

Chapter 4 "A Taste of Honey" written and performed by *Herb Alpert & the Tijuana Brass*

Chapter 5 "Karma Police" written and performed by Radiohead: *OK Computer*

Chapter 6 "Know Your Chicken" written and performed by Cibo Matto: *Viva! La Woman*

Chapter 7 "Every day is exactly the same" written and performed by Nine Inch Nails: *With Teeth*

Chapter 8 "The Galaxy Song" written and performed by Monty Python: *The Meaning of life*

Chapter 9 "Give Me a Pig Foot" written by Wesley Wilson, performed by Billie Holiday: *The Blues Are Brewin*

Chapter 10 "Mother Popcorn" written and performed by James Brown: *It's a Mother*

Chapter 11 "I Put a Spell on You" written and performed by Screamin' Jay Hawkins: *At Home with Screamin' Jay*

Chapter 12 "Eh Cumpari" written by La Rosa & Bleyer, performed by Julius LaRosa: *Cadence Classics*

Chapter 13 "Everybody Eats When They Come to My House written and performed by Cab Calloway & His Orchestra: *Are You Hep to the Jive?*

Chapter 14 "Bar b que" written and performed by Wendy Rene: *Stax Volt: The Complete Singles 1959- 1968*

Chapter 15 "Chocolate Jesus written and performed by Tom Waits: *At the Terminal-Burbank Airport '99 Live*

Chapter 16 "Sausage and Eggs" written and performed by Tom Waits: *Nighthawks at The Diner*

Chapter 17 "Ain't No Rest for the Wicked" written and performed by Cage the Elephant: *Cage The Elephant (Expanded Edition)*

Chapter 18 "Pour Some Sugar on Me" Written by Def Leppard, performed by Emm Garner: *The Side Street Project Live*

Chapter 19 "Crawfish" written by Wise & Weisman, performed by Elvis Presley: *King Creole*

Chapter 20 "I'm Wishing" written by Larry Morey, performed by Tiger Darrow: *Youtube*

Chapter 21 "Peaches and Cream" written by Venet & Boyce, performed by Beck: *Midnight Vultures*

Chapter 22 "One Meatball" written by Zaret & Singer, performed by Bing Crosby & the Andrew Sisters: Bing and Friends 3

Chapter 23 "That Cat is High" written by J.Mayo Williams, performed by The Ink Spots: Swing High, Swing Low

Chapter 24 "Red Beans and Rice" written and performed by spearhead: Spearhead

Chapter 25 "Gunning for the Buddha" written and performed by Shriekback: Big Night Music

Chapter 26 "Pass the Peas" written by Brown, Starks, Bobbit, performed by The J.B.'s: Food for Thought

Chapter 27 "Southern Fried Chicken" written by Brown & Durrette, performed by Bill Thomas & the Fendells: *Southern Fried Chicken Single*

Chapter 28 "Gooey" written and performed by Glass Animals: *Zaba*

Chapter 29 "Tempest" written and performed by Jill Alikas St Thomas & Glenn Neff, performed by Sonic Fleur featuring the author -Jill Alikas St Thomas: *Sonic Fleur*

Chapter 30 "Brose and Butter" original poem written by Robert Burns, performed by Eddi Reader: *The Songs of Robert Burns*

Chapter 31 "The Right Side of Me" written by Paul Bartlett, performed by Lowrider: *Why Can't We be Friends?*

Chapter 32 "Take Me Out" written and performed by Franz Ferdinand: *Franz Ferdinand*

Chapter 33 "Favorite Crime" written and performed by Olivia Rodriguez: *Sour*

Chapter 34 "Cake by the Ocean" written and performed by DNCE: DNCE

About The Author

An early passion for poetry, singing, and writing, Jill Alikas St. Thomas annoyed friends, family, and neighbors alike with a distinct desire to perform that led her to Florida, where she attended but did not complete studies at the University of Tampa with a full, classical music scholarship. Jill became the singer of a local Tampa band, The Flower Sermon, in '85, and in '87, she met Ray Carroll in NYC, and they created The Waterlillies. They were signed to Reprise/ Sire Records by Seymour Stein, with three songs breaking the top 10 charts in 1994 - 1995 and "Never Get Enough", reaching No. 1 in the U.S. She continued to compose, record, and perform with Suicide Lounge in 2004 and Sonic Fleur in 2011. Love struck in the summer of 89' she met her life partner, Thomas St. Thomas, a fine artist from California and they married in '94 in Hawaii. A year later, her mother, Margaret (Peggy) Ann Rankl -Alikas, who was an emotional and supportive benefactor in Jill's life, died of cancer, and The Waterlillies broke up. Navigating reinvention, Jill moved to Madrid, New Mexico, with her husband in '96, and they opened the fine art gallery, Margeaux Kurtie Modern Art, named in homage to her mother and a friend of her husband's, both of whom died the previous year.

After years of writing songs and poetry, she ventured into essays and artists' statements with a keen eye for marketing. This led her to an assistant field position to Siegfried Halus, the Chairman of Arts for Santa Fe Community College, for the publication of *Idea Photographic; After Modernism*, in conjunction with the San Francisco Museum of Modern Art and Princeton University Art

Museum collections which was published by the University of New Mexico, New Mexico Museum of Fine Art, and SFCC.

Navigating global, financial duress after 9-11, she co-founded Mad Hatter Coffee & Tea, a cannabis infusion company, in 2007 with her husband. Together they have pioneered cannabis and CBD beverages. Considered a Green Queen of cannabis, she has been profiled by *The New York Times*, *Time Magazine*, and *Newsweek*.

In 2015 Jill began writing larger fiction than songwriting could contain, The Stephanie Beroe Chronicles are based on surreal experiences in the cannabis industry, life in a ghost town, and the explosive social and political landscape of its time. This series continues, and is a collaborative venture between music and words with chapter song playlists that combines the author's passion for music and a sentient, interactive experience for writing fiction in a media-based world.

Having home-schooled her daughter through Covid and several years prior, Pot Luck A Home School Murder Mystery is a culmination of the cathartic process of raising children in a brave new world.

Jill continues to live in New Mexico with her husband of 34 years, their daughter Elektra, who is also a writer, and their dog Mr. Darcy.

For more information about the author please visit and follow.

www.JAStThomas.com

To support this author, please review this book on Goodreads, Amazon, google, Barnes & Noble and the author's website.

Cat Tales Publishing

Written word by J.A. St. Thomas:

A Walk in the Park, Book I of The Stephanie Beroe Series.

Class 7, Book II of the Stephanie Beroe Series

Pot Luck, Home School Murder Mystery, Book III of The Stephanie Beroe Series.

Prytania – Volume 1 – The Rathbone Mansions – Coming soon!

http://www.CatTalesPublishing.com

Musical works by J.A. St. Thomas

LP Sonic Fleur – Sonic Fleur

LP Suicide Lounge – Suicide Lounge

LP Envoloptuousity – The Waterlillies, *Sire/Reprise Records*

LP Tempted – The Waterlillies, *Sire/Reprise Records*

www.ingramcontent.com/pod-product-compliance
Lightning Source LLC
Chambersburg PA
CBHW020459310726
48979CB00016B/2727/J

* 9 7 9 8 9 8 8 6 1 8 8 0 5 *